"Run!" Helicron said. "We've got to run!"

"We?" Navis Redling asked.

The tavern's doors swung open to reveal an enormous figure framed between them, and several similar forms waiting behind it. Redling suddenly saw the reason for the urgent tone in his subordinate's voice.

He began to run. There didn't seem to be much choice. He was armed, but there certainly wasn't time to draw any weapon that would be effective against what confronted him now.

Behind him, six times four booted feet slammed against the asphalt pavement and made rolling waves of thunder. To his left, Helicron Daas's two feet, wearing soft leather shoes, made somewhat less noise as he kept pace with Redling's long, loping strides. The boy was in good shape, but his breath was coming in ragged gasps now. Even Redling was beginning to feel the strain.

The thunder grew louder.

The centaurs were drawing closer.

"Get the two-legger and his friend!"

"Cheat! Foul!"

"Give us back our money!"

He began to run faster.

MARC MILLER'S
TRAVELLER®

GATEWAY TO THE STARS

PIERCE ASKEGREN

BYRON PREISS MULTIMEDIA COMPANY, INC.

NEW YORK

POCKET BOOKS

NEW YORK   LONDON   TORONTO   SYDNEY   TOKYO   SINGAPORE

An Original Publication of POCKET BOOKS

POCKET BOOKS, a division of Simon & Schuster, Inc.
1230 Avenue of the Americas, New York, NY 10020

Copyright © 1998 by Imperium Games, Inc.
A Byron Preiss Multimedia Company, Inc. Book

Traveller® is a registered Trademark of FarFuture Enterprises. Used under license by Imperium Games, Inc.

Byron Preiss Multimedia Company, Inc.
24 West 25th Street
New York, NY 10010

The Byron Preiss Multimedia World Wide Web Site Address is:
http://www.byronpreiss.com

ISBN 0-671-01188-X

First Pocket Books paperback printing June 1998

10 9 8 7 6 5 4 3 2 1

POCKET and colophon are registered trademarks of Simon & Schuster Inc.

Edited by Keith R.A. DeCandido
Cover art by Chris Foss
Cover design by Steven Jablonoski
Interior design by MM Design 2000, Inc.

Printed in the U.S.A.

For my father, Kenneth Askegren, who bought me my first books, and always expected me to write some, as well.

PROLOGUE

Some two-and-one-half centuries after stumbling upon the secret of atomic power, humanity made its second watershed discovery: the Jump Drive that allowed its representatives effectively to exceed the speed of light. Filled with the heady spirits of accomplishment and ambition, they cast themselves into the sea of interstellar space, eager to take the stars.

They found that the stars had already been taken.

The cosmos was filled with countless worlds, spinning beneath suns that were similarly without number. On those worlds, a near-infinite quantity of variegated intelligent beings ate and drank, fought and loved, lived and died in environments that seemed strange and alien to the explorer. Some welcomed the Terran vanguard with open arms; some did not.

The explorers from Earth had expected that, too.

The worlds they found were bound together by commerce and custom, and contended against one another in conflict and competition, all on a scale geometrically greater than anything Earth had ever known. One empire alone comprised more than eleven thousand worlds, roughly equivalent in size and assets to Earth. This was the Ziru Sirka, or Vilani Empire, the dominant political entity of its age, but not quite the end-all and be-all of the cosmos. Even an empire that large could not encompass everything; it had rivals and rebels, foes and friends.

If the explorers from Earth had not expected the

Ziru Sirka, they had at least anticipated the possibility of it, or something similar. The sheer size of the culture they faced came as a surprise, but not the fact of its existence.

What they had never imagined, and what no one on Earth had ever anticipated, was that the most denizens of the Vilani Empire—and of all the lesser federations and republics and systems and dominions—were human beings, too. There were other intelligent species, but those were the minorities, both in terms of power share and cosmological distribution.

Other races shared the cosmos, but humans ruled it.

Some found the situation funny. Humanity had sent forth its best and brightest to take the stars, only to find that they had been beaten to the punch by their own progenitors. Credit, or blame, belonged to the Droyne. Some three hundred thousand years before, the inhuman Droyne—the first star-faring race known to history—visited ancient Earth. When they left, they took with them several thousand hominids, humans and near-humans. No one knew why, or whether the specimens were pets or servants or entertainment or food—the actual reason was long lost to record. Those hapless creatures, isolated, frightened, and powerless, were the ancestors of the half-dozen or so human races that would one day reshape the galaxy in their image.

A day came when the Droyne fell and were no more. Humankind took their place, growing to a kind of maturity amid the ruins of that extinct people's empire. The Droyne had been a powerful people, by turn both industrious and warlike. They left wreckage and remnants in their wake, to be studied and salvaged and misunderstood by those who came after them.

The Velani Empire would be remembered by history as the First Imperium. It fell, in no small part because the Velani themselves underestimated the drive and tenacity of their distant cousins, the armies of the Terran Confederation.

The end of the Ziru Sirka meant the beginning of the Second Imperium, bearing the conceited but mostly accurate name, the Rule of Man. The Second Imperium was to be less widespread than the first, and less enduring. When it, too, fell, so did the Long Night, a nearly two-millennium era of barbarism and despair that stretched throughout what had been the civilized galaxy.

Then came the new age of expansion and conquest, of challenge and adventure that was the Third Imperium...

CHAPTER ONE

A dozen planets in a dozen different systems bore the name Farworld, bestowed upon them by a similar number of unimaginative explorers. Each of those people had been equally certain that he or she had carried the frontier as far as it would go and defined the farthest reach of humanity's expansion through the galaxy.

Events had proven most of them wrong.

Nine of those planets were heavily occupied urban worlds now, nestled deep inside the boundaries of territories and jurisdictions that had grown up around them. Two others hung between competing, hostile systems and were the sites of frequent territorial squabbles. Ultimately, each would find itself the prize in some final battle, and later be integrated and tamed as human civilization marched without pause along the paths between the stars.

Only one Farworld remained a frontier planet. It was a scruffy little ball of arid rock perched in orbit around a dying star along the outer reaches of the galaxy's northern spiral arm, where space itself was stretched thin and habitable worlds are few and far between. Between it and the galactic core lay the burgeoning jurisdiction of the Third Imperium; beyond it lay worlds uncharted and untamed.

On that Farworld, in the city of Farport (also one of far too many), in a cluttered office, a grotesquely fat man named Tithe sat behind a desk that was much too small for him and reviewed his accounts. Close at hand was a stack of tattered plastic sheets, the kind used by businesses for temporary records, each page nearly covered with parts numbers and prices, both received and paid. Tithe's concerns were many and varied, but his favorite among them was one that amounted to a combination storage facility and junk-yard—with the former giving rise to the latter. That bifurcate business was near and dear to Tithe's labor-ing heart, and running it involved considerable record keeping.

Now, he narrowed watery eyes and read from the first sheet, then typed laboriously on an antiquated keyboard that he had purchased from an itinerant ped-dler. The handwriting on the sheets was his own, too sloppy and idiosyncratic for even him to read easily, and the subject matter was mostly numeric: currency amounts and exchange rates. The end result was that the documents were unsuited by format and content for data entry by either reader or speech vocoder, but important enough to justify transcription by hand. It was hard, slow work, yet fascinating to a man of Tithe's pecuniary bent, and so it commanded his entire attention. So intent on his task was he that he did not notice another man enter the crowded space, pick his way though a maze of file cabinets and boxed hard-ware, and then pause before Tithe's desk.

"You've got a ship in a storage bay out at the 'port," the man said, "a Cadmus Far Trader." He sounded vaguely annoyed or perhaps amused as he named the spacecraft's make and model, as if disdaining the man-ufacturer's lack of imagination.

"Yuh," Tithe grunted. He did not look up, but continued typing as he spoke. "The *Gateway*. Been there a standard year now."

"I'm here to take her off your hands."

"Nuh." Tithe peered at another plastic sheet and kept typing.

"'Nuh'?"

"Nuh," Tithe affirmed. "Gonna part her out. Low market value. She's old. Drive's still good, though, and some other stuff. Worth more 'n pieces than she is whole."

"Can't let you do that, old boy," the man responded. His tone, though light and jocular, nonetheless suggested that he meant business. "Set a bad precedent. What would you do if someone felt the same way about you, and decided to act on it? Why, there'd be little pieces of fat junkman spread across the entire Imperium, and we couldn't have that, could we?"

A look of sudden anger flowed across Tithe's round, oily features as he finally looked up from his work. "Look, y'wanna do business, you talk nice, or I'll—"

His words trailed into silence and he blinked eyes that were buried deep in the fleshy rolls of his face. When he spoke again, he looked more annoyed than pleased. "Know you," he said, but his voice still held a note of doubt, as if he were not totally certain that his words were true.

"Of course you do, Tithe, old chum," the other man said as Tithe looked at him. He was very nearly the junkman's opposite, tall and lean and casually elegant, with a stance that suggested self-confidence so total as to border on arrogance. Baseline human, such as might have walked on Earth itself, his most notable features were his gray, twinkling eyes. They gazed out from regular features framed by medium-length black hair. "We're the very bosomiest of bosom buddies," he continued in a japing tone that stripped his words of any real meaning. "At least, you are. I've got my weight under control."

"Huh. Redling," Tithe said. He still sounded a bit doubtful. "Didn't think I'd ever see you again."

The man Tithe had called Redling nodded and grinned, his features parting in a buccaneer's smile. "So I gather," he said cheerfully. His voice was deep and pleasant. "But no need to be so formal—you can call me Navis." The words were a lie, but he delivered them with utter sincerity.

"When'd you get back?"

"I blew into town a few days ago," was his response. That much was true, at least. "Took a Low passage on the *Black Covenant*." More lying; he had ridden that ship, but he hadn't ridden Low. Only a desperate pauper or fool would ride that way, drugged and frozen and stowed in a cargo hold like so much meat. He liked to think that he was neither, so, he'd ridden Middle instead, where a man could eat and breathe and talk with civilized folk. He would have preferred the luxuries of High, and he could have afforded them, but Navis Redling would never have considered spending that kind of money. Even riding Middle was stretching a point. "I've been keeping a low profile since."

Tithe grunted again, a sound of disgust this time. "I can understand that," he snorted, then ran his fingers along the keyboard. The aging computer hummed softly to itself, and then the liquid crystals of its display rippled and flowed, until several dozen lines of abbreviated text coalesced out of the chaos. "Heard you were dead, Redling," Tithe said. He read from the file he had summoned from his records. "Freighter captain, out of Draen, came by here three months ago. Needed a full set of integrated flux modulators. Real distress case. We did some business." He smiled at the memory. Ship components could be hard to come by, this far out, and men like Tithe could make a lot of money on others' misfortune.

The man who looked like and claimed to be Navis Redling paused a moment, and sorted through memories that were his only by right of purchase. "Someone's got a busy mouth," he said. "The fellow lacked your generous dimensions? Out of Draen? That would be Skelder. I don't imagine you gave him a fair deal."

Tithe nodded. "Skelder Treph. A real skinny-bones, that one," he said. Two of his too-many chins rippled and shook as he spoke. "Told me you'd overdosed months before on crystal."

"Hardly," his visitor said. He settled into Tithe's guest chair, moving so gracefully that he seemed less to sit than to flow into the seat's greasy embrace. "Hard to overdose on something as nice as that." He grinned again. "Won't say I didn't try, though." He sighed, but the sound was like an actor might make, a mock acknowledgment of a regretted past that had never happened.

Tithe grunted again. The inarticulate sound seemed to constitute most of his vocabulary.

The new Navis Redling continued. "Euphorinol is wonderful stuff, Tithe, the very ticket out of workaday reality. You really should try it. It might show you what it feels like, to be smaller than a planet." He suddenly sounded a bit less lighthearted. "The only hitch is that leaving one place means you have to go another, and in my case, that other place was a rehab colony on Carter's World. I checked in there after you and I cut our little deal, and I've been there ever since." He paused again, and then beamed. "Until now, of course."

"Shoulda stayed there," Tithe said. "Nothing for you here." He pressed a key and the computer drooled out some plastic film covered with close-set characters. Tithe passed it across his desk. "Read the print. There's no grace period. You waited too long. Storage fees ran out today an' the *Gateway* is mine. Worth more—"

"*Run* out," Redling amended, interrupting.

"Whuh?" Tithe grunted.

"Run out. The storage fees run out today, not 'ran' out. No grace period, true enough, but one full standard year, paid in advance." Redling's left hand slid under his tunic and he drew forth a wallet made of blue leather, then snapped it open. It was filled with documents, sheets of plastic and metal foil and even paper, all marked with densely set type and elaborate seals. He selected a single sheet and unfolded it. "I know how to read, Tithe, even the inarticulate drivel that flows from your fat fingertips. Review the original deal, not your jerried-together little reprint, and you'll see that the year runs out at midnight." Redling glanced at the personal com unit on his wrist. It was a cheap model that did little more than provide place and time data and that would have been hardly worth stealing. "Five standard hours to go, three point seven, local time." Ignoring the document that Tithe had proffered, Redling tossed his own on the desk. "And we'll work from this sheet, thank you. That way, we don't have to worry about any little changes that might have crept into your copy, right?"

Tithe glared at him some more.

"That should be enough time for even you to sign your name, don't you think? I've already spoken with the 'port administrator and told her I'll take possession of the *Gateway* in the morning."

Tithe shook his head, making rolls of fat quiver like jelly. "Nuh," he said. "Didn't wait a whole year just so—"

"That's right, you didn't. Not for another three point seven hours."

"—some spazzed out crystal-head can come crawling back to take what's mine," Tithe continued, as if he had not been interrupted. He reached for a desk drawer with one pudgy hand, moving rather fast for someone of his bulk and build.

Redling moved faster.

He moved much faster, in fact. One moment the dark-haired man was seated, and the next, he was on his knees atop Tithe's desk. The first moment gave way to the second so quickly that there seemed to be no period of transition between them. Redling reached his right hand out in a slapping motion that ended when it intersected with the left side of Tithe's hairless head, even as his left hand snaked toward the fat man's neck. One set of fingers grabbed Tithe's ear, gripped and twisted, while the other found his throat and dug deep into the rolls of oily flesh there.

Tithe made a gurgling noise, but he quit moving.

"Slowly," Redling said. He spoke calmly, in tones that suggested he attached no particular importance to the present situation. The only emphasis he gave his words was a gentle twist to Tithe's ear. "Slowly, slowly, slowly."

Tithe's hand emerged from the drawer, gripping the

butt of a body pistol. It was a small gun, intended for concealed carry, but it fired large bullets that could punch even bigger holes in a person. It didn't fire any now. Once the compact weapon came completely into view, Tithe released it and let it fall to the floor.

Redling reduced the severity of his grip at the fat man's throat by some fractional increment, enough to permit speech.

"Hurts," Tithe croaked. His eyes were trying to climb out of their sockets now, and tears of pain trickled from their corners.

"Good," Redling responded. He twisted the fingers of his right hand, the one that grasped Tithe's left ear, and smiled. "It's supposed to hurt. Otherwise, I wouldn't bother doing it."

"No cash here," Tithe said, choking out the words. His face was purpling. "Not much, anyhow. Nothing worth taking."

"I doubt that very much," Redling said, "but it doesn't matter. I'm not here to take what's yours, just what's mine. All I want out of you right now is your signature and particulars." He released Tithe's throat and tapped one finger on the release form. "Sign the quit-claim and I'll be off." He grinned wolfishly. "Don't sign it, and your ear will be off, instead."

Tithe grabbed a stylus. He scrawled his name across the plastic sheet and then pressed his thumbprint against the appropriate blank space. He pressed down hard enough to activate the specially treated film's memory. When he lifted his hand again, his thumbprint remained behind, permanently embossed in the document surface. "There," he said, gasping. "There! Take your damned rustpot tub and go."

Redling shook his head and squeezed the captive ear again gently, but hard enough that something red oozed from between his fingers. "Registry seal, too," he said, "and make the transfer. Make it now."

The fat junkman said nothing as he complied. His breath came in ragged gasps and the skin of his throat still bore the angry marks made by strong fingers.

"You're going to have yourself a nasty bruise there," Redling said, glancing at the discoloration. "Might want to buy yourself a nice scarf. People do talk, you know. Scarf won't work for the ear, though."

Tithe glared at him but said nothing as he pushed the button that sent an electronic version of the quit-claim form to the local spaceport's computer network. The computer chirped as it concluded the action, and then Tithe's ear was suddenly free again. He rubbed it sullenly, making it bleed a bit more, and looked reproachfully at Redling, who had already poured himself once more into the guest chair. "You didn't used to be like this," the junkman said.

"The rehab colony offered an impressive slate of self-improvement courses," the other man said lightly. "All the basket-weaving sections were full, so I took Self-Assertiveness Training, Applied Interpersonal Social Dynamics, and a refresher in How To Strong-Arm Recalcitrant Goons." He looked utterly at ease, relaxed and tranquil, and not at all like a man who had been poised to kill his host a moment before. His face split in a grin that was very nearly elfin, making his face an incongruous study in benevolent innocence. "Things change, and people change, too," he contin-ued, in a tone that suggested his words held more than one meaning. "You might remember that, next time you try to go back on a deal."

"Not going back on it!" Tithe said angrily, still wheezing. "Standard year expires today, at the beginning of the day, not at the end—"

Redling looked at him quizzically, one eyebrow raised. The fingers of his right hand curled and writhed bonelessly, like anemone fronds in an ocean current.

Tithe noticed, and composed himself. "Get out of here," he said. "You got what you wanted, now go."

"Nuh," Redling said, repeating his imitation of Tithe's trademark grunt. This time, practice made it perfect. "We're not quite done yet, after all."

Tithe looked at him warily.

"Things change," Redling repeated. "People do, too, but you haven't. You've still got a spoon in every pot on this backwater world. All *my* contacts are dead or offplanet, or they've written me off as a 'spazzed out crystal-head.'"

"Don't believe it," Tithe said. "You want to do business? You want to do new business? After cheating me? After *this*?" He caressed his bruised throat, pained outrage giving some definition to his gelatinous features.

"Of course I do," Redling said. "I've got a Far Trader to outfit and a crew to sign, and I need cargo to haul, and I've got money to buy services. Are you telling me you'd let a little thing like a bruised trachea get between you and a commission, now that we've renewed our cherished acquaintance? Tsk, tsk, tsk, Tithe. Nobody changes *that* much."

Tithe looked at him, blinked. He scratched one of his chins for a moment, and then shrugged. Finding a clean sheet in the chaos of his desk, he took up his stylus again, and began writing. "What is it you need?" he asked. "When?"

Smiling again, the man who was now Navis Redling told him.

The hotel was a respectable one, at least according to some standards; certainly, it was respectable enough that it catered to a clientele a few ranks above working class. The place rented rooms on a sliding scale—the more credits the guest was willing to pay, the fewer questions that guest would be asked. Redling had settled on an intermediate fee and a corresponding level of inquisitiveness for several reasons. Simple economy was the least of them; much more important was experience's hard lesson that paying extra for fewer questions almost always yielded more, instead. True, those questions tended to be spoken behind the subject's back instead of to his face, but that was hardly an improvement.

Redling's room, per his request, was a windowless one on the inn's fifth floor. Now, as he returned to it, the first thing he did was to review the scanner box he had left on the dresser's top. The unit had detected no monitoring devices in the room, nor unauthorized visits during his absence. He had expected neither, but another lesson that life had taught his was to be certain, whenever possible. He clicked the scanner off, smiled tightly, then knelt to slide his weapons case from its temporary home under the bed.

The case and what it held constituted one of the few compromises he had made during his current scheme, and ranked among the very little he had brought forward from his old life to his new one. His years before becoming Redling had been profitable ones, filled with challenge and adventure, but he had set most of that aside for the nonce. He had left behind his name and his face and his history, but not the tools of his trade, even though they were clues that pointed to the man he had once been.

The case was a good one, secure and custom made, and much too expensive for a man of the real Navis Redling's hard-scrabble means and pedestrian tastes. Beneath the battered plastic exterior, its body was crafted from collapsed-molecule steel, as dense and tough as a starship's hull. A paired grav unit and inertial compensator inside the case worked together to shoulder a substantial portion of its mass, but the remainder was still too heavy for most people to lift comfortably. Redling pulled it out and placed it on the hotel bed's mattress in one easy motion.

Only his current fingerprints would open the case. He pressed his thumbs against the appropriate sensitized pressure points, waited a second for the seal to disengage, then swung back the case's top. He smiled again as he beheld the contents, and then he began to inventory and inspect them methodically.

First came the laser pistol and rifle, a matched pair he had appropriated from an unwary Imperial Security Officer during a raid on a pirate base in Ethilion's outer asteroid ring. The pirates' leader had been a friend of the man who now wore Navis Redling's face, but not a business associate; the Security Officer had made the mistake of assuming the contrary, and paid dearly for the misapprehension. The weapons were Imperial issue and looked it, but Redling had spent considerable credits having their interior electronics upgraded. The pistol, especially, was much more powerful than it had been when the overconfident agent had pointed it in his direction. The external battery packs for both weapons rested in nearby compartments, trickle-charged by the same fuel cell that drove the grav unit. Redling took a moment to check power levels and run a diagnostics check, and then proceeded to the projectile weapons.

He liked them better than the energy weapons, as a general rule. He had been in enough scrapes to earn a sincere appreciation of reliable tools, and of devices he could maintain and repair personally. Projectile weapons, pistols and rifles alike, fell into that category.

First came the magnum revolver, a smoothly curved and contoured handful of steel that could spit seven rounds on a single reload, each bullet ten millimeters in diameter. Seven shots was far fewer than the laser pistol could muster on a charge, but more than he was likely to need in any single encounter. Next to the pistol was a compact submachine gun, with a collapsible stock that folded to reduce the gun's overall length by nearly half. In another recess near the guns' niches were twenty packages of ten-millimeter ammunition, fifty shells each, manufactured by experts to his personal specifications. The submachine gun was chambered and bored to accept the same rounds as the pistol, but they weren't a matching set. Whereas Redling had bought the long gun on Carter's World, the sidearm had been a gift. It had come with an oath of undying gratitude from one Milos Grogan, the Imperial Governor of the Mariposa System. Redling supposed that Grogan had, by now, forgotten the incident completely, as governors had a way of doing.

Mariposa was a confederation of twenty industrial-ized worlds that lay somewhat closer to the Imperium's heart—and closer to the Imperium government's heart, too. Five standard years before, while pursuing certain goals of his own, Redling had encountered the gover-nor's runaway daughter. He had retrieved her from renegade data smugglers, reprieved her from the pro-verbial fate worse than death, and harvested a healthy reward for his work. More than once since those days, Redling had wondered just how effusive the governor would have been had the silly fop realized how many different warrants bore Redling's real name or other aliases, or how little the daughter had minded her stay with the outlaws.

Redling really couldn't blame her for that. He had felt a certain kinship with the data smugglers, him-self—and had done business with them since, under another name, while wearing another face. That was the way of his life, drifting from world to world, from one identity to another, moving wherever the twin siren songs of money and adventure called him. It was easi-er to lead such a life here, in the Imperium's borders, where civilization's interlocking matrix of law and cus-tom were slightly less constricting.

Such considerations didn't really matter right now, of course. The revolver he held did. It was a good one, precisely the sort of top-shelf item that the Imperium's higher-ranking toadies esteemed as badges of office, without ever appreciating their values as weapons. To Redling's certain knowledge, Governor Grogan had never fired a single shot from the weapon's precisely machined barrel, and would have recoiled in cultured distaste at any suggestion that he do so. Redling was all too familiar with that kind of mindset. He had encountered it a thousand times on a hundred worlds—a love of symbolism and power, paired with a blissful ignorance of the way life should be lived. That kind of thinking was why Grogan's daughter had run away in the first place. Redling half-hoped that she had fled his paternal embrace again since. Whether she had or not, he had the gun, and, more importantly, the other reward that Grogan had offered—one million standard credits, tucked neatly away in one of Redling's many secret accounts.

Padded sheaths lined the case's lid. They held knives of various sizes, shapes, and compositions. Redling inspected each carefully, to verify its keenness, and then selected one for the evening's use. He settled on a spring-knife with a plastic blade, razor-keen but transparent to scanners, and tucked it inside his left tunic sleeve. A moment later he peeled the five miniature blades from his left hand's fingertips. There were plastic, too, as invisible to the naked eye as to most technology. Glued to his nails, they had been more than sufficient to cow the bovine Tithe, but tonight's business called for slightly sterner measures, albeit still discreet ones. He wasn't expecting trouble, but if it came, it would not come from anyone as clumsy and ineffectual as Tithe.

Another compartment held a half-dozen pieces of electronic apparatus—scanners, coms, and a few other carefully chosen items that had come in handy from time to time in his adventurous life. He pulled the com unit from his wrist and traded it for another, more expensive personal communicator. The one he had worn to the junkman's nest had belonged to the real

Redling, until a few months before, and there had been the small chance that Tithe would recognize it. That wouldn't be an issue for the remainder of the evening, so he donned another it its place, a gleaming unit that fit his wrist as if custom-built to ride there—which was, in fact, the precise truth. He snapped the buckle shut, and the com unit instantly came to life. Redling smiled, and pressed one of the gadget's keys.

"Front," a bored voice said from his wrist.

"This is Redling, on five."

There was a brief pause, apparently to allow the clerk to review his guest log. When the com unit spoke again, the man's voice sounded suddenly more attentive. "Yes, sir! Service needed?"

"Just directions," Redling responded. The room came with a com, too, but he preferred using his own equipment, whenever possible. "Whereabouts can a respectable traveller find a decent place to eat, and maybe make a few acquaintances?"

"Um." Another pause, as the attendant estimated how much tariff the market would bear. "That would be Og's Palace of Otherworldy Delights, two blocks over. I can call a ground car, if you want, or plot you a track."

"Not necessary," Redling responded. He had seen Og's during the ride in from the spaceport. It looked to him like an overpriced tourist trap, not that this world was likely to attract many tourists. "How about a less than respectable spacer, just looking to do a bit of business? Where would *he* go?"

This time, the response came instantly, born of casual familiarity. "You're looking for fun? Try Blith's, over on Star Street. Anything you can't find there, you won't find anywhere else, either."

"Star Street it is, then," Redling said. He thanked the other man and broke the connection. After a moment's thought, he drew a body pistol from another of the trunk's recesses. There were no memories or anecdotes attached to this gun; it was big enough to be lethal, and cheap enough to be disposable, which suited his purposes for the evening. He stowed the gun beneath his tunic, reactivated the scanner, and headed for the door.

The town of Farport was as unexceptional as its name. The settlement was laid out like countless other spaceport towns on countless other planets. It was only seventy or so standard years old, young enough that the bare bones of its functional design were still evident, as yet unmasked by softening, "civilizing" influences, such as churches, schools, slums, and such. The spaceport proper lay some fifty kilometers to the east. That was not as close as some would like it, but too close for Redling's tastes. He had been on Ekton, one of the core worlds, when a Patrol Cruiser's guidance systems had failed, ten standard years before. That was when two hundred-plus tons of hull and cargo had come down, screaming and burning, in the heart of that planet's capital city, killing thousands and, of nearly equal concern to Redling, interfering with certain business initiatives of his own. The crashing craft had missed its designated landing site by much less than the fifty kilometers that stretched between Farport's blast apron and its city limits.

Unfortunately, this Farport was still more or less a frontier world, and economy and safety were only rarely companions on the frontier. Redling had long since become inured to situations where pragmatism took precedence over prudence, so he was able to put such considerations from his mind as he ambled along the dozen or so blocks to the tavern on Star Street.

Every planet with a spaceport had a Star Street, whether by that name or another. Star Street was where the spacers went when they weren't in space anymore. Scattered across the cosmos, living on literally thousands of different worlds that spun beneath different suns, humanity had made many adaptations to various environs, but certain characteristics remained constant to all races: the need to eat and sleep, the desire for companionship and entertainment and information. Star Street was where cheap lodging and cheap food could be found, both suitable for denizens from hundreds of different planets. Travellers could exchange messages and news, and search, most likely without success, for news of any home they might still care to claim. Deals could be cut and contracts signed—whether written contracts or quiet handshake deals, backed by powers more binding than any jurisdiction's law. On more heavily trafficked worlds, Star Street would be the Registry Hall's address, where spacers could pay their guild dues and taxes, file their credentials, and be tried by courts of their peers for regulatory violations. Many minor worlds, however, and worlds with little interstellar commerce, found themselves with too little demand to support a Registry Hall. Instead, business was done in more informal venues.

Places like Blith's Tavern.

Blith's was at the end of a fairly narrow alley that stretched between a cheap inn and what was probably a bordello—prime real estate for a Star Street tavern. A totally hairless man more than two meters tall and nearly as wide stood next to the place's doorway, obviously on guard duty. He appeared to be girderlike bones and slabs of muscle, and nothing else—likely the product of a heavy-gravity world, where the human genome had compromised with the local circumstances and built out so that it could build up. He wore a green leather vest, leggings, and boots. A large, open sack of similar leather rested on a shelf at his side. The big man looked sleepily at Redling as he approached, and then, suddenly, he didn't look sleepy anymore.

"You're armed," the gatekeeper said. His rumbling voice cut though the pounding music that seeped out through the door behind him.

"People tell me that all the time," Redling said. "No matter where I go, they say it. I must bear a really remarkable resemblance to this fellow Armed." He didn't try to walk past the big man, though.

"Nuh," the gatekeeper said.

"Oh no, not you, too," Redling responded.

The guard looked at him quizzically, as if about to ask a question; then he apparently thought better of it. "You got a weapon," he said.

"Yes," Redling said, positively beaming. "Something we can agree on."

"No weapons," the guard said. "Not tonight, anyhow. Good crowd inside, and good money, and the barkeep wants them coming back for more." He raised one broad hand. It had had five fingers, but only three had nails; then even those three were lost from sight as he opened the hand and extended it, palm up.

Redling placed a local currency twelve-credit bill in it.

"Nuh," the big man repeated, but he tucked the

money in his vest's outer pocket before extending his hand again. "Gimme."

Redling paused and made a great show of considering the demand. While he pondered, the music faded, and muffled chatter took its place. He grinned, and shrugged, and drew the body pistol from beneath his tunic and handed it to the gatekeeper.

"You can come back for it later," the big man said. He dropped the gun in his sack, then extended his giant hand again. "That, and the other one."

Redling grinned again, but he didn't move.

The giant grunted, and stepped closer. "You're still carrying," he said. "I can tell. Gimme."

"Come on, fellow," Redling said. "You've done your job; now let me pass."

"Nuh. You've got a second piece. I know your kind."

"I know your kind, too," Redling said. He purred the words. "A man your size can let his girth do the work for him. A man your size, living on a midgrav world, probably doesn't have to do much fighting."

On the giant's face, the hairless patches of skin that would have been eyebrows on another man rose quizzically.

Redling continued: "Even in a town as cosmopolitan as this, you're hardly likely ever to chance upon someone who realizes just how slow that much muscle and bone can make you. Why, I'd bet that a man half your size who knew what he was doing could take you down—certainly, it wouldn't take a man any bigger than me." He grinned, but it was a smile that was suddenly anything but amiable. "If it's the right man."

The big man made another grunting noise, an angry

one this time and stepped closer. Redling stepped closer too, then back, moving with the liquid speed and silence of a shadow. He had played this game many times before. As he took the first step, he brought both hands forward, touched one to the bouncer's vest, and the other into the open sack at his side. They did not seem to pause in either place, not even for the briefest of instants, before he drew them back again, even as he took his second step, backwards. By the time Redling completed his second step, the hairless giant was a quarter of the way through his first, rocking forward and closer to the smaller man. He was still in midstride when the heel of Redling's left foot found the arch of the big Man's right one and smashed into it, hard. There was a flat, dry sound, the kind of noise breaking pottery makes. The traveller followed through on his kick, smashing the target foot down to the pavement, and then Redling used the force of his blow to drive his own body further back.

"See?" he said, not even breathing hard. "Slow."

The bouncer limped forward again. He extended his arms and reached for Redling, but the smaller man easily evaded his embrace.

"The problem with goobs like you is that you won't learn, but you're willing to teach," Redling said. "You won't learn that I can outfight you, but you're willing to teach the same fact to anyone who watched you try to do the dance."

The big man paused, a sudden glimmer of concern in his deep-set eyes. Behind Redling, there were the sounds of more patrons—footsteps and voices, both getting louder. The big man's thought processes were evident on his brutish features. It simply wouldn't do to be seen trying unsuccessfully to subdue a man who was so much smaller, and yet, that seemed to be precisely what was about to occur.

"Good evening, my man!" Redling said loudly, playing a part for the benefit of his new audience. He tried to make it sound as if he'd just arrived. "Wine, women, and song inside, I assume?" He shot a pointed gaze at the bouncer.

"Wine we got, an' song," the other man said, looking confused and then annoyed. "Women are the next door over." He stared balefully at Redling, suddenly aware of the role he was supposed to play. His audience was getting closer. "You got to check your weapons though."

"Of course, of course," Redling said, with mock sincerity. His left hand held his body pistol again, the same one he had taken from his weapons case, then taken again from the satchel at the bouncer's side. He extended. "And a claim check?"

"Y' don't need one," the giant said. He took the gun. "I'll remember you."

"I'm sure you will, chum," Redling purred. His right hand made a movement so fast that it seemed slow, and the same twelve-credit bill as before unfolded with a crisp snap, an inch from the other's eyes. "Here you are, my good man, something for your troubles."

The big man took the money again and pocketed it again, then nodded. He stepped aside to allow Redling to pass. "Enjoy the evening," he muttered, already turning to face the newcomers. "But don't forget to pick up your piece on the way out. I'll be looking for you."

"I'm sure you will," Redling said over his shoulder as he drifted inside.

Blith's was bigger on the inside than it looked on the outside, a vaulted hall framed in dark native timber, but built of durable synthstone slabs. Luminescent strips traced bright lines along some of the support beams and angled walls, casting omnidirectional light to clearly define the obstacle course of broad tables, benches, and chairs, but little enough light that there were still pockets of shadows.

The place's clientele was entirely human, at least as far as Redling could see, and the air was filled with chatter in a dozen or more languages. At one end of the tavern's main hall was a low stage littered with unattended drums and stringed instruments, apparently the source of the din he had heard earlier; now, other, softer music bubbled out of ceiling speakers. Running along the far wall were a bar and stools, and beyond them, a porcine fellow served drinks to his motley assortment of patrons.

To Redling's immediate left, on a second, smaller stage, a nearly naked woman with blue skin danced sinuously to the strains of the canned music. Presumably, she was an employee and not a patron. Redling smiled at her, winked. He had retrieved his twelve-credit note a second time from the hulk outside; now, he deposited it at the woman's feet. She smiled and leaned down to pick up the money, and the silken fringe of her golden mane slid along his forehead as she returned to her dance. Redling stepped past her, heading for the bar. He was looking for drink and information and business, in that order.

It didn't take him long to find them. A minute after

he entered, he was sipping a scant measure of what purported to be Mariposa brandy and chatting desultorily with a pinch-featured man named Koth, who claimed to be a fully qualified navigator, just in from Ekton and looking for work. Unfortunately, someone had stolen his credentials, and since there was no Registry Hall on this backwater world, well, he was sure a man of Redling's obvious discernment would understand—

Three minutes after that, still working on the same brandy, he chatted with one Dawn F'Ral, a handsome, strong-featured woman who was, in fact, from Ekton—she had the papers to prove it—and who had come to Farworld as an apprentice engineer on the *Waltzing Spider*. That was a luxury liner that hailed from the Red Nebula. Ordinarily, such a vessel would not pause, even briefly, at a port as rural as Farworld. However, there had been trouble between her and the captain and a passenger, and a blown Jump Drive coil had offered a convenient resolution to the problem— convenient for the ship captain, at least. Following emergency repairs on Farworld, Dawn had found herself cut from the crew and put ashore with a healthy severance payment. That money had not lasted long at the starport city's inflated prices. Now, Dawn wanted desperately to secure transportation to a more trafficked section of the galaxy, and would accept any billet for which Redling thought her qualified. She was still a few courses shy of full certification in Jump Drive technology, but she knew all of the essentials. Certainly, she knew enough to handle a Far Trader's engines, especially if that Far Trader was just a Cadmus. If Redling could just overlook or ignore certain piffling requirements, she was certain that—

Ten minutes later, a beefy fellow with mismatched eyes and a jagged tracing of scars on his forehead that suggested cranial implant surgery gone wrong spoke urgently to Redling about ten small crates, five kilos each. He needed them taken from a nearby warehouse and to some place called Keppleman's Folly. The beauty of the situation, the scarred man explained eagerly, was that the mood prions in those crates weren't even illegal in most jurisdictions. He claimed that the pseudolife, subviral particles were too new for legislators to regulate. He had been trying to arrange transport for weeks. The local connections were big on promises, but that fat pig Tithe wanted too big a cut for his services. Surely Redling—

Gustylyu was next, a retired businessman whose catlike attributes marked him as one of the Aslan, a nonhuman race whose members moved freely through the Imperium. The Aslan were leonoids, descended from four-legged carnivores and vaguely resembling the lions of old Earth. Gustylyu was perhaps a head taller than Redling and far more heavily muscled, and he moved with a liquid grace that made the blue-skinned dancer seem almost clumsy. The Aslan were a tribal race, driven by genetic imperatives to claim new territories, and organized according to pride, clan, and tribe. Redling had to wonder if Gustylyu was his people's only representative on Farworld, but he knew better than to ask; the Aslan were notoriously hostile to questions they viewed as inappropriate. Which questions might those be? There was no way that any human could tell.

Whatever his status, or his reason for being so far from home, Gustylyu wanted desperately to leave the frontier world. Redling didn't inquire into that, either, and Gustylyu didn't offer an explanation—but he offered money, and plenty of it. Unfortunately, he did not have the requisite sum with him, but if Redling could only wait until—

None of the supplicants knew Redling personally, or knew the man they thought he was, but they all knew about him—at least as much as they needed. The word was out that he had a starship, that he was looking for a crew and that he had space for available for cargo and passengers alike. News and rumor moved faster on planets like Farworld and in places like Blith's than light did in normal space. Information, good and bad alike, dispersed through the crowd the way oil spread across water, but countless times more swiftly. Perhaps a hundred thousand men and women presently resided on this particular Farworld. Apparently, at least half that number wanted very much to go somewhere else, to leave behind a world they called a "backwater abscess" or "rural way station" or "pleasant but unpromising little place." Most of them didn't care where they went, as long as it was to someplace busier and more heavily trafficked, and offered to serve as a stepping-stone on the way to a more desirable world.

Redling could take his pick, and he did. In only a few hours, he had found four potential crewmembers to his liking. The first was the woman, Dawn, who was almost qualified to serve as ship engineer and more than qualified to serve as medical officer. Helicron Daas, a bluff and hearty local kid, eager to ship out for the first time, was ready to accept a reduced salary, but had the proper certifications for navigation duty— earned from local tutors, and good enough for Redling's purposes. Pikk Thyller was a dusky giant who had been the gunnery officer on a Free Trader whose drive had suffered catastrophic failure almost immediately upon planetfall. Now, what was left of that ship languished in Tithe's care, while Thyller looked for a way off the world—a way that Redling could provide. That same craft appeared on the résumé of one Catra En'Elt'En, a stocky man from Draen whose skills ranged from cookery to environmental science, with many stops in between. He had served on Imperial Navy ships and on private vessels, before the vagaries of travel had brought him to Farworld. He was looking for work, and Redling had it for him.

It was a buyer's market; Redling was the only spacer working this particular crowd tonight, or the only spacer with billets and cargo space available.

As had been the habit in each of his lives, Redling based his selections less on credentials, certifications, and résumés than on instinct and empathy. Both had served him well any number of times, and he had learned to trust them. An existence as adventurous as his was filled with risk and gambling, and he had long since given up regarding anything as definite or reliable—credentials and certifications included. He applied very much the same principles to judging prospective cargo and passengers—he took what and who he liked and didn't bother with anything or anyone he didn't, no matter how much money was waved in his direction. He made agreements and reviewed proffered documents and shook hands. All the while, the real Navis Redling's memories, implanted inside his skull, muttered in protest as established techniques and priorities fell by the wayside. He ignored the borrowed perspective and went about his business with a distant grin; this life was his life now.

He had certainly paid enough for it.

"My husband says that you owe him a lot of money. He says he'll have you killed if you don't give it to him soon," a new voice whispered in his ear. The announcement, delivered in a slippery contralto, came from his left, as Redling concluded business with a (literally) bug-eyed man on his right.

"Do tell," he drawled, turning to face the new speaker. The words had come from the blue-skinned dancer, dressed now in a belted robe that was surprisingly effective at hiding her charms. She had perched on the stool next to him and was gazing at him with an expression midway between bemused and speculative. "Silly me. I didn't even know you were married," Redling continued. "Who's the lucky man? I guess this means I don't get to buy you a drink."

The woman shook her head, making blonde hair ripple and flow. He could see now that her skin hue was a dye job, but the face under it seemed to be her own—elfin features, limpid green eyes, strong white teeth that were set now in a mocking smile. "I don't think that would be wise," she said. "You're in enough trouble already."

Redling smiled, too, but he was suddenly glad for the reassuring presence of the tapered blade hidden in his left sleeve. "I've been in trouble before," he said, "but never enough." He gestured at the porcine barkeep. "Another for me, and one for the lady."

"Y'wanna brandy, Sascha?" asked the bartender.

The dancer shook her head. "No."

"Two of them," Redling ordered. He put some more money on the counter.

"Something doesn't quite add up, Redling," Sascha said. "You don't look to me like the 'phorinol has rotted your brain away completely, but I might be wrong. I've been watching you—"

"Funny. I can say the same thing," Redling interrupted, lying. He had scarcely noticed the blue woman after his first, brief encounter with her. His attentions had been directed toward more financial matters.

She continued as if he had not spoken. "—watching you conduct business, and you seemed to have your wits about you. I didn't even realize who you were at first; you seemed too competent. And you look in pretty good shape for a guy my sources say had a ten-crystal-a-day habit a year ago. They must do good work on Carter's World." She turned and stared at him, her previous expression giving way to contempt. "It came as quite a surprise when word got out that you were back. I can't figure out how anyone, even a spazzed-out crystal head, would be stupid enough to come back to a planet where he owed more than ten megacredits to a man like my husband."

While she spoke the barkeep had set two glasses of amber liquid on the counter between them, and Redling had lifted his to take a sip. Now, he felt the brandy try to escape through his nose as he controlled his reaction to the woman's words. Ten megacredits was a tidy bit of money, only slightly less than half what he had paid the real Navis Redling for the *Gateway* and all the other trappings of this new life—nearly a third of what a Cadmus Far Trader would cost new. That sum had been about as much as he wanted to spend on this particular caper, and the woman's quiet announcement of a new and enormous liability wasn't good news.

Redling took a quick look through his purchased memories, trying to find some stray datum that would support or undermine Sascha's claim. He tried and he failed—but that didn't mean anything. The technology that had given him his counterpart's memories wasn't perfect, and he couldn't reasonably expect to have the other man's entire life at his beck and call. Whoever Sascha was, the real Navis Redling had provided no remembrance of ever meeting her.

"Ten million credits?" he said softly. The sum didn't sound any better when expressed that way, but he had wanted to try, anyway. It was a lot of money, not beyond his means, but certainly beyond the means of the role he was now playing.

Sascha nodded. She shrugged, picked up her brandy, and drained it. "It wasn't ten when you left, but it is now," she said. "Penalties and stupidity fees, mostly. And interest. Blork is very fond of compound interest." Her voice took on a poisonous sweetness. "He likes compound fractures, too; at least when they happen to someone else."

Blork. Alarms rang inside Redling's head. The name meant something to him. What? Who was Blork? Once more, another man's memories slithered through Redling's brain, slippery and swift, like foreign fish swimming in familiar waters. He knew that name—but not from experience.

At least, not from his own personal experience.

Redling—the real Redling—might not have recognized Sascha, but he certainly knew Blork, knew who he was and what he wanted. Now, a face that his own eyes had never seen suddenly drifted up from Redling's purchased memories. It brought with it other memories, images of crystals, metallic and shimmering green, that some alien part of his mind found hypnotically attractive. He knew what it was—Euphorinol, in its condensed crystalline form. A single gram of the drug was enough to short circuit the pleasure centers of the human brain for an hour. Double that amount, and the brain would access memories and create hallucinations to justify the near-orgasmic ecstasy washing through it. Triple the dosage, at least for anyone with even a smidgen of psionic potential, and the drugged brain would access other people's memories, too, then weave them into elaborate collages of sensation and emotion. By every account, it was the meanest drug on record, as addictive as air and always leaving its users crying for more. The man who was now Navis Redling had tried a lot of things in his life, but never Euphorinol; he was smarter than that.

The same couldn't be said of his predecessor in this life, however. That man had tried Euphorinol, and soon found that he wanted more—lots more, so much more that he could never have enough. The real Navis Redling was a wizened little spider of a man now, wire-thin and wracked with spasmodic tics, choking out what was left of his life in a rehab colony on Carter's World. How he had ended up there remained unclear. His present lot in life was that of a desperate fugitive from debtors who was cut off from his chief asset in life, the *Gateway*. He had been a charity case, without the means to buy even the most basic of medical care. Then, one day, the man Tithe and Sascha both justifiably referred to as a spazzed-out crystal head had looked up from his hospital bed to see a smirking stranger standing over him, a stranger who offered a way out of the horror his life had become. The stranger had offered to buy his ship, his life and memories, and more—

His history.

His troubles.

His debts.

His enemies.

Suddenly, the world looked a bit less amusing, and became a place that was, if not altogether grim, then at least busily taking steps in that general direction. Redling had anticipated some difficulties in his new life, but nothing quite on the scale of ten megacredits. There had been limits on his ability to research such matters, of course. That was one of the chief problems with interstellar commerce in general—in a universe where the speed of communication was limited by the speed of transportation, doing research on both ends of a deal was nearly impossible. Such concerns didn't matter right now, however; the matter at hand did. He pushed the other man's memories from his mind and made himself smile. There would be time to fret later.

"So *you're* Mrs. Blork?" he said. "Not quite what I would have expected. Old Blork has come up in the world. Crystal peddling must pay well."

She glared at him. "Their customers sure don't," she said tartly.

"So why are you here?" Redling asked. He was honestly curious. "To offer a deal? A way out?"

She shook her head. "I'm here to tell you that my husband says you owe him a lot of money," she said, "and he's going to kill you if you don't give it to him soon. And he'll kill you if you try to slip offworld again."

"Well, you're right about one thing," Redling said. "Ten megacredits *is* a lot of money."

Sascha smiled sweetly at him again. "Eleven megacredits is more, and that's what you owe, come midnight," she said. "Twelve, the midnight after that. Now that you're back on planet, you qualify for the accelerated rate." She set down the glass she had been toying with, then laid the twelve-credit note on the bar and gestured for the attendant to keep the change. "I pay for my own drinks," she told Redling. "Now, excuse me, my next set is about to start." She let her body flow from the barstool and undulated her way back to the stage.

Redling watched her go, but he was already thinking about other things.

CHAPTER TWO

Even prior to making the acquaintance of the remarkable Mrs. Blork, Redling had not intended to stay very long on Farworld. He had said as much to Dawn and Helicron and the rest—they had to be ready to leave, and soon, and he had a corresponding obligation to them to embark in a timely manner. Redling's plans were to stay planetside for another week at the most, and there was much to be done in that time.

There was a ship to ready. The *Gateway* had sat, unused, in a storage bay near Farport's blast apron for more than a standard year. Her power plant was cold, her Jump Drive long since out of calibration. Redling directed Dawn to tend to those concerns, with some assistance from Helicron. Once underway, the two would need to work together closely, and be intimately familiar with the *Gateway*'s workings, and the prep would give them a start on both. The ship's computers needed upgrades and its add-on meson cannons needed a complete overhaul. Redling set Pikk to overseeing those tasks, with worker services brokered through Tithe's organizations. Catra, he sent to market, to lay in complete supplies for the coming voyage into space. All four crewmembers took to their assignments eagerly; working for Redling meant that they were working for money again, whether on the surface of one world, or in the gulf between two.

There was cargo space to sell. Farport saw enough

interstellar business that someone who was willing to settle for many small consignments rather than one large shipment—someone like Redling—would easily find enough to fill his hull. Redling's personal agenda called for working the general direction of the Red Nebula; he let the bills of lading determine the *Gateway*'s specific intervening itinerary, as long as those bills didn't feature destinations too far off his chosen track. Tithe handled most of the bookings, for a commission that was surpisingly reasonable, perhaps because freight rates and tariffs on most goods were set by Imperium decree and aggressively enforced. Redling elected to stick with relatively respectable stuff for the *Gateway*'s hold—brandy, exotic grains, business correspondence, and the like.

He would take no contraband, despite Tithe's not-so-subtle overtures. Those consignments that were illegal or looked like they might be, he declined absolutely. The mood prions that the man with mismatched eyes was so eager to ship would have to remain on Farworld, at least for now. He had no particular objection to smuggling in principle, but not this time out. There was no point in attracting unnecessary attention from the authorities.

In fact, a big part of Redling's general outlook on life was that there was *never* much point in attracting attention from the authorities.

There were passengers to book. Redling took a more active hand here, personally interviewing potential travellers before allowing them to book passage. Space was at a premium on the *Gateway*. Far Traders were small ships, relatively speaking; their design and construction worked toward three goals: speed, capacity, and economy. Unfortunately, those goals lay in differing directions, to one degree or another, and so the basic design was an essay in compromise.

The end result of the compromise was that the *Gateway* had space only for six Middle or High passengers, though Redling thought that anyone expecting genuine High passage on such a scruffy tub was doomed to disappointment. In fairly short order, Tithe managed to broker four Middle berths to passengers that Redling found acceptable. In theory, fully twenty individuals could book Low passage in the craft; Redling declined to sell even a single such billet. That stance prompted anguished squawks from Tithe, who knew that Low berths meant high profit. He stood to earn a commission on each space sold. Redling was adamant in his refusal, however.

He had his reasons, and they were good ones. Once, and only once, he had travelled Low. That had been in his youth, when he was desperate to leave the world of his birth, a planet so obscure that he had long since forgotten its name. After many long weeks of dreamless sleep, the boy who would one day be Navis Redling had awakened to find himself the only survivor of fourteen Low riders. The other men and women were all dead, the victims of a failed hibernation support system. Since then, he would have nothing to do with Low travel, whether to partake or provide.

Now, he directed Tithe to tear out the hibernation pods, dispose of them, and reconfigure the space to hold more cargo. The directive assuaged the fat junkman's anger over missed opportunity by providing him with an ample, windfall profit from reselling the equipment.

Redling didn't really care. He wasn't overly concerned about making the trip profitable. His real business was on a world in the Red Nebula, involving some cached artifacts based on Droyne technology and held by religious zealots. He had spent several years piecing together clues and hints of that mysterious treasure trove, which was rumored to be worth credits beyond reckoning. Even if that specific trove proved to be nonexistent (and such things often did), he was certain that other opportunities would make themselves available to him.

For now, however, the Redling subterfuge was a convenient way to go about his business with only minimal interference from the so-called authorities. He knew from bitter experience how many of the self-righteous were all too eager to punish independent entrepreneurs such as he. Of course, most were even more eager to execute the many warrants and earn the many rewards that his exploits had prompted. There were limits to his largesse, but he was quite willing to spend a bit of money on buying a lower profile.

There was always more money to be had, after all, at least for one who knew how to make it.

Besides, there were other matters to concern him. Many interesting things happened during the week that stretched between his interview with Tithe and his intended launch date.

One Wonday, two armed men braced him in an alley and threatened him with laser pistols and hammers. They attempted to use their disparate tools to demonstrate just how eager Blork was to pursue his claim on any and all monies in Redling's possession. After convincing the hapless duo of their folly, Redling sent one back to his masters, to report the failure. The other assailant he left sprawled unconscious on the alley floor behind Og's, next to a waste disposal unit.

On Tuday, the giant bouncer from Blith's dropped by Redling's hotel. The big man, whose name was Eddie, wanted to return the checked body pistol that Redling had left behind after his visit to the tavern. Off-duty, Eddie proved to be an amiable sort, eager to learn a bit more about the gliding step maneuver Redling had used on him. The two men enjoyed a casual lunch together, during which Eddie made an interesting comment.

"There's a lot of chatter out about you on the street," the giant said. He was munching on a fried piece of some kind of bird purchased at Redling's expense. "Money talk, mostly."

"Oh?"

"Yeah. And Sascha asked me what I knew about you. I told her I didn't know anything."

"That was considerate of you," Redling responded. He wondered how much of a bribe Eddie would request for the service.

The giant shrugged. "Hey, just being honest," he responded. "But I know that if I were you, I'd watch my back." Eddie paused, as if deciding just what to say, and how. "I'd watch out for fat men, too. A lot of those guys, they aren't popular, but that doesn't mean they don't have friends."

"I see," responded Redling, not sure that he did. The intent of the other man's words was obvious, though, and he would have been hard-pressed to disagree. Tithe wasn't exactly his favorite person. He nodded. "Thanks, Eddie. I'll watch out."

"Yeah, I figure you can take care of yourself, but we're talking a lot of money here."

"We are?" Redling asked, but he was able to get no substantive response from his dining companion.

On Thirday, the com unit he wore on his wrist began buzzing, using an alternate, secure access ID he had reserved for personal business. Only a select few on Farworld were supposed to have that number, but none of them responded when he answered. Instead, the dead hum of a carrier wave reached his ears. This happened at precise fourteen-minute intervals for the remainder of the day, until the call at midnight, when a familiar voice responded to his irritated, "Hello?"

"Fourteen million, Redling," a woman chirped. A second passed, and then, so did midnight. "Fifteen million, now," she continued.

"Hello, Sascha," Redling said easily. "Shouldn't you be on stage?"

"It's my night off," she said. "I wanted to spend this part of it with you." She laughed then, an acid giggle that went a long way toward balancing out her remembered charms. "It's not like we'll have many more opportunities." She laughed again, and broke the connection.

On Forday evening, Redling dealt with another of Blork's goons. This one came with a face he knew. Redling was ambling along a secluded side street that stretched between Star Street and his hotel when two meters of steel-spring muscle surged silently at him from the shadows. One giant hand lashed out and a set of needle-sharp claws raced toward his face.

Redling dropped back and down to one knee just in time to avoid nearly all of the sudden attack. Four thin lines, red and stinging, traced a short path along his left cheek even as he ducked and rolled from the path of his attacker. When he came to his feet again, he was holding today's knife. This one had a surgical steel blade and a jeweled hilt. It had been a gift, too, but Redling could not remember from whom.

"Hello, Gustylyu," Redling said. The brief, almost subliminal glimpse he had taken at his attacker had been enough for recognition. Besides, there couldn't be very many Aslan on Farworld; they tended to travel in packs. "Still looking for transit?" The lion-man's only reply was to leap at him again. The legs of the "retired businessman" were proportionally longer than a human's legs and much more heavily muscled. Those muscles were more efficient, too, strong enough to give the Aslan speed and power that were surprising for one of his bulk. The force of the lion-man's leap was great enough to lift Gustylyu bodily from the dirty pavement and send him flying in Redling's direction.

Redling dodged again, this time ducking low enough to let the Aslan pass above him. That was when Redling made his move. He brought the butt of his knife's hilt up and slammed it, hard, against the knob of bone behind Gustylyu's ear. There was a popping sound, a noise like a full bottle breaking, and the Aslan made a growl of pain as he came to ground again.

"There's no need to do it this way, Gustylyu," Redling said. By now, he had drawn his magnum pistol, too, and thumbed back its hammer. "We can still talk." His words were false; he knew too much about the Aslan and their nature to think that one would ever drop a fight at this stage.

The lion-man growled. He balanced on the balls of

his sandal-clad feet and bent his legs again, tensing their long muscles. "Put away the gun, and we'll talk," he said. He blinked feline eyes at Redling. The pupil of the left one was big now and getting bigger; Redling's skull-cracking blow had produced some effect, but not enough to stop the assailant. "You can keep the knife."

"That's mighty generous of you," Redling said, "But—"

Instead of leaping, Gustylyu brought his left leg in a lightning kick towards Redling's legs, hard enough to break either or both.

Redling danced backwards and dodged again, though not without effort. The fingers of his left hand twisted and his left arm moved the way a snake's body moves when it strikes. The knife he held left his hand and found a new home below Gustylyu's right kneecap. It sank into the muscle and bone it found there with a meaty thumping sound, and then came to a vibrating halt.

This time, the lion-man made no sound of pain, but he staggered backward and fell against a supporting wall. His left eye, plainly visible in the light from a nearby street lamp, looked worse now, but his right one followed Redling's every move.

"—but I'll let you have it, instead," Redling continued. He was breathing more quickly now, from a combination of physical effort and emotional tension, and the cuts on his borrowed face had become wider as the wounds opened slightly. He pointed with the gun. "I'll keep this."

Gustylyu glared at him. The knife was imbedded in the Aslan's leg deeply enough that only its hilt was visible. Gustylyu bent slightly and reached for the weapon's handle.

"No," Redling said. He gestured with his pistol. "None of that. Just tell me why you're doing this. It certainly won't get you a berth on the *Gateway*." He had declined to sell the Aslan passage, in part because the lion-man had lacked the funds and in part because Redling didn't like him. Now, despite the situation, Redling grinned slightly; it was always good to see that his gut instinct had been right.

It almost always was, of course.

"Money," Gustylyu said. He drew his hand away from the embedded dagger. "Bounty." His words were barely recognizable as such, and came close to being growls.

"Bounty?" Redling asked, but he knew the answer. "More of Blork's shenanigans, I assume."

Gustylyu's reply was to roar and leap again—or rather, pounce. The damage that Redling had inflicted on his leg wasn't enough to keep it from doing its job. The Aslan's long, muscular arms moved in mirror-image arcs, and the claws of both hands came racing towards his target's throat.

Again, Redling dropped back. As he did, his right wrist bent and his right hand twisted, bringing the muzzle of his gun to bear on the underside of Gustylyu's jaw. He pulled his index finger back, and the weapon's trigger came with it.

The gun roared now, and so did Gustylyu—but this was a death cry, a final paroxysm of lung and larynx as a ten-millimeter bullet crashed through his brain. The cry was followed by another kind of thunder as his body fell to the dirty pavement, even as Redling nimbly stepped to one side to avoid being pinned by him.

For a long moment, Redling stood silently over his

assailant's remains, taking one deep breath after another and willing the tensed muscles of his body to relax. Then, calm again, he retrieved his knife, cleaned it, and returned it to its hiding place. A pouch at his belt yielded a small mirror, and he used it to inspect the damage that Gustylyu had done to his face. The series of red lines were shallow but distinct, and a film of blood oozed from them. It was enough to draw unwanted attention, so he took a moment to repair the worst of the damage before resuming his stroll to the hotel. When he started walking again, however, there was a bit less of a spring in his step.

He was tiring of the steady stream of distractions.

By Fiday, even Redling's ebullient spirits were quite a bit worse for the wear. Blork and his agents wanted money, and lots of it; Redling had money, but intended to keep it, and Blork's efforts to convince him of the contrary were undermining his own business initiatives. Twice, he had offered to meet with the dancer's husband and discuss the matter, and twice, he had been told that no discussion was necessary—only payment.

The continuing distractions were taking up too much of Redling's time, and he found himself allowing Tithe an entirely inappropriate degree of autonomy in refitting the *Gateway*. He was on his way home from a confrontation with the junkman regarding fuel stores and weapon system upgrades when his com unit buzzed again.

"Redling," he snapped, expecting to hear Sascha or another of Blork's agents respond.

"Colonel Johanssa Tressler here," came the reply. He knew her; she was the spaceport administrator. He hadn't expected to hear from her today, but he didn't mind, either. Sascha's dunning calls had long since ceased to amuse.

"Yes, Colonel," Redling said. He had been on the third-floor landing of his hotel stairwell when the call came; he was exiting onto the fifth floor as he spoke now.

"I've been trying to reach you all day, Redling."

"Sorry; com unit problems." Sascha or another of Blork's underlings had managed intermittently to jam Redling's codes as part of the campaign of harassment.

"I was reviewing your case file when I noticed that you've put in for launch clearance next Wonday," she said. "Do you still intend to make that date?"

"That's the plan."

"Bring proof that you've cleared your liens, then," she said. "Or I won't be able to grant—"

"Liens?" Redling stopped dead in his tracks, less than a meter from his room door. "What liens?"

Tressler's voice took on a clipped and officious tone. "Are you certain you weren't notified? The 'port court has granted an injunction against your launch, until you satisfy two liens against your craft and goods issued by the same court."

"This is the first I've heard of any liens. Who filed them? For how much?" Redling asked, reasonably certain he knew the answers.

Tressler didn't even try to hide her annoyance this time. "Merchantman and Commerce Council Member Chim Blork, along with his corporation, Blork Associates. Together, they total twenty-seven megacredits. Really, I don't know how they do things wherever you come from, but we try to follow procedures on Farworld."

Blork again. Redling was very tired of hearing that name. Heaven only knew what kind of strings the drug pusher had pulled to execute this maneuver, but Redling had some idea. He made his apologies and excuses, then broke the connection. He strode toward his room, his mind filled with unpleasant thoughts.

Even if he had wanted to pay Blork, he couldn't; twenty-seven megacredits was not only more than the *Gateway* was worth, it was more money than Redling could access at the moment. To his mind, that left only one solution to the Blork problem, and that solution could be a messy one.

Very messy.

The real Redling's memories said that Blork's organization was a big one, with security forces that were significant in quantity if not quality. Besides, Blork was apparently a prominent citizen, in his own notorious way, and any abrupt disappearance would be investigated. However, once said vanishing was accomplished, a few well-placed bribes would make the liens go away. The expense would be less than seventeen megacredits, even if it remained more than Redling really wanted to spend. Unfortunately, that was the only course of action he could see that offered promise of success.

Two steps from the door, his com unit buzzed again—a different signal this time, on that came from the scanner unit he had left on his desktop.

Someone was in his room.

Redling let the dagger he carried drop into his left hand again. He used his right to cock Milos Grogan's magnum pistol. He had taken to carrying it with him in recent days. He took one step to his left, hugging the wall for concealment. Then, in one smooth motion, he pressed his right index finger against the door look, drew the pistol, and used the heel of his hand to push open the door. He peered around the door frame's edge.

What he saw beyond it made him blink.

Redling had hunted sky sharks on Guldenfall. He had hung in that gas giant's stratosphere for a long time, held aloft by an antigrav harness and protected by an environment suit. He had seen the buoyant monsters move in silent packs through the inhospitable sky, and he had seen the creatures that preyed on them—giant pterosaurs, with leathery wings and slashing claws.

Something very much like a miniature version of those creatures sat now in Redling's hotel room, seated awkwardly—very awkwardly—in a guest chair that had not been built for its kind. Standing, his visitor would probably be more than two meters in height. Its skull looked very much like that of a pterodactyl and so did the folded wings that sprouted from its back, but it had arms and legs and a torso that were more like a human's. Redling recognized the species, though he had never actually met a member of it before.

"I hope that you will pardon my reluctance to rise," the Guy-troy said. The voice that came from the leather beak was raspy, as if wrapping itself around phonemes to which it was unaccustomed. Dark eyes stared unblinkingly at him. "It was very difficult, composing myself in this way, and I would not care to repeat the exercise. I am willing to do so, however, if courtesy so demands."

"No. No, don't trouble yourself," Redling said, still in the doorway. He meant it, too. Even seated, the other was an imposing figure; he probably need to stoop, once standing. The Guy-troy was obviously trying to present as little apparent threat as possible, short of assuming a totally submissive posture. His hands were open and empty, and he was alone. Redling considered the situation for a moment, then holstered his pistol and stepped into the room.

He held onto the knife in his left hand, however.

"Your culture nods to signal agreement or the willingness to agree, correct?" the inhuman voice croaked again. "I know it is common in your species, but not universal."

Redling wondered just how the entity formed the words. Its mouth was a beaklike construction, lacking lips to shape labial sounds. He supposed the Guy-troy had vocal chords similar to birds he had encountered on other planets, winged creatures that could imitate human speech and that were kept as pets.

His visitor, imposing even in his seated posture, was obviously no one's pet, however. It was always risky to ascribe human qualities to members of another species, but the seated winged man nonetheless had an air of power about him.

Redling nodded in response to the Guy-troy's question, then realized that he had not really answered it, at least not using terms that his visitor was likely to understand. "Yes," he said. "A nod means yes." He was still startled enough to feel confusion.

He was not accustomed to feeling that way.

The winged man nodded. "Good, then. I am Ku-Ril-La, of the Guy-troy." He paused. His fingers, obviously adapted talons, drummed on the chair's armrests, for no apparent reason. They made a sound like rattling bones. A sign of impatience? Hostility? Amusement? Redling couldn't guess, so he ignored the motion and the sound. "Please, be seated, and forgive my own intrusion in your quarters," the Guy-troy continued. "I believe that we can be of aid to each other."

Redling nodded again. He entered the room and closed the door behind him. He glanced around, then returned his dagger to its sheath. Ku-Ril-La appeared to be alone, and Redling was confident in his ability to deal with almost any individual, no matter what his species.

That this was the first Guy-troy Redling had ever met was significant, considering how many worlds he had visited. However, his travels had always tended towards the rough-and-tumble worlds along the frontier, or in the border provinces, where the Guy-troy were known more in anecdote than in fact. They were a cosmopolitan and well-travelled race, but they were known to be fond of luxuries and comforts. Most members of their species who had emigrated from their home world dwelled now in the more "civilized" areas of the Imperium. By nature, they were gregarious and social, but fond of their own kind, and tended to live in enclaves or colonies that catered to their own needs and tastes. Most of the major cities on the Imperium's core worlds had Guy-troy sectors or towns or quarters, where they lived and did their business. To see one alone was a surprise; to see one on a world as rough and unpolished as Farworld was very nearly a shock.

He settled into another chair and faced his visitor. Dark eyes met his gaze and held it. "The intrusion is forgiven, but I'd like an explanation. How did you get in here?" Redling asked.

"Money can accomplish much," the winged man

said. The tone of his voice was flat and neutral, perhaps because the speaker had not evolved for human speech. Ku-Ril-La's word carried the full content of his message, with no coloring inflections or accents. "I have quarters here myself," he said. "I was able to secure access to your spaces by bribing the hotel staff, and then I bribed them again to buy their silence." He paused. "I bribed them a third time to buy their silence about the second time."

Redling nodded. He had expected that, or something similar; it fit in remarkably well with his assessment of the hotel's management. "Expensive," he said, "and probably inconvenient. Why not just call me, or my agent?"

"As a matter of courtesy, I prefer to speak directly to those with whom I do business," the Guy-troy said. "And the man Tithe is, in my considered opinion, untrustworthy."

The blunt assessment comported well enough with Redling's own that he found himself smiling. "He certainly is," he said. "But his and mine is a temporary arrangement, and it will be done soon."

Ku-Ril-La essayed another nod. The effect was incongruous, and brought agreement to mind less than it did the image of a predator striking its prey. "Tithe's arrangement with Chim Blork is of somewhat longer vintage, however," he said, "and likely to continue, even after your business with him has concluded." The winged man's clawed fingers scrabbled and rattled again. "Perhaps even after the ending of your life."

Redling muttered a word under his breath, but not quite softly enough.

"Repeat, please, and translate," Ku-Ril-La said.

"The term is unfamiliar." He shifted in his chair and the folded membranes of his wings made a sound like rustling leaves.

"Hmph?" Redling asked. "No, no, never mind that." He was suddenly very angry with himself. A connection between Tithe and Blork made so much sense that it should have been obvious. Sascha and her husband obviously knew that Redling had money to spend; equally obviously, Tithe had been the source of that information. Redling had given Tithe his com unit's reserved access code, and Sascha had begun calling it a few days later. Even the two attacks by Blork's underlings made more sense if he assumed that Tithe had told them where to look for him, and when. The bit of news that Ku-Ril-La had given him carried far-reaching ramifications.

The Guy-troy was waiting for him to speak, he realized.

"I'm in your debt for that information," he said. He meant it, too. "I didn't know that Tithe and Blork were partners."

The Guy-troy made a clicking sound deep in his throat. Redling thought that it might have been his race's equivalent of a laugh. "Partnership is not the correct term for their arrangement," Ku-Ril-La said. "I believe your kind calls it *networking*."

"Close enough," Redling said sourly. "How did you come to this information?"

The response was one the Guy-troy had used before. "Money," he repeated. "A simple review of Freeman Tithe's business filings for the last three years. His name appears alone on the charter, but the various merchant licenses are to Blork Associates."

"You've shown ample interest in my business," Redling said, "and some degree of consideration in bringing this matter to my attention. May I ask why? My people have a saying—'nothing for nothing.'"

Ku-Ril-La's throat clicked again. By now, Redling was reasonably sure it was a signal of amusement, if not an actual laugh. The Guy-troy said, "All peoples have that saying, Redling. Those that don't are soon drained to extinction by those who do."

"I would still like to know the reason why."

"Because I desire to book passage with you on the *Gateway*, of course. Yours is the only craft on this planet headed in the direction I wish to go. I investigate everyone with whom I do business, and apparently, I do a more thorough job than is your custom." The Guy-troy's vocal inflections were as neutral as ever, but they nonetheless managed somehow to communicate an element of derision.

Redling couldn't argue with it. This was not the first time he had ever tried the assumed identity ploy, but certainly the first he had made such a problematic choice. In his mind's eye, he visualized a white sheet of writing film, and then added to it the letters that spelled his assumed name.

When all of this was done, he had a score to settle with the real Navis Redling.

"Well," he said lightly, "since I don't have the time to investigate you, why don't you do the job for me? Tell me what it is you want, and what's in it for me."

Ku-Ril-La nodded at the question. "Your people have a term for a type of academic endeavor, the 'Grand Tour'," he said. "Are you familiar with it?"

This time, Redling nodded. "I've heard it bandied

about, though not lately, and not hereabouts. You don't get many academics in the hinterlands," he said. "In the core worlds, or in one of the more settled outer provinces, however, and among people with entirely too much money, I've heard of the term."

The concept of the Grand Tour was simple enough: wealthy patriarchs who couldn't be bothered with the task of rearing their children farmed them out instead to other worlds. This was done in the lofty name of "broadening their horizons." A typical Grand Tour could last ten years, and involve a dozen different institutes of higher learning on as many different planets. The idea was to partake of new perspectives and disciplines, and then bring those perspectives and disciplines home. In theory, a young man or woman who had completed a Grand Tour returned to his family better for the experience and better educated, more ready to take the reins of power and authority.

Personally, Redling had his doubts about the whole setup. It struck him as a way to get the kids out from underfoot, and also to produce spoiled young scions with too little allegiance to their homeworlds and too much time on their hands.

He wondered for moment about his guest, and about the winged man's relative maturity, always difficult to assess in an unfamiliar nonhuman species. "Please don't tell me that you're taking one now," he said.

Ku-Ril-La made the clicking sound again, louder and longer. "No, no, no," the winged man said. His talons fluttered and bent, then fluttered again, and his wings rustled again. "So I look to you like a hatchling, do I? I am much more than adult by the standards of my people, and my years are many by the standards of your race."

"I'm not overly familiar with your people," Redling said stiffly, suddenly embarrassed. "I meant no offense."

Ku-Ril-La clicked some more and shifted in the ill-fitting chair. "Oh, no offense was taken. Only amusement, much amusement." He paused. "Among my folk, this—" he clicked again, now with a more deliberate air "—indicates recognition of an inappropriate incongruity, and an invocation of emotional distance. Yours would call it laughter."

Redling smiled, honestly pleased that his original guess about the sound had been correct. It was a bit of knowledge that might come in handy later. "Good, then—I amuse you. You must want more than that, though," he said. "What's this about the Grand Tour?"

"My species in basically avian in nature," Ku-Ril-La said. "Our home is not the land, it is the sky, and we were born to roam. We are not as territorial as the Aslan, but we have an inborn desire to journey, to range beyond the known horizon. It is a vestige of our ancestry, the legacy of generations gone by. Like the Aslan, we are to some extent the prisoners of our biology."

"Not humans," Redling said. "I like to think we're a bit more than that."

The Guy-troy clicked some more, softly this time, and then continued. "Perhaps," he said. "However, my people also have a saying—'the monkey can live so long in a cage that it cannot see the bars.'"

Redling wasn't sure how to respond to that.

"At any rate," Ku-Ril-La said, "the instinct to roam is strongest in the earliest years of maturity, when our fledglings venture forth and seek new winds for their wings. That is *our* Grand Tour, and for some of us, it can encompass more worlds than one. My own Grand Tour was many Standard Years ago."

"There's not much wind between the stars," Redling said dryly, "at least, not the kind that your wings could use."

Ku-Ril-La nodded. "True enough. But it is the drive, the imperative itself, that matters, not the means of its execution. I do not know as much about you as I would like, but I recognize that you are enough of a wanderer to understand what I mean."

"After a manner of speaking, I suppose," Redling responded. His feet had known the soil of more than a hundred planets, but there were so many places he had never been. "If this isn't your personal Grand Tour, why did you bring up the subject?"

Ku-Ril-La told him. He spoke a bit of his own youth, in the opulent Guy-troy enclave on Mariposa. He spoke of growing up as the child of a moneyed merchant, a trader in exotic spices whose robust business had made him a player in local politics. Ku-Ril-La, as his only child, had been able to take his father's success and build upon it, creating a network of commerce than was, in some ways, more expansive and powerful that the civil authority that supported it. The spice concern had become the foundation of a multisystem financial empire, one that took its name from the Guy-troy word for *prosperity*—the Kaal Combine.

The name made Redling come to sudden attention. "You're behind Kaal?" he asked, startled. It was a famous name, and an even more famous logo. His own histories included some dealings with the sprawling conglomerate, and he had never realized that its head was a member of the Guy-troy. He knew that the winged folk were supposed to be expert and aggressive businesspeople, but the Kaal—

"A modest enterprise," Ku-Ril-La said. This time, for whatever reason, he did not nod. "I am pleased to call it mine."

"I'd feel the same way," Redling said. The Kaal Combine had its fingers—talons?—dug deeply into at least a hundred different pies he could name, and doubtless many more that he couldn't. He had seen the name associated with products and services that ranged from babysitting to heavy arms manufacture. Its operations were so varied and omnipresent in the human-dominated cosmos that he had always assumed its owners were human, too. The news that its head and founder, at least, was not came as a bit of a surprise.

Of course, ignorance of the Kaal's origin had never kept him from dealing with it. More than a little of the loot hidden in his various accounts had once belonged to the Kaal or its subsidiaries.

There was no reason for Ku-Ril-La to know that, of course, and many reasons for him not to.

"How does someone with your means end up on a dirtball like Farworld? I haven't noticed a Kaal office here."

Ku-Ril-La made no direct response, but continued his story. He had spent much of his adult life—a span that he measured in decades—building and running the Kaal. He had issued many of his directives through the lips of human lieutenants, because of his own preference for privacy and because his travels had taught him that the Guy-troy were not eagerly received in all quarters a galaxy so thoroughly dominated by various breeds of the human race.

"Maybe so, but the kind of money you're talking about can buy a lot of courtesy," Redling said. He had been listening to his visitor carefully, studying his speech patterns and word choices. He fancied now that he could detect some variations in the winged man's intonations and inflections, and assign some meaning to them.

To Redling's only slightly trained ears, the Guy-troy sounded tired, and it did not sound like a passing fatigue. Rather than being of the moment, it seemed to be born of the many moments that had come before—the kind of world-weariness that came, at least to some, with advancing age.

"I am not interested in courtesy I can buy," Ku-Ril-La answered. "There is a saying among my people—" He paused, as if considering his words. His talons drummed again on the chair's arms, and he sighed. "But you did not ask for aphorisms, only for information, and I shall comply."

Ku-Ril-La's story took on a surprisingly human aspect now. He told of several childless marriages—whether sequential or simultaneous was unclear—and the growing sense of frustration and emptiness his business endeavors gave him. Two standard years ago, he had grown tired of his duties, and handed certain of his responsibilities to a loyal steward. The long months since had been filled mostly with travel, as he sought to retrace—at least roughly—the path of his own Grand Tour, some sixty years before.

"We have a word for what you feel," Redling said. "*Nostalgia.*"

"My third life-mate had a word for it, too," the winged man replied. "It's roughest equivalent in your dialect is *idiocy*."

Redling wasn't sure how to respond to that, so he didn't. Instead, he asked, "Your Grand Tour included Farworld?" He shook his head; that was hard to believe.

"The lateral motion—that indicates doubt, or denial, or disagreement, correct?"

Grinning openly, Redling nodded.

"It's a more consistent element of your race's body language than the nod," Ku-Ril-La noted. "It has its origins in the motion an infant makes when declining nourishment from its mother."

"And what do your babies do? Close their beaks and let the stuff fall where it may?"

Ku-Ril-La clicked a bit more, a sound that Redling found increasing familiar and easy to interpret as their conversation progressed. "Something like that," he said. "But I understand your doubts. I have them, too. I was very young then, and all I know is that my track took me to this sector, and to a young world, and of a level of development appropriate to this one's current status."

"So you're chasing memories, but you aren't entirely certain of them."

"Something like that. The details do not matter, only the broad strokes. Even if I retraced my route precisely, I could not truly recreate my Grand Tour. The worlds that are, are no longer the worlds that were. Do you understand?"

Redling thought he did. He thought for a moment, as he rarely did, of a desperate and penniless youth, eager to leave the world that had birthed him. That youth had found out the hard way just how very difficult it could be to earn such sums, at least though honest labor, on the humble world of his birth. Pickpocketing and petty theft had proven much more effective at yielding the funds necessary to buy passage offplanet. He thought of the Low passage he had bought so eagerly, and the months of dreamless sleep.

He thought of thirteen failed hibernation modules and the unmoving forms within them, the unlucky travellers whose dreamless sleep had become permanent. He remembered them, better than he remembered the world of his birth. In all the years since, he had never returned there—but if he did, would he recognize the place?

He couldn't be sure.

"I understand, I think," he said. "But again, I have to ask you—what brings you to me?"

"There is not much to see in Farport—"

"I'll say."

"—and I have been here long enough. It is time I was on my way. There are seven more worlds in this general sector I wish to visit, all convenient to the itinerary of a ship that has the Red Nebula as its final port of call," he said.

"You've done your research," Redling said. Not many knew the *Gateway*'s full travel plans. He tried to think where Ku-Ril-La could have learned them. From shippers? From Tithe's organization? From the spaceport administrator? He set the questions aside, at least for the moment, since they all had the same answer: money.

"Worlds you've been to before, or just worlds like them?"

"Some of each," the Guy-troy said. "But my own needs are quite specific. I know where I wish to go, and no further substitutions are acceptable. The diversions from your chosen course are minor."

"Even if we can do business, why not book passage on a better ship? Some come through these parts. Not many, but some. I happen to know that the *Waltzing Spider* swept though within the last few months. Others like it will be along. You could find accommodations more to your liking. Wait long enough, and you could probably book a charter. The best that the *Gateway* can offer is High passage in name only."

"I care little for creature comforts, and I do not wish to wait."

"You'll wait a long time for the *Gateway* to leave, I think," Redling said. "Two rather considerable liens have been placed against it."

"To the sum of twenty-seven megacredits," Ku-Ril-La said. "Substantially more than the vessel's present resale value, even if Tithe reduces the craft to its individual components and charges his inflated price for each." One clawed hand reached into a pouch that hung at his belt. Redling watched him attentively, but felt no real sense of apprehension; he was reasonably sure now that the winged man was looking to do business, and not to make trouble.

The fact that he knew the relative values of the lien and the *Gateway* was something of a surprise, however.

The Guy-troy drew forth a battered leather wallet, not unlike the one that Redling used to carry his own documents and local currency. He began sorting through its contents. His talons were surprisingly nimble as they explored the wallet's various compartments.

"I know you're rich," Redling said, "but I would hate to think you're crazy. If you offer me twenty-seven million credits for pseudo-High passage on a Cadmus Trader, however, I'll have no choice but to decline your bid and report you to whatever mental health authorities this backwater has to offer." He shrugged. "I don't know much about them, but I'm sure they're not very good."

Ku-Ril-La made more clicking noises, longer and louder. By now, they sounded very much like laughter to Redling's ears, and he laughed, too.

"Don't be absurd," the winged man said. "I do not intend to pay at all, at least, not in credits." He had found the item he was looking for and passed it to Redling. As he did, one talon grazed Redling's fingertips. It was surprisingly cool to the touch.

Redling looked at what the Guy-troy had given him. It looked like a standard Universal ID, the wafer-thin bit of personal electronics that was standard issue for Imperium denizens. The ID's circuits held detailed identity information about its owner—date of birth, place of birth, tissue types, and so on. They were omnipresent little gadgets, distressingly reliable and quite expensive to counterfeit. Redling knew that from personal experience; his weapons kit held four different Universal IDs, each identifying him quite conclusively and reliably as someone else entirely.

None of them was quite like the one he held now, however.

Redling examined the ID carefully. He squeezed the appropriate pressure point on its surface. The holo-image of Ku-Ril-La faded from the crystal display, to be replaced by background data. He squeezed again, and paged through all of the display's various screens. He saw a half-dozen different Imperial certifications and seals, each with countersignatures that he recognized from his travels. Each name and title was more impressive than the one before it, but the implications they carried were even more impressive.

If the ID he held were real—

It *looked* real.

Abruptly, he realized why a businessman as powerful and wealthy as Ku-Ril-La could feel safe, travelling alone in the galaxy's hinterlands.

"I've heard about these," Redling said, "But I've never seen one." He was sincere, and an unfamiliar emotion that felt uncomfortably like respect for authority swept though him as he spoke. He wished very much that he could keep the ID long enough to investigate the possibility of fabricating a duplicate. Instead, he returned the Universal ID to its owner.

Of course, it was suddenly apparent that other opportunities might present themselves.

"There are not many such to see," the Guy-troy replied. He seemed pleased with himself.

"May I ask how you qualified for such a thing?"

Ku-Ril-La put away his wallet. "Another saying among my people," he said, "is, 'Power is always eager to nest with money.'" He paused. "And I have a great deal of money, after all."

There wasn't much that Redling could say in response to that. Compared to the wealth of the Kaal, his own hidden hoards became abruptly inconsequential.

"Now," the Guy-troy said, "to business." He drew

papers and stylus from his pouch, along with a small device that seemed to be his race's equivalent to a top-line com unit, with advanced data processing capabilities. "Let us negotiate."

CHAPTER THREE

The Far Trader was a very popular model of starship, especially among those of relatively limited means—small businesses, lone entrepreneurs, and the scruffy type of low-revenue/high-risk capitalists that fell somewhere between the two classes. That said, it was hardly surprising that it had been the real Navis Redling's craft of choice.

As an exercise in design, the Far Trader scored high on functionality, but low on appearance (a negative) and on cost (a positive). The base-model, generic Far Trader hull was squarish, with plenty of flat surfaces and sharp corners. Cadmus Shipwrights had licensed the design from its originator and made some minor changes before adding it to their product line. Atmospheric streamlining, never great, became virtually non-existent, and the takeoff footprint became larger, to accommodate slightly less efficient engines. Thus, the *Gateway* was even boxier than Trader models from other manufacturers. The gray steel of its hull showed the marks of many takeoffs and landings, as well as the peculiar moiré pattern that a high-mileage ship's hull could get after many years of Jump Drive use. Now, after slightly over a year in the storage bay, the battered craft stood instead on what spacers still called the blast apron. The name was a legacy of the days before applied gravity manipulation, when people had used fire to launch themselves to the stars.

Farworld's lone spaceport was more advanced than

some, but that really wasn't saying much. In Redling's personal experience, dry lake beds on some planets qualified as spaceports. Farport's founders—pragmatic businesspeople and those who worked for them—had broken ground for the blast apron on the site of their initial planetfall. The 'port was little more than a few acres of reinforced stressed-matrix concrete, divided by traffic lanes into an erratic mosaic of launch slips. The blast apron, in turn, was fringed with a variety of support structures—observation towers, maintenance and storage facilities, fuel depots, and administrative buildings.

Navis Redling had an appointment in one of those administrative buildings this morning. Said building consisted of five utilitarian floors crafted of commercial-grade concrete and steel divided into storage spaces, hallways, offices, and hearing rooms. Redling was seated in one of those hearing rooms now, on one side of a long table, along with Dawn F'Ral, Helicron Daas, and Ku-Ril-La. The woman was looking at the judge attentively, the young local was fidgeting with some kind of gaming piece, and the Guy-troy looked—at least to human eyes—utterly oblivious to his surroundings. Seated across from Redling's party were a few other individuals whose presence he found less pleasing.

There was Sascha, her skin a slightly darker shade of blue today, her blonde hair neatly coiffed, and her trim, dancer's body clad in a severe suit that made her look remarkably businesslike. She was seated next to a muscular, almost simian fellow whose face was filed in Redling's memories under the name "Blork." Right now, he stared unblinkingly at Redling's party, but said nothing.

Tithe did, however. He had wrapped his obese bulk in some kind of decorative caftan and sat perched on the edge of a chair that was much too narrow for his prodigious proportions. A smirk flowed across his features like scum on a stagnant pond as he glanced in Redling's direction and said, "Nothing personal, Navis. Just business, you know." The smirk broadened. "Money."

"I imagine there's very little in your life that's personal and doesn't involve the exchange of money," Redling responded.

Sascha smothered a laugh and even the taciturn Blork looked amused; Tithe, for his part, flushed angrily and fell silent.

"This may not be a formal court," Judge Crondor said, "but I require a certain degree of decorum." She was a woman of indeterminate but clearly very advanced years, her wizened features bearing many marks put on them by time and none by cosmetic surgery. She wore the same quasimilitary uniform issued to the spaceport staff, but her shoulder insignia was the interlocking circle of the local court system. Right now, she was reviewing screen after screen of data on the terminal at her bench. To one side sat a stack of plastic film documents.

"Of course, Your Honor, of course," Tithe said, a veritable study in obsequiousness. "My apologies."

Crondor looked up from the screen. "Frankly, this action doesn't make much sense to me," she said. "I can't imagine how you got it past the lower court."

"Money can accomplish much," Redling said.

The judge looked at him sourly. "Decorum," she repeated. She glanced in Tithe's direction. "Freeman

Tithe, I've reviewed the particulars of your lien, and I find them a bit lacking. The fees charged to the *Gateway* account are unconscionably high—"

"Inflation, Your Honor. It's the bane of our otherwise healthy economy."

"—but that's between you and your conscience, I suppose."

Tithe beamed, his round features splitting in the easy smile of a man unburdened by such things.

"What I can't understand is why you signed a quitclaim and uploaded it last week, if, as you say now, Redling owes you this much money."

"It's all in the records, Your Honor. That alleged agreement and fee schedule pertained solely to basic services, which were paid in advance. It didn't cover our more advanced attentions, such as weekly engine inspections and electronic integrity inspections—two services that set my operation apart in a field of inferior competitors. Those are the services he hasn't paid for."

"Didn't get, either. Those engines were inch-deep in dust," Dawn hissed in Redling's ear. "And I had to relay most of the control yoke by hand."

If the judge heard Dawn's comment, she didn't indicate it as she said to Tithe, "You have an exclusive franchise at this 'port, Freeman. You don't have any competitors."

"I was speaking in the general sense, Your Honor."

"Furthermore, your complaint lays claim to the accused's vehicle, the *Gateway*, in order to discharge that debt. Your lien alone is far in excess of any reasonable valuation of a ship that age and condition."

"Only if that ship is whole, your honor. I can charge

appropriate prices for its main components and still achieve a modest profit."

"As I said, that's between you and your conscience." Crondor paused. "The other lien, however, for 'unspecified services and products.' That sounds outright suspicious. Would either plaintiff care to explain?"

"Redling has a problem—" Tithe began.

"That's me," Blork interrupted. His voice was deep and rumbling, and he seemed to regard each word as a hard-won treasure, too valuable to give up easily. "Was surprised to see him back on planet. He owes me. We did business."

"The complaint doesn't specify what kind of business," the judge said. She didn't quite make the words a question, but her intent was clear.

Perhaps not clear enough; Blork didn't respond.

Crondor looked at Redling. She held up a printout film. "This earlier promissory note bears your signature and print," she said. "Care to provide any details?"

"I've never seen this man before in my life, Your Honor," Redling said, grinning broadly. "My dealings have been entirely with the ineluctable Mrs. Blork." Technically, that was true, if one counted a hastily guzzled glass of brandy. "Though I suppose that if she's ineluctable, he's inevitable, so it's about time I made the acquaintance." He extended one hand. "Nice to meet you, pal. How's the wife and all the little Blorks?"

Blork ignored the gesture and stared stonily back at Redling until he withdrew.

"Decorum," Crondor said for the third time. "But I'm ready to hear the defendant's arguments."

"You have them," Redling said. He gestured at the documents on the judge's bench. "The note that's been satisfied bears Tithe's print. I don't suppose the others bear mine."

"Actually, they do."

"Mmph," Redling said. He backpedaled a bit. "Prints can be forged."

"Yes! Yes, they can! I was just coming to that!" Tithe seemed positively elated by Redling's observation. He heaved himself out of his chair and waddled towards the judge's bench, where he pointed eagerly at the quit-claim that he had signed and printed a week before. "Prints can be forged, Your Honor. Why, that print, there—"

"I repeat: I insist on certain minimal standard levels of decorum," Crondor said, her voice abruptly becoming an angry snarl. "Plaintiff will sit down and plaintiff will shut up, or this hearing will come to an immediate end, and plaintiff will not care for the outcome."

Tithe sat.

"I believe," Redling said carefully, "that examination with appropriate instruments will verify that the thumbprints on the plaintiff's original notes did not come from my hand." He wiggled his fingers for the others to see.

What he said was true, of course; his fingerprints matched those of the real Navis Redling, but his genetic structure did not, and one function of the sensitized forms was to retain DNA samples large enough to analyze and compare. Presumably, Tithe's second claim was a forgery. Blork's certainly was; not even the real Redling would be foolish enough to sign a promissory note to his own drug dealer. Still, the ploy was a dangerous one, since it could also prove that the print on the ship's title wasn't his, either.

It could expose him.

"We're a humble little backwater world, Redling," the judge said. "We don't have that kind of equipment. Even if we did, I don't have the budget to authorize its use."

"So I can't use my first and best defense?"

Crondor shook her head. "No, you can't. I don't suppose you'd care to explain the nature of Blork's previous, personal claim against you? I don't know how he got the lien granted, but we might, and I stress 'might,' be able to dismiss it."

Redling briefly considered just telling her that he was an Euphorinol addict and that the money allegedly owed was for illegal drugs, making the debt itself illegal and thus beyond the 'port court's authority. Ultimately, he decided against it. He had no doubt that the judge's reaction would be amusing in the short run but problematic in the long one. "No," he said. "No, I can't explain that."

"You're not giving me much choice, then," Crondor continued.

"There is no choice to be had." Ku-Ril-La's words came as a surprise to most of the hearing's participants; until now, the winged man had remained so silent and restrained that the initial novelty of his presence had long since worn off. Despite his outré visage, he had faded into the background; now, he strode forward from it, to great and startling effect. "You will dismiss the liens and grant *Gateway* full clearance."

"Oh?" Crondor abruptly became more formal, even contentious. "You'd best identify yourself and your standing in this matter, sir."

Ku-Ril-La handed her his ID. Crondor looked at it,

blinked, then looked at it some more. Nearly a minute later, she had reviewed the last of its screens and then passed it back to the Guy-troy. When she spoke again, she was remarkably more subdued. "I beg your pardon. I had no idea we had a citizen of such prominence in our midst."

"No pardon is necessary; there was no offense," Ku-Ril-La said. He opened his pouch and began to return the ID to it.

"What is it? Who is he?" Tithe demanded angrily. "Give me that!" He reached for the ID.

Tithe had proven previously to Redling that he could move rather fast for someone of his bulk, but Ku-Ril-La moved faster. The Guy-troy's talons were a blur as his free hands slashed out and raked at Tithe's clutching fingers. The torn flesh of Tithe's hand pulled back, to reveal red muscle and white bone. The fat man shrieked in pain.

"My hand!" Tithe said, dropping into his chair. His words were almost a sob. "You've cut me!" He clutched his injured fingers in his other hand. Blood trickled from the gash, glistening like liquid rubies beneath the hearing room's stark lights.

"Do not touch your betters, groundling vermin!" The Guy-troy spat the words. The winged man's claws were still clean, Redling noted. Apparently, they had moved too fast to be stained with the junkman's life-fluids.

Ku-Ril-La was fast. That was something to remember.

Tithe whimpered.

"He's a lot more emphatic than I am, Tithe, old chum," Redling drawled.

"Protest!" The two Blorks spoke as one, then looked at each other quizzically. The big man nodded, and Sascha took up the part. "I protest, Your Honor! I demand that you charge the alien with contempt of court, with assault, with—"

"Nothing," Crondor interrupted. She sighed. "He'll be charged with nothing. The esteemed Ku-Ril-La is beyond my jurisdiction."

The plaintiffs, all three of them, blinked. Redling grinned. Ku-Ril-La's beaked features made no expression that any of them could read.

"I—I don't understand," Tithe muttered. "He hurt me, I'm cut."

"What Her Honor is saying," Redling said with more than a small degree of smugness, "is that Ku-Ril-La's Universal ID is also a Universal Passport, a Universal Writ of Habeas Corpus, a Universal Pardon, a Universal Grant of Amnesty, a Universal Holo Club Card, a Universal Library Card, a Universal—"

Crondor gestured for silence. "The Guy-troy," she said, nodding respectfully at Ku-Ril-La, "is an Imperial appointee, a designated Diplomat at Large. He moves through the Imperium—"

"And all allied worlds," the winged man interjected. His wings shifted and rustled.

"And all allied worlds," Crondor continued, "with a grant of total diplomatic immunity, with exemption from all provincial complaints. He can be tried only after impeachment by the Imperial Council." She sighed again. "He can do anything he wants, with impunity, until and unless that immunity is revoked by appropriate Imperium authority."

Tithe whimpered some more.

"I protest, Your Honor," Sascha repeated, but the words sounded weaker now.

"Frankly, so do I," Crondor acknowledged. "But this is just a 'port court, and there's no way I can challenge the matter, at least not in the time available to me." The limits of interstellar communications had interesting ramifications for local law. "You can protest to the Council."

"The Core Worlds are more than a year away! He's not going to stay here and wait for a decision!"

"True enough, Sascha," Redling said with honest pleasure. "And you can't be sure when the next ship headed in that direction will blow through these parts. Of course, you could always try an in-system com laser. The signal should reach the Core Worlds in—oh—seven thousand and two Standard Years."

Sascha spat at him, forcefully enough that he could barely dodge. It was becoming increasingly apparent that she was the dominant partner in the Blork marriage. Chim Blork might or might not have the muscle, but Sascha had the brains, looks, and venom it took to run a successful crystal operation.

"Decorum," Crondor said softly. Her voice had the sound of futility now.

Redling ignored her, too pleased with the way things were going to stop now. "Tell you what, Sascha. The ways of a Free Trader captain are unpredictable and erratic, but you might just see me again someday. I promise, if I'm ever in this quadrant again, I'll make a point of checking with you. If your complaint has been processed—"

"No! No! No! This, this," Sascha paused, pointed, "this *thing's* immunity doesn't extend, can't extend to a lawful debt incurred by a smooth-talking con artist!" She stamped a foot. "It *can't*!"

"A lawful debt?" Redling said softly. He was still smiling.

"She's got a point," Crondor said. "Citizen Tithe's injury is one matter, but your legal status is quite another."

"Not if I'm part of the Guy-troy General Diplomatic Mission," Redling said. "Ku's immunity extends to me."

Crondor drummed her fingers. "That's not the intent of the law," she said. "The intent of the law is to further higher causes of policy, commerce, and interstellar relations by freeing the diplomats from the petty entanglements of local jurisdictions." She sounded particularly unhappy as she said the last words. "The esteemed Guy-troy's status was not intended to serve as a passkey to a jail cell, or as a blanket exemption from all regulations. It certainly was not intended as a free pass for a low-line commercial tub, just because you make a lucky choice of passengers."

"My people have a saying," Ku-Ril-La said to Judge Crondor, pointedly refraining from the use of any honorific. "'The heart deals in intents, but the whole deals in reality.' This is your reality: for legal purposes, I am an Imperial Diplomat at Large. Navis Redling is a member of my entourage, and the *Gateway* is, for the nonce, an official vessel of the Guy-troy Diplomatic Corps. We completed and filed the appropriate forms yesterday."

"But—but he's hauling cargo," Tithe said. He was still bleeding, but thoughts of commerce seemed to have taken his mind off the injury. "He's making money—"

"With my assent, groundling," the Guy-troy said. "Would you question my authority to grant such?"

Tithe didn't say anything, but just stared desperately at his business partners, a look somewhere between shock and nausea on his face. Neither Blork made any audible response, but the expression that Sascha, especially, wore was one of unrestrained fury.

"Good, good, now that we're all understood," Redling said, "let's get down to business. If Your Judgeliness will just close the hearing, Dawn and Helicron have some certifications to present, and then we'll be off." He grinned at Sascha. "Unless you'd like to discuss passage? We've got a few cabins left. Since you're low on cash, I'd be willing to let you work for passage. Even if you don't have a head for business, you must have other marketable skills." He smirked. "I can think of several things you should be good at."

Sascha shook her head. "No, not now. Not ever." She grimaced. "Don't ever come back to Farworld again, Redling. If you do, you won't leave."

"I'll be back," he promised. He looked at her thoughtfully. "But you won't know I'm here until it's too late."

An hour later, the Gateway drifted lazily up from the blast apron, freed from Farworld's pull by antigravity engines and driven aloft by reaction motors. From his station on the bridge, Redling watched the video feed from a hull-mounted camera, displayed on the bridge's main screen. He smiled as Farworld's rotation and the Gateway's trajectory took the spaceport from his field of view. The whole effect was actually quite pleasant. First, the view of a grubby little spaceport gave way to one of a grubby little city, and then to the visage of less-developed rural territory, and then the untamed wilderness that covered most of Farworld's single continent. The frontier planet was still, for the most part, an empty world. He supposed that would change, one day.

Someday, he knew, Farworld might well be as crowded and cluttered as Draen or even Plimbo, but for now, it was a nearly empty world. Farport was the only settlement of any real size, and was likely to remain one for some time to come. At present, Farworld's only business was business itself. The place existed primarily as a stopover point for travellers going to and from more prosperous planets, and remained relatively unspoiled. The worst thing he could think about it was that it was home of Tithe and the Blorks, and, as flaws went, that one wasn't much—at least not on a planetary level.

"We'll be out of Farworld's jurisdictional area in about seven minutes," Helicron said. He wasn't looking at the main viewscreen anymore, choosing to ignore the receding view of his birth world and gazing instead at an instrument display. He had his gaming piece out again and was rolling it back and forth between cupped hands on the navigation console's worn surface. The piece was a dodecahedral die and he seemed to view it more as a lucky piece than anything else. Certainly, he paid no attention just now to the markings that its face presented. "After that, four standard hours until we're far enough up the gravity well for our first Jump."

"Shouldn't you be plotting a track, then?" Redling asked. The Jump Drive was what made interstellar travel possible, by allowing the transition of normal matter to a parallel, nonrelativistic subcosmos. Thinking about the math behind the process made Redling's head hurt, but he knew that there were considerable calculations involved in determining the points for exit from and re-entry to normal space. Those calculations had an undeniable payoff, however. Without the Jump Drive, travel between the stars took decades or even centuries; with it, the span was measured in weeks or months.

"Already plotted," Helicron responded. He didn't bother with a "sir"; Redling's views on shipboard etiquette were more liberal than those of a typical starship captain. "It's just a matter of asking the box the right questions." The single die clicked some more as he rolled it back and forth.

"You can't ask the right questions if you don't have the right data," Dawn interjected. She was at the opposite end of the small bridge area, behind the squat console of the engineering station. Until now, she had seemed to be paying no attention to Redling and Helicron's discourse, focusing instead on her various readout displays. "You better pull up those files. It's time to make some changes."

"Problems?" Redling asked. His tone was casual, but his concern was genuine. He lacked detailed knowledge of the mechanics of space travel, but he knew enough about the subject to be aware that risks were always present. It was the job of Dawn and people like her to minimize them.

"Not really," the engineer said. "This is an old ship with an old pile, and it sat cold for a long time. The ground crew ran a complete recalibration sequence, but Farport's facilities have their limits. Power output is fluctuating a bit and Helicron needs to compensate for that."

"Problems?" Redling repeated, but even more casually this time. Neither of the others seemed especially concerned.

"Not really," Dawn said. "Everything's still within acceptable parameters. It should just be a matter of making a few minor adjustments to the Jump coordinates."

"You'll need to keep me posted, too," Pikk said from his gunnery station. His voice was a deep rumble, but it was overlaid with the worlds-weary tone of a man who had seen everything and done everything. "This boat's weapons and shields are in pretty good shape—the shields better than the weapons—but they've got their limits, too. I'll need to compensate for any power surges. Let me know the numbers when you're done."

"That's assuming we run into trouble," Dawn said.

"It's safe to assume that we're never completely safe," Pikk said.

Redling smiled at that. It was a cleverer turn of phrase than he had expected to hear from the other man. He filed it away mentally for future use.

"Dawn's right about the Jump numbers," Helicron said. He had pocketed his worry piece and was reviewing his own console's display. His fingers began to dance along the computer's keyboard as he entered new command sequences. "Won't take a minute, though and we've still got nearly sixty."

"Okay," Redling said. "Go to it. I'd like to leave this system far behind, and as soon as possible."

Dawn made an amused sound, the first he had heard from her. "Oh?" she asked. "I thought you were quite taken with Mrs. Blork."

Redling shook his head. "No," he said. "But not because she didn't try."

Dawn made no response.

Redling shrugged, and returned his attentions to the main monitor, where Farworld had receded enough now that he could see its entire profile. The ship's track took it outward at an angle, so they were moving now into the world's shadow. The planetary profile was little more than a silhouette now, an orb of darkness against the starfield. Then, as they continued to move out, Farworld's young sun peered out from behind one horizon, and light spilled across the vast seas that made up most of the planet's surface. He had seen the sight— or similar ones—perhaps a thousand times before, and it never failed to impress him with its beauty.

For a moment, he considered bringing the view to Helicron's attention, to give the younger man his first offplanet view of his native world, but then he decided against it. The young navigator was deep in conversation with Dawn. The two were speaking some kind of mathematical dialect of which Redling could understand only every third word, and both of them made adjustments to their instruments. The time did not seem ripe for interruption. Redling had spent much of his career working alone, but he knew quite a bit about being a leader—and one of the things that he knew was that sometimes the best way to lead was to let other people do their jobs.

He glanced at Pikk again. The big man was sitting almost motionless behind the gunnery controls. His eyes were the only part of him that moved, as he trained them on one display and then another, and then back again.

Pikk still struck Redling as something of an enigma, difficult to know and assess. That wasn't entirely surprising, however. Even in an age of computer-assisted firing systems, a ship's weaponry officer relied heavily on insight and intuition, especially on a ship as small as the *Gateway*. Piracy was an established fact of life in the space lanes, and the buccaneers who prowled the areas surrounding developed systems were often very heavily armed and shielded indeed. In the face of such odds, maneuverability and guile counted for much. The need for such traits, coupled with the simple fact that gunnery officers killed for a living, meant that they tended to be individualistic and standoffish.

Redling turned his attention to his own instrument panel, to the banked displays that presented summary versions of his crewmembers' screens. Numbers spooled indicators flashed, and graphic displays presented trajectories that looked like abstract art. He absorbed that percentage of the information that he could understand and ignored the rest, but acted on none of it. He couldn't; that fell to Helicron and Dawn and Pikk, but his primary role now was to wait.

So much of space travel was waiting—waiting for launch clearance, waiting to clear planetary space, waiting to enter Jump space, and waiting to leave it again. He thought back again to his single Low passage, to the long months of dreamless sleep that had shielded him from the tedium and boredom of shipboard life.

There were times when he understood Low travel's appeal.

CHAPTER FOUR

Dozens of communications satellites and navigation beacons followed various orbits through the star system that was Farworld's home. The *Gateway*'s initial jump came approximately three minutes after the spaceship passed the last of them.

That was appropriate and even symbolic, Redling thought. One of the peculiarities of interstellar travel was that communications were absolutely limited to the speed of transportation. Conveying a message from one planetary system to another meant taking it there physically. In a peculiar sort of way, commerce between the stars reduced aspects of human existence to a pretechnological level—like the natives of old Terra, or the occupants of any world that had not yet mastered radio, dealing with distant people meant dealing with them face to face. A locker in the *Gateway*'s cargo hold was nearly filled with sealed documents, data chips, and other correspondence meant for destinations either on the ship's itinerary, or near it.

"Twenty-seven seconds to Jump," Helicron said. "Twenty-six, twenty-five—"

Redling glanced at Dawn. Once again, she looked amused, and even rolled her eyes slightly as she caught his gaze.

"I think we can dispense with the countdown, Helicron," Redling said.

"Uh—yes, sir. It's just, this is the first—"

"Let the computers do their work," Redling continued. He looked again at the main monitor, at the glistening star field displayed there. "Just sit back and enjoy the ride."

Less than a third of a minute later, a slight, almost imperceptible shudder swept though the ship, as the surrounding fabric of space opened, folded itself around the *Gateway*, and then closed again. As he had so many times before, Redling felt phantom sensations of touch and taste and smell and hearing dance along his nervous system, as his senses tried to process an event that was utterly alien to them. Then the sensations passed, and he looked at the main monitor again.

It was blank now, and not the kind of blank that came from an open switch or a failed camera. It was blank because there was nothing outside the ship to see.

They were in Jump Space now.

This was what made interstellar travel possible, at least in human terms. A ship in Jump Space could sidestep the rules imposed by conventional physics. It could cut across the curvature of normal space, to reach its destination in a fraction of the time that any other means would demand. In a very real sense, at this specific moment, the *Gateway* was the only occupant of a pocket universe, an enclosed bubble of folded space and time that followed different rules. A stardrive physicist had once tried to explain the process to Redling, only to give up in futility when both men realized that his mathematical skills were not even remotely adequate to the job of understanding.

One thing he did understand, however, was that the Jump Drive allowed a ship to travel long parsecs in mere weeks, instead of decades.

"We're on our way," Helicron said. He sounded very pleased with himself.

Redling nodded. "Dawn?" he asked.

"One hundred-sixty-three hours until emergence," she said. "Elapsed distance should be six light years. That's one fourth of the way to Draen."

"Only six?" Redling asked. "The engines are rated for Jump-2." The distance she had named was a half-light year shy of two parsecs.

"They're old engines," she said, repeating what she had said earlier. "We need to operate well within their tolerances, at least until I have the feel of them. I want a margin of safety."

That seemed reasonable. Redling had heard rumors and reports of Jump Drives driven beyond their rated energy levels, or powered up without careful calibrations. The results were unpredictable, and almost always dangerous. Most ships that dropped into Jump Space under such circumstances never dropped back into the normal cosmos.

Redling nodded. "Your call," he said, "and a good one." He paused, thinking. "There's not much more to do here while we're underway." Once in Jump Space, there was little a ship could do to direct itself; all navigation and power adjustments had to be made beforehand. "Keep your com units handy, but I don't see any need to linger at stations. I'll take the first—"

"Request permission to take the first watch!" That was Helicron again, his boyish eagerness lending a respectful note to his voice. "I want to familiarize myself with the nav deck a bit more."

Redling shrugged. He had been young once. "Fair enough," he said. He glanced around the cluttered bridge area. Pikk had already shut down the gunner station and was signing his name to a log sheet. That made sense, too; his weapons and shields were useful only in normal space.

Pikk caught his gaze. "I'll take second, if you want," he rumbled.

"Sounds good," Redling responded. "Dawn? Third or fourth?"

"Third, I think." She paused. "But right now, I want to check some readings in the cargo hold," she said. "Maybe you'd care to join me?"

Redling didn't much like artificial gravity. He recognized its utility and even necessity, but he didn't like it. Specifically, he didn't like the way it felt.

Fellow travellers from all walks of life had told him many times that there was no way that the human nervous system could detect the synthesized and directed gravitons at work in a controlled-grav environment. He was sure they were wrong. There was something different about how the *Gateway*'s deck plates tugged at his feet when the craft was underway. Moving from one level of the ship to another, especially, produced a disconcerting sensation as one monodirectional field surrendered his body and the next took charge of it. The effect was especially noticeable now, as he rode one of the *Gateway*'s two powered lifts with Dawn. He could feel the plane of transition pass through his entire body like wave of mild nausea—but nausea he could feel everywhere, even in his fingers and toes. He had felt it before, on other spacecraft, but it was more pronounced here and now.

"Can't you do anything about this?" he asked.

Dawn glanced up at him from her work. She was reviewing a series of plastic checklist sheets on a clipboard she held in one hand. "Something about what?" she asked.

"The gravity." The lift dropped another level, and he felt the unnerving sensation move through him again. This time, the disorienting wave almost made him hiccup. "There, that."

Dawn looked suddenly thoughtful. "Um," she said. "Same situation as with the power plant. The field casters are as close to spec as I could get them, but they're still slightly out of alignment. The alignment is worse when we're in Jump Space, since the drive uses so much energy, but even so, I can barely feel the effect. You must be especially sensitive if it bothers you."

"Maybe." The lift stopped and so did the unpleasant sensations in Redling's stomach. He led her from the lift and into the passageway beyond. They were on the cargo deck now, where a curved corridor wider than it was high led past interior hatches set flush into the bulkheads. They, in turn, opened on the various controlled environment holds. Behind the hatches were the various cargoes and consignments that Tithe had arranged. One door also hid the compartment where Low passengers would have travelled, stowed like so much frozen meat; now, instead, that space was occupied with bundles of Pellenethian cigars. "Can you do something about it?"

Dawn had paused in front of one hatch cover and accessed a crystal display set in its frame. She pressed a button and recorded in her notes the numbers the screen displayed. When she was done, she looked at him and shook her head. "Not here," she said. "Not when we're underway. Even after planetfall, I probably won't be able to improve things much. This isn't a luxury liner like the *Black Covenant* or the *Waltzing Spider*. It's an old ship, and an economy model, to boot. Plus, it sat idle a long time." She paused a moment. "The title certificate says you've owned the *Gateway* for seven years. Are things really so much worse than they were before you put her in storage?"

"No," Redling said easily, but he felt some irritation with himself for raising the issue.

"Oh. Anyway, you let a ship sit idle for a year and all kinds of glitches creep into the electronics." She tapped the clipboard. "Right now, I want to see what the power output is to storage systems, and I'm not sure I can trust the bridge console. That's why I'm validating these readings." She stepped to the next display and started writing again.

"No, it's not," Redling said. "There's more to it than that."

Dawn stopped writing. She looked at him and blinked. She was a handsome woman, not a pretty one, but there was something about her strong features that Redling found attractive, in a businesslike sort of way. Right now, framed by Dawn's short-cut reddish hair, those features bore a thoughtful expression. "Explain," she said. The word sounded more like an order than a request, and it came in a tone that was significantly different from any other she had used in his presence.

"I don't need to. You're the one with something else on your mind," Redling said. "We don't need two people to read meters, after all." He hadn't minded joining her as she made her rounds, since there was very little for a ship's captain to do while the craft was in space, and even less when it was in Jump Space. Still, he had known that there had to be a reason for the request to join Dawn. "What is it that you want to talk about?"

Dawn nodded, and hung the clipboard from a chain attached to her belt. She leaned against a bulkhead. "The Guy-troy," she said.

"You mean Ku-Ril-La, unless there's another one lurking about somewhere on board," Redling said. "A prospect I find unlikely." He had personally installed the winged man in on of the two remaining High/Middle staterooms on the passenger deck and directed the crew to do everything they could to make his ride an easy one. Catra En'Elt'En, particularly, had been assigned to prepare meals that were suited to the Guy-troy's taste, and serve them in his cabin.

Catra had complained a bit about the extra attention the bird-man required. Neither he, nor the rest of the crew, nor the other passengers had exactly welcomed the winged man with open arms, either—but their concerns were of remarkably little concern to Redling. He owed Ku-Ril-La for facilitating the court hearing back in Farport, and intended to pay the debt.

"No," Dawn said. "But I don't mean just him, either. What do you know about the Guy-troy?"

Redling rooted through his memories, both earned and purchased, but part of his mind was busy wondering why Dawn was asking such questions. Until now, she had struck him as competent but unexceptional; now, he was beginning to suspect that at least a minor mystery lurked behind her sea-green eyes.

"Descended from some kind of pseudopterosaur species," he said. "They can fly, in the right gravity and atmosphere. First encountered the human race during the First Imperium, I think, and our peoples have been trading ever since. I don't know much more than that; I've never been a big history buff. They're successful but cliquish. There's a good-sized enclave of them on Mariposa, I know. They're very successful in business, or so people say. That's too general a statement for me."

"You've been to Mariposa?" Dawn asked the question nonchalantly, but something made Redling pause a moment before answering.

He had been to Mariposa, of course, several times and on various kinds of business—and under several names.

None of them had been Navis Redling.

To the best of his knowledge, the real Navis Redling had never set foot on Mariposa.

It was something of an effort to keep track of which of him had done what. Presumably, Dawn had reviewed the ship records and logs, and could find discrepancies in his story, if she was of a mind to do so.

Was she?

Suddenly, Redling had to wonder.

He watched Dawn's face carefully as he answered, and even as he spoke, he realized that she was doing the same to his. "Not in person, no," he said. "But I hauled a few tons of exotic allotropes for some minor functionary in Grogan's cabinet. He'd been to Guytroy town and liked to talk about it. That was years ago, though."

Dawn didn't look as if she cared, which probably meant that she did. "Just curious," she said. "I hadn't heard you mention the place before."

Redling could almost hear the gears in her head turn

as they stored away the bit of information. He wondered why she was so attentive to his words. Nothing in his interview with her, or his quick review of her papers had suggested that she was other than she claimed to be—a not-quite-fully certified apprentice starship engineer, fully qualified for some vessels. She had done a fine job overseeing the *Gateway*'s engine overhaul and power up, proving herself quite a bit more competent than he had expected. Even her smooth expertise at explaining the minute power fluctuations had come as a bit of a surprise.

Was she *too* competent?

He was suspicious now, if only because she seemed to be. It was not a state of mind he enjoyed. He had questions now, and no easy way to resolve them.

"What about the Guy-troy?" he asked. "Why do you ask?"

She shrugged. "I don't know," she said. "I was just curious. I've never met one before—"

"That makes two of us," Redling said dryly, with more than one meaning to his words. "But Ku-Ril-La did do us a favor."

"How did you meet him?"

"Same way I met the rest of you," Redling said. "A man with a spaceship tends to be very popular among people who want a ride." He hadn't told his crew precisely how he had met the Guy-troy, nor the precise nature of their arrangement.

"It's just—I haven't had much contact yet with the nonhuman races," Dawn said.

Redling suddenly realized that he didn't believe her.

"You will," he said. "Especially if you're going to make space travel your business."

"I know that," she said. "There was a pride of Aslan on the *Waltzing Spider*, headed for Draen. They're more like us, though. They're paramammals, kind of like cats. Friendly."

"I'm quite familiar with the Aslan," Redling said.

"But the Controlled are dif—"

Redling interrupted her, startled by her choice of terms. "The 'Controlled'?" he asked. "I've never heard the Guy-troy called that before."

Dawn didn't say anything.

Redling looked at her levelly. "Showing our xenophobic tendencies, are we?" he asked, not bothering to hide his irritation. He didn't have much patience with sweeping generalizations about entire peoples—not even about species where such sometimes seemed justified. Liking and disliking people on an individual level kept him quite busy enough without adding the judgment of entire races to his workload.

"No." Dawn retrieved the clipboard from her belt and walked towards the next hatch cover. "It's just a word I heard, onboard the *Spider*," she said. "I don't know what it's supposed to mean."

Redling still didn't believe her. The conversation, as brief as it had been, nonetheless disturbed him deeply. Dawn had asked only a few questions, but her words had raised many more—too many, really, considering how many he had already.

Redling had never been to Draen before. The homeworld of the remarkably slender Skelder and of Catra En'Elt'En, it wasn't an address on the original itinerary so lovingly prepared by Tithe, so Redling hadn't expected to visit the planet this time around, either.

Despite that, it was close enough to his chosen course to make stopping there reasonable when a passenger requested that the *Gateway* do so.

More than reasonable, actually, considering who had made the request. Ku-Ril-La had certainly earned his gratitude, if not his understanding.

The Guy-troy continued to be a bit of a puzzle. The trip from Farworld to Draen had taken about four standard weeks; during that time, Redling and the winged man had spoken many times, conversations that ranged from brief chats about dinner to long dialogues on Imperium politics. None of the other passengers or crew had expressed much interest in their mysterious benefactor, and the winged man had reciprocated. Redling, however, found Ku-Ril-La fascinating. Already, he had developed a ready familiarity with the Guy-troy's cadence and vocabulary, and even (to some degree) with his body language and physical expression. Despite Ku-Ril-La's occasional condescending remark, Redling genuinely enjoyed his company, and thought he detected an element of reciprocity there, too.

Given that, he had been a bit surprised when the Guy-troy had declined his company after planetfall on Draen.

"Sure you don't need the companionship?" he had asked. "I was hoping you could show me the sights."

Ku-Ril-La had made his sound of amusement again. "You sound bored."

"Not much on the schedule here, for me nor for anyone else on board."

"Nonsense; your personnel are enterprising creatures. They can find productive ways to fill their time during the day or so I need here. I am certain that there is business to be had and cargo to be consigned, even if such was not your original intent. At any rate, our lay-over shall be but a day or two."

"Looking up old friends?" There was a Guy-troy enclave on Draen, albeit a small one. A single sky-scraper high-rise, with its top twenty floors occupied entirely by members of the Guy-troy, perched at the capital city's edge.

Ku-Ril-La had nodded. "Friends, and less than friends. 'Classmates' would be your folk's term."

The winged man had been correct on one point, however. Draen was a much busier place than Far-world, with a far more active commercial sector. Several of the *Gateway*'s cargo holds had been empty upon the ship's departure from Farworld and arrival at Draen. Such would not be true when they left again. Already, Redling had cut several deals, more out of boredom than of any need for the money he could earn. Now, he strolled along Draen's version of Star Street, a thoroughfare that rejoiced in the name of Glom Boulevard. It was a broad avenue that ran though Spacer's Quarter, crowded with restaurants, taverns, and shops. He hoped it also held something that would occupy his restless mind—or at least, a promising restaurant.

He was gazing thoughtfully at a menu posted in one bistro's window when the doors next to that window opened and burped out Helicron Daas.

"And stay out!" someone yelled from inside. "No more trouble, see!"

"Helicron?" Redling said to his navigator.

"Redling?" Helicon asked in response. His voice

was filled with fear and confusion, and empty of respect or formality. "What are you doing here?"

Another voice rang out from the bar—a rumbling thunder that had an inhuman quality to it. "Trouble! I'll show him trouble! We'll show him trouble!"

"Run!" Helicron said, as Redling helped him to his feet. "We've got to run!"

"We?"

Then the tavern's doors swung open again, to reveal an enormous figure framed between them, and several similar forms waiting behind it.

Redling suddenly saw the reason for the urgent tone in his subordinate's voice.

He began to run. There didn't seem to be much choice. He was armed, but there certainly wasn't time to draw any weapon that would be effective against what confronted him now.

Redling, under all his names and in all his adventures, had learned a scant handful of what he was willing to acknowledge were universal truths, truisms that applied in all situations. They were few in number, but varied in nature.

There were things in life that were supposed to hurt.

Cold beer was better than warm beer.

Drawing a gun without being willing to fire was foolish; firing a gun without being willing to kill was crazy.

Sure things never are, but hopeless odds usually live up to their billing.

All other things being equal, people with four legs can run faster than people with two.

The last was at the forefront of his mind a moment later as he ran through the alleys that branched from the main avenue and made of Spacer's Quarter a complex maze. Behind him, six times four booted feet slammed against the asphalt pavement and made rolling waves of thunder. To his left, Helicron Daas's two feet, wearing soft leather shoes, made somewhat less noise as he kept pace with Redling's long, loping strides. The boy was in good shape, but his breath was coming in ragged gasps now. Even Redling was beginning to feel the strain.

The thunder grew louder.

The centaurs were drawing closer.

"Get the two-legger and his friend!"

"Cheat! Foul! Meat-eater!"

"Tickle us, will you!"

"Give us back our money!"

He began to run faster.

The shouts and demands came from their pursuers, six members of the K'Kree, a race of militant vegetarians who resembled the half-man, half-horse creatures of old Terra's legends. Right now, their equine parts were doing horse work—running—and their human parts were doing human work—shaking fists and shouting threats. Each centaur was as large as Redling and Helicron put together. They all seemed quite ready to do some damage, and they had the muscle to accomplish that goal.

Redling knew the K'Kree as an insular bunch who tended to stay within their own borders. They were very social within their own species, however, so much so that those members of their race who operated alone were viewed as dangerous and insane. They did not travel much; when they did sally forth, however, they tended to journey in groups. Redling had been surprised to encounter six of them, but he would have been stunned to meet only one.

Just now, however, he would have preferred being stunned. One angry centaur would have been easier to deal with than six.

"Left," Redling said as a corner came close. "Now!"

He took the turn first, leaning into it and pushing hard against the pavement as he changed directions. He did not slow as he turned, but Helicron did, if only slightly.

"Now right," Redling snapped. He executed the second turn. This time, the younger man fell a step or two behind, only to pick up the pace as they entered the new passageway. Apparently an access alley serving a long row of eateries, it was narrow and smelled bad, but they had it to themselves. No one blocked their path.

No one was behind them, either, at least for the moment. The two rapid changes in direction had been too much for the centaurs to duplicate. The few who had been able to match the first swerve had failed with the second.

Another truism consistent in Redling's experience was that big things moving fast couldn't hope to turn as swiftly as smaller things that were moving more slowly. A twisting, turning trail was a great equalizer when it came to pursuit.

"Here!" The long muscles in Redling's legs were beginning to sting and burn, and his breath was punctuated with gasps. To his left, an unlocked and slightly ajar door beckoned. He accepted the invitation eagerly and gave Helicron a split-second to do the same; a moment later, he slammed it shut and drove the bolt home. He drew a deep breath. His lungs filled with the aroma of cooking meat.

"Patrons' entrance is in the front, gents," a sardonic rumble said. "Better turn around and go back the way you came."

Redling glanced in the voice's direction. It came from a big man, nearly as big as one of the centaurs. He wore a butcher's apron and a white chef's cap, and was holding a rather large cleaver in one hand. Before him, on a cutting board, lay a sizeable joint of meat. Apparently, the big man had been working on it with the cleaver when Redling and Helicron entered his workspace.

"This is Og's, right?" Redling asked. "Og's Palace of Otherworldly Delights?"

The butcher shook his head and waved the cleaver, in approximately equivalent arcs. "No Og in these parts," he said. He pointed with the big blade at the door behind Helicron. "Now take off," the big man said. "Use the way you came."

"I was sure this was Og's," Redling said. He mustered his most winning smile. "And I had my buds set for a big plate of sand hydras."

The big man snorted. "No hydras here. You find your Og, you might find your them, too. Now, look." The blade in his hand glinted menacingly. "You want to eat here, you come in the front."

"Uh oh," Helicron said softly. He had recovered his breath enough to speak, which Redling supposed was encouraging, even if his choice of words was not.

"But we had such a time finding even the back door," Redling said smoothly. "I don't want to think how long it would take us to find the front."

The butcher made no response, but seemed unimpressed.

Through the door and the walls, Redling could suddenly hear familiar, drumming footfalls. They passed the building once, grew distant, and then loud again as the feet that made them retraced their path The centaurs had backtracked and were continuing their search. They couldn't exit now, not without coming face to face with more than a ton of fighting-mad herbivores.

The big man behind the chopping block shook his head again. The motion made him look somewhat like Eddie, back on Farworld. "That's your problem, not mine." He had evidently heard the sounds of pursuit, too; he pointed the cleaver again, this time directly at Redling. "I don't want any trouble," he said, "and I don't want you in here anymore."

Redling's hand dropped an inch or two, towards the pouch at his belt, even as he gauged the distance between himself and the butcher. It wasn't far, but the breakneck chase had been enough to tire him, and had taken the edge off his speed. Yet, even with his knife, the big man didn't seem all that dangerous—

The butcher hefted the cleaver and then tossed it upward. It spun so fast that it was little more than a silver blur as it dropped back down. Without even looking, the butcher reached his fingers into the spinning blur and caught the cleaver's handle. He gripped it and brought the big knife's business end down, fast and hard. He struck so hard that the big knife sheared instantly through the bone and meat on the board before him and even cut deep into the scarred surface underneath. The two pieces of meat that had been one a moment before jumped apart, and then the big man drew the cleaver up again. He pointed its blade in his visitors' direction.

The entire series of movements took less than two seconds.

"No trouble," he repeated. The lightning demonstration hadn't even made him breathe hard.

"How about some money, then?" Redling asked.

"Money?"

"Yes," Redling said, with a mock cheeriness that became genuine as he saw the other man's expression change to one of interest. Redling drew a wallet from his belt pouch. "Would you like some money? I have plenty."

A moment later, both men stepped through the another door and into the restaurant dining area.

"Thanks," Helicron said. "Thanks for helping me." He looked quite chastened.

Redling shrugged. "I need a navigator," he said.

"Uh—that money, how much—?"

"We'll talk about that later. You should know that I have a firm policy regarding bribes," he said. "Pay them when necessary, but always try to get someone else to pay them for you." He grinned. "The big man's new suit is coming out of your wages, but dinner is on me."

"Dinner?"

Redling nodded. "I haven't eaten, and this place is as good as any. We certainly aren't going back out there until I'm reasonably sure that the thundering herd has given up on us."

"Won't they search for us?"

"Not in here," Redling said. "They're K'Kree, remember? Militant vegetarians. The smell of cooking meat sickens them. That's why I picked this particular establishment." The fact that its door had been the only one ajar had helped, too.

The restaurant proved to be a busy one, and somewhat more upscale than the fairly minimalist kitchen had suggested it would be. Thirty or so tables shared the floor of an expansive hall, and diners of a dozen different races and species ate beneath subdued lighting. They had to wait for a table to become available, and then wait longer for one that met with Redling's approval.

Finally, they settled in at a corner table. Redling, with his back to the wall, grinned as a stocky woman with greenish-blonde hair set plates piled high with food before them. Thick slices of meat dripped heavy gravy that pooled out and found the mounds of vegetables that surrounded them. A moment later, and the server returned with their drinks.

"They really don't have sand hydras," Redling said as she left. He tried a sip of his brandy. "Pity."

Helicron didn't say anything, but lifted a forkful of puffed grains to his mouth. Even ebbing, panic had apparently lent strength to his thirst; he had already drained a quarter of his stein of ale.

"You should try the roast," Redling said. "It's good, and it's good for you." His real concern was to keep the younger man from getting drunk before explaining a few things.

"I don't eat very much meat."

"Well, that might explain why you were able to get close enough to the horse-men for them to hate you," Redling said. "They're usually nauseated by the breath of carnivores. Even the more outgoing among them have only a limited tolerance. They've fought wars over things like that."

Helicron ate some meat. He didn't look as though he liked it.

"So, tell me how you came to be providing entertainment to a bunch of centaurs, most of whom sounded pretty drunk to my untutored ears," Redling said.

Helicron looked at him quizzically, the fork poised to enter his mouth again.

"Now," Redling said firmly.

"We were gambling," the younger man said. "That tavern had a gaming room in the back, and I was a bit better at Spindledrift than they had expected." Spindledrift was a game popular among spacers; it involved dice, cards, and a patterned playing board. "I was winning and they were losing. They didn't like losing."

"Can't say as I blame them," Redling said. "Were you cheating?"

"They thought I was."

"But were you?"

A long pause, and then: "I don't think of it as cheating. Just evening the odds up a bit."

"Which means you were cheating." Redling sighed. He knew all the tricks. "What was it? Card counting? A shaved die? Tickle the board?"

"You know how to tickle the board?" Helicron asked eagerly. "Can you teach me how?"

Redling took a mouthful of food. He shook his head as he chewed. "Nope. I know how it's done, and I know how to do it—but I don't, and I won't help you," he said, after swallowing. "I'm not a big believer in gambling, but I don't see the point in cheating at it." That was true, after a fashion; the real Navis Redling had bent the rules in an occasional round of Kimble, but other vices had soon displaced such games from his recreational repertoire.

Helicron snorted derisively. "You have to take risks to—"

"I take risks," Redling interrupted. "Plenty of them. I hired you, didn't I?"

Helicron didn't respond.

"The risks I take just aren't associated with gaming." He looked levelly at Helicron. "Is that why you were so eager to leave Farworld behind you? Did you think you were going to make a killing in the casinos of the galaxy?"

Helicron fidgeted a little, and pushed the food around on his plate. "It's one way to get ahead," he said.

"It's also one way to get a head handed to you by a bunch of wine-crazy centaurs—*your* head. You almost found that out the hard way."

Helicron shrugged. "They should get used to losing," he said. He spoke with the easy confidence of youth.

"That's not the way," Redling blinked in surprise as he saw something over Helicron's shoulder, "the worlds work."

Dawn F'ral was seated at the bar.

Helicron mumbled inanities as Redling discretely studied Dawn. He almost hadn't recognized her, and not just because he was seeing her in such an unexpected setting. She looked quite different; her short reddish hair was longer and darker—extensions? a wig?—and the strong lines of her features had been softened by the skillful application of makeup. Instead of the utilitarian jumpsuit she typically wore while at her duties onboard the *Gateway*, she was clad in a smartly cut dress that fell somewhere between the high end of casual and the low end of formal. It was the kind of outfit that was good for most social occasions.

"—was a great gamer, and I'll be one too," Helicron was saying. He drank some more beer. "That's what he wanted."

"If your father was such a great gamer, how did he end up on Farworld?" Redling asked. His mind was only half on the conversation, but that was more than enough, when it came to talking with Helicron. "Not many casinos there."

Helicron blushed, which made him look even more boyish. "He didn't end up there. Just a stopover. My mother told me about him."

"Ah."

Was Dawn just in a social mood? Redling supposed that was possible, but he doubted it. She had changed her appearance too much, and too skillfully, to constitute preparation for a simple night out on the town. She looked less like a woman looking for companionship than she looked like a woman who didn't want to be recognized.

Redling knew a bit about not wanting to be recognized.

He said something in response to a half-heard question from his navigator and kept watching. Dawn apparently had not spotted them; most of her attention was focused on a set of swinging doors that led to the establishment's private rooms. She sipped a drink, declined a conversational gambit from a neighbor, and sipped her drink again, some portion of her gaze always directed at those doors.

She was behaving very much like an undercover law officer on surveillance, Redling realized. He had been the target of such stakeouts enough times to recognize them. He didn't like the thought, and he liked even less how well it fit in with certain questions that Dawn had asked on board the *Gateway*.

He was beginning to think that his engineer might have a few certifications that weren't on her résumé.

"You're not listening to me," Helicron said. He sounded petulant, but he was right.

"Sorry," Redling said, not meaning it. He glanced back at the kid. "My thoughts were elsewhere." He didn't want the navigator to notice Dawn. It was unlikely that he would recognize her—Helicron's observational powers were not exactly at their peak just now—but if he did, he would no doubt feel compelled to make his and Redling's presence known. At the moment, that didn't strike Redling as a particularly good idea. Dawn had made of herself a puzzle to solve; the fewer who knew about that aspect of the situation, the better—at least for the time being. "Tell me more," he said to his dining companion.

Helicron told him. Between bites of food and gulps of ale, he nattered on about growing up in the backwaters of a backwater world. He talked about his mother, an indentured waitress, and the man she said was his father. He talked about putting himself through endless rounds of correspondence coursework and computer-based training to earn his navigator's certification, eager to leave Farworld behind and make his mark on the cosmos. What he didn't talk about very much was his interest in gaming, other than to make snide references about clumsy-fingered centaurs who should know better than to bet with the odds.

Redling wasn't sure whether the younger man's reticence on that particular topic was an indicator that he had learned his lesson, or if it simply proved that he had not.

"Hey! Hey, miss!" Their server had come into view and Helicron had noticed that his glass was empty. He had given up on his food and was concentrating instead on drink, and on the gaming piece that he had again drawn from his pocket. The worn die clicked on the table top as he fidgeted with it. "More beer, miss!"

Redling ignored him. He had noticed something else.

The paired doors that had been the subject of Dawn F'Ral's clandestine scrutiny had swung open, and a familiar-looking figure strode through them. He had greenish skin, large dark eyes set in a beaked skull, and folded wings.

Ku-Ril-La?

No; Redling had spent enough time with the winged man to recognize him. This was another member of the same race, however, which he supposed wasn't all that surprising. Draen was home to a number of the species, after all, and they weren't exactly reclusive.

Dawn had abruptly set her drink aside and settled her tab, Redling noted.

A second Guy-troy emerged from the private dining room. This one *was* Ku-Ril-La, Redling was certain. The two winged men were talking to one another, conversing in a series of clicks and whistles that carried intermittently across the main dining area. The sounds were presumably words in their native tongue. Redling couldn't tell what they were saying, and not just because of the background noise; he wasn't wearing translation equipment.

He wondered if the same could be said of his engineer.

Ku-Ril-La and his companion were leaving the restaurant now. Dawn F'Ral, to Redling's educated eyes, was poised to follow. She was standing now, and gathered her cloak about her as the two Guy-troy approached the exit.

Redling watched carefully as the scene unfolded.

The doors opened. The two winged men stepped through them, and they whisked shut again.

Dawn waited ten seconds, then began moving toward the exit herself. She moved quickly, but with some attempt to look casual. Redling watched with a faint smile as stepped around a table full of well-dressed tourist types, then almost bumped into a server and apologized, then reached for the door actuator, and then—

That was when he decided he had watched enough.

"Dawn! Dawn F'Ral! That's you, isn't it?" Redling called out the name with reasonable volume, certainly loud enough to cut through the restaurant's background chatter. "Dawn! Over here!"

She flinched and looked in his direction. Her typically confident green eyes were blue now, he noted, and as she recognized him, they suddenly looked like those of an animal caught in a ground car's headlights.

"Dawn! Over here! It's me, Redling! Join us!"

"Dawn?" Helicron asked. "Dawn's here?" He looked around, saw her, waved. "Ahoy, shipmate!" he sang out.

People were beginning to stare now, and Dawn was one of him. Shock and surprise had become irritation and resignation, but she still managed to shoot Redling a glare as she sidled towards the table.

"Dawn!" Helicron said. The words sounded mushy in his mouth. "Almost didn't recognize you! You're boo'ful now!"

"He's trying to say 'beautiful,'" Redling said, grinning. "Having a bit of trouble with his consonants at the moment." He suspected that the next morning wouldn't be much fun for the young spacer, and that the next leg of their trip would be even less. However inadvertently, Helicron had just insulted the woman who sat next to him, and their duties meant that he would need to work closely with her for the remainder of the trip.

It could have been worse, Redling realized. The younger man could have found a way to offend Pikk, instead.

"So I gathered," Dawn said. She looked from one man to the other, and then back again. "What are you two doing here?"

"Enjoying what the menu calls roast pit sloth with steamed floogle shoots," Redling said. "And having a bit of a man-to-man with our young Helicron, here."

"Well, I wouldn't want to—" Noticeably pleased to have an excuse, Dawn made as if to leave.

"Nonsense! I insist you join us," Redling said. He could sound quite jovial when he chose to. "Captain's orders! I'm going to need some help getting young Helicron back to the *Gateway*."

Dawn looked at him, a hint of speculation in her eyes.

"We're talking about gambling," the younger man announced eagerly. "Do you play Spindledrift?"

Dawn sighed, the sound of resignation. Redling wasn't sure what she had been up to, but whatever it was, he knew that he had wrecked it. Even so, she was doing a reasonably good job of concealing her own annoyance. "I know Spindledrift," she said. She glanced one last time at the exit, and then sat in the empty chair between Redling and Helicron.

"Do you know how to tickle the board?"

"I know the theory, but not the practice," she said. She glanced again at Redling. "I don't believe in spoiling someone else's game."

"I do!" Helicron said beerily.

"Me, too," Redling said, doing his best to look innocent. "At least, some games."

"I have a bit of business for you," Ku-Ril-La said to Redling, approximately forty-three hours later. The two of them were seated at a bar in the spaceport terminal. Draen's facilities for starfaring folk were far more elaborate than what was available on Farworld, and they served a more cosmopolitan clientele. The place's other patrons included another Guy-troy— apparently not the one that Redling had seen at the tavern—and representatives of several different nonhuman races. In such a setting, Ku-Ril-La looked much less out of place than he did in an exclusively human gathering place.

"Good. I could use the additional revenue," Redling said. He was serious. Draen had not been a terribly profitable stopover for him. He had come here solely out of courtesy to the Guy-troy dignitary. None of the cargo in the *Gateway*'s hold was bound for Draen, and the passengers that Tithe had booked for him had complained about spending two days on an unscheduled stop. He had blunted their concerns by discounting the fare schedule a bit, which offset what little cargo and correspondence he'd been able to pick up. The idea of making some extra money sounded attractive.

Of course, it usually did; Redling liked money.

"I just hope it's on our current route," he continued.

Ku-Ril-La clicked. "Carstair's World," he said.

Redling nodded. Carstair's was a moderately urban planet that hung on the fringes of the Red Nebula. He had several thousand Pellenethian cigars bound for there, and a sizeable sealed pouch of business correspondence. "We're going there, all right," he said. "What's the deal?"

"Many Guy-troy live on this world, in this city. We have an enclave of our own," Ku-Ril-La said. He seemed to be watching Redling a bit more carefully than usual. "I met with a classmate and dined with him. We did a bit of business."

Redling nodded. That explained Ku-Ril-La's presence in the bistro, if not Dawn's. That was still a mystery that needed solving.

"Kaal business?" he asked. The interstellar combine had several offices on Draen, and he had supposed that the Guy-troy would be spending much of his time there.

"No," Ku-Ril-La responded. "This is a holiday of sorts for me; I was not entirely pleased when matters of commerce arose."

The Guy-troy's eyes shifted in their hooded sockets as he gazed in Redling's direction. Redling found himself wondering precisely how much Ku-Ril-La knew about what had happened at the restaurant.

The Guy-troy continued. "My classmate has some items he wishes taken to Carstair's World, for reshipment to Plimbo." The second planet he named was on the same primary trade route as the first. "He will pay competitive rates, and there need be no broker's fee, which should increase the profit margin considerably. I told him of your vessel, and that cargo space was available."

"*Might* be available," Redling said. Something about the Guy-troy's choice of words made him hesitate. He was still trying to keep a relatively low profile, and carrying contraband could work against that, diplomatic immunity or no diplomatic immunity. "Depends on what he wants moved."

"Droyne droppings," Ku-Ril-La said. He sounded less than impressed.

Redling shook his head. He knew a bit about the Droyne, at least as much as any layman did. The Droyne had been something of a super-race, both inhuman and prehuman, long since extinct but still very much the subject of study by interstellar archaeologists. According to some of those scholars, a single bloodline of the Droyne had been responsible for literally dozens of technological advances that still baffled those who had inherited their domains. Ultimately, they had turned that genius upon themselves, making war with one another until they had obliterated their own race and left an empty cosmos for other races to inhabit. The Droyne had been master builders who had left their mark on many worlds, but the specifics of many of the wonders they had worked remained shrouded in mystery. The rare technological items that had survived and surfaced in working condition were prizes beyond price.

Certainly, the cache his sources said awaited him in the Red Nebula promised to be worth the ransom of a good-sized system.

"Everyone and his brother says he has functioning Droyne artifacts," he said. "My experience is that such are few and far between. The ones that do surface are too hotly contested to make desirable cargo, especially for a Free Trader like the *Gateway*." He paused. "We're far enough out that piracy is still a problem, after all."

Ku-Ril-La clicked again, and drummed his talons on the bar's polished surface hard enough to make his drinking glass dance. "Any brigands who target this consignment would too foolish to remain in the business," he said. "I've seen it myself. It's little more than rubble—shards of polyceramic, a few of those offset hinges that the Droyne liked so much, broken bits of machinery with unknown functions. As I said, droppings."

"Why go to the trouble of shipping them, then?"

"Faddishness and fashion. There is a vogue among my folk for things that carry the stink of age," Ku-Ril-La said. "Every hen demands her mate procure her some dusty relic of a forgotten people to clutter the family nest." He picked up his glass and drank. "I sometimes wonder what that says about my species."

"Or about wives."

"We are an ancient people, Redling, but we know remarkably little of our own past. History is an old and respected discipline among your folk, but it was evidently unknown to mine before our races encountered one another. Certainly, no primary records or reliable accounts of Guy-troy history from before that date sur-

vive. We have so little of our heritage. The broad outlines are clear, of course, but there are no textures, no
nuances to study."

"That was during the Ziru Sirka, right?" That was
the name that the First Imperium had used for itself.

Ku-Ril-La nodded. "And, of course, your forebears
were too busy conquering the cosmos to take much
note of the civilizations they elbowed aside."

"That's one way of looking at the situation, I suppose," Redling said. He wasn't sure he agreed with the
winged man's views, but decided to keep his reserva-
tions to himself. "There have been a few upheavals
since then, too, of course. I suppose they've muddied
the trail even more."

"The First Imperium was a remarkable social construct, arguably your people's finest moment," Ku-Ril-
La said. His voice took on a quality that might have
qualified as wistful, if coming from a human. "It rose
with such remarkable speed, and it took so very long to
fall. But fall it did."

"I don't know much about that," Redling said. He
was sincere, too; his adventurous life had been too
much in the here and now to allow much time for study
of those who had come before him.

"An ancient drama, acted out with different players
again and again through the ages. But for this production, there were no watchers—only participants. Fat
and complacent, the people of the Ziru Sirka were easy
prey for their more aggressive cousins from Terra."

"You sound like you've made quite a study of it."

"I have. As a hatchling, I already knew more about
your people than you are likely to know now. My people came late to the study of history, but many of us

have made a fetish of it. We study what legacy of our own we have, and, as if to compensate for the shallowness of that draught, we study others, as well. Guytroy universities even offer advanced degrees in human history."

"I've never focused much on the past."

"That's because you have one to focus upon," Ku-Ril-La said. "My people do not." He ordered another drink. "But enough of this. Perhaps you are right to view things as you do; we live in the present, after all."

CHAPTER FIVE

Sending a ship into space, even a ship as relatively simple and utilitarian as a Far Trader, requires an immense amount of preparation. There are foodstuffs to take onboard, and waste recycling units to replace. There are fuel tanks to fill and nuclear engines to recharge. The Jump Drive must be recalibrated between each use, and its circuits and processors demand careful inspection whenever the facilities are available. On a planet like Farworld, most such preparatory work is done by a ship's crew; on a more developed world like Draen, it's done by franchised specialists who charge stiff fees, and require close supervision by ship personnel. With so much to do on such a tight schedule, processing cargo—a freighter's very reason for existence—sometimes takes a surprisingly low priority, and becomes almost an afterthought, especially when that consignment is a small one.

Eleven standard hours before the *Gateway*'s scheduled launch, a ground car forklift rolled from a warehouse onto the spaceport's blast apron, bearing six full-size cargo modules. Each of them bore a distinctive seal. Redling looked up from some forms that Dawn had presented for his thumbprint and watched as the clumsy vehicle rolled awkwardly up the *Gateway*'s cargo ramp toward the hold. Each of the cargo modules on its front end was the approximate size and shape of a very large coffin, which gave the vehicle a slightly macabre look.

"Those should be Ku's Droyne droppings," he said. He gestured at the forklift driver and pointed the way to the appropriate hold.

"There sure are a lot of them," Dawn said. It was nearly three days after shared drinks and dinner with her and Helicron. Her hair was red again, her eyes were green, and she was dressed once more in her work clothes. Now, she took her copies of the proffered forms and handed the rest to a squat, square-faced man.

"Thanks, Miklos," she said to him. "I'll upload the file versions before takeoff."

Miklos grunted. "Still need a memory flush in the online processor, if you ask me." He sounded like a man who didn't like losing arguments.

"Maybe next time we're in these parts. What we've got will keep for now," Dawn said, a note of steel in her voice.

Miklos grunted again, then ambled off to join his own crew, which had spent the preceding six hours overhauling and recalibrating the *Gateway*'s Jump effect generators. Dawn had insisted on having the work done, as soon as the Draen facility became available. As Miklos left, Redling began walking in the same direction as the forklift, and Dawn walked with him.

"Problems?" Redling asked lightly, nodding in the general direction of Miklos and company.

"They'll sell you the moons if you let them," Dawn said. She spoke with such casual authority that it was easy to forget that she was relatively new at her job. "I knew what we needed done, but Miklos wanted more."

Ahead of them, the six modules had been deposited

in the appropriate section of the cargo hold, and the forklift driver was preparing to secure them, using the stasis clamps that protruded from the bulkhead.

"I'll take care of that," Redling said.

"I gotta do it," the other man said, frowning. He had yellowish skin and a caste tattoo stretched across his forehead. "Guild regulations."

Redling shook his head. "Guild regs say that we pay you to secure anything you bring onboard," he said cheerfully. "Nothing says you have to earn the money—"

"Hey!" the driver interrupted, bristling at the condescending tone in Redling's voice.

"—when I certainly don't earn mine," Redling continued. He smiled disarmingly and plucked a small clipboard from the ground car's dash. He glanced at the plastic sheets. "Top copy's mine?"

"No, second one, but—"

It was too late. Redling had already 'printed both sheets, taken his, and returned the clipboard to its hook. He drew a note in local currency from his pocket, made it snap between his fingers, and then tucked into the driver's coverall pocket. "There you go. Buy yourself something nice, but not too nice, and let me worry about the Guild, won't you?"

"What was that all about?" Dawn asked as the forklift rolled away. "The guy was just trying to do his job."

"He was just trying to do what someone else had decided was his job," Redling said. "And I get tired of rules sometimes."

"Who doesn't?" Dawn asked. "But if you think life's regulated here, you should try the Core Worlds."

Redling thought a moment before responding, something he had found himself doing fairly often in conversations with Dawn. Had he been to the Core Worlds? Had the real Redling? The answer to both questions was the same. "Done that," he said. "Why do you think I'm here?"

Dawn's head moved in a barely perceptible nod.

Why? Had the comment been an innocuous one? Or a disguised interrogatory feint, intended to produce a verifiable response? Redling wasn't sure, couldn't be sure, and that uncertainty annoyed him.

He liked things he could understand, and he didn't like second-guessing himself every time he opened his mouth. Dawn F'Ral was becoming a bit of a problem, or, at least, his impression of her was. He knew that he had to do something about that, and fairly soon.

He looked at the six modules, stacked in a convenient recess. They were standard issue, made of matte-finish plastic with alloy reinforcement and thick layers of insulation. The only thing that set the boxes belonging to Ku-Ril-La's associate apart from dozens of others in the hold were the top-line security seals affixed to their access panels.

"I hadn't expected to open the hold at all, actually," he said. "Nothing was bound for here, and I wasn't looking for any new business."

"We've got pretty close to a full ship now," Dawn said. She sounded curious. "Whatever this stuff is, he's paying good rates to ship it. We'll show a profit this trip, yet."

"Maybe," Redling responded. He had already decided that it was time to put a bit more effort into playing the role of an independent freighter captain, and display some fretfulness about money. "We won't, if we keep making unscheduled stops, though. The fare discounts are eating me alive."

"Don't look at me," Dawn said dryly. "This was your idea. I'm just the engineering officer."

"True enough," Redling said, even though he was reasonably certain that there was more to Dawn than that. Right now, he was hoping to find out how much more. "I just hope this is the last favor Ku asks of me this trip. He was a big help, getting us off Farworld, but—"

He let his words trail off, in hopes that Dawn would give voice to the misgivings that she clearly held about the Guy-troy.

Dawn glanced at him but declined to rise to the bait.

Redling sighed inaudibly. It had been worth a try, but if the conversational gambit wouldn't make Dawn open up a bit, perhaps it was time for a different approach. He reached into the pouch that hung from his belt and drew forth something he had taken earlier from the weapons case in his private quarters. "Pick a module," he said.

"Huh?" Dawn looked startled, and easily as surprised as she had been the night he had spotted her in the restaurant. "What do you mean?"

"Pick a module," Redling repeated. He was sliding his right hand into something like a cross between a wrist com unit and a three-finger set of brass knuckles. As he pushed his fingers through the metal rings, leatherlike straps unfurled from the gadget, extended themselves like pseudopodia, then tightened snugly around his wrist and palm.

Dawn's green eyes suddenly grew larger as she

watched the override configure itself to Redling's grip. "What the Drog is that?" she asked.

"Just a little toy that I picked up in my travels," Redling said. The ring at the base of his index finger had split into two, and now the new one slid along the length of his digit, trailing a narrow probe. When it reached the tip, the ring contracted slightly and anchored itself in place. Redling felt the hairs along his forearm stand on end as the device he called the override charged itself.

He looked at Dawn again. "Pick a module," he repeated. "It's inspection time." He paused. "You don't think I'm going to risk hauling contraband on my ship, do you?" He smiled tightly. "I'm not a criminal, after all."

Judging by the expression on her face, it seemed entirely possible that Dawn had thought the contrary. "These are under Ku-Ril-La's personal seal," she said slowly, but he could tell that she was interested. "You open them, he'll know. He's the only one who can—"

Redling sighed, audibly this time. Sometimes, if you wanted a job done, you had to do it yourself. He stepped to the most convenient of the six modules and pressed his metal-ringed index finger to the coppery surface of the Guy-troy's identity-specific security seal. The marker was a fairly sophisticated bit of hardware, proof against tampering and incognizant of any touch but its owner's.

Redling tapped his fingertip against it once, twice.

The seal split and swung back, and the cargo module's access panel opened.

"What the Drog is that thing?" Dawn repeated. This time, the question had a commanding sound to it.

"How did it open the case?"

Redling held up his hand and wiggled his fingers so that she could get a better look at the device. By now, the override had conformed itself so completely to the contours of his palm and fingers that it looked little heavier than a glove. He knew from experience that if he wore if for an hour or more, the device would even change its color to match his skin. "Droyne droppings," he said, grinning.

"Not the cargo; that piece of equipment you're wearing."

"Droyne droppings," Redling repeated. He was searching the cargo module's interior now. It held a series of hinged trays made the absolute maximally efficient use of every bit of the big container's interior. Each tray held various-sized niches, and each niche held a wrapped item, secured in place by short-range pseudo-gravity fields. The override he wore on his hand was light and flexible enough that Redling could forget about it as he reached for the most convenient item in the module's interior. It was a hand-sized piece of something, and the padded wrap enveloping it cracked as the tugged it free. "Or, if you want to be technical, a functioning technological artifact from the pre-First Imperium Droyne Empire," he continued.

"The Droyne made burglar tools?"

Redling looked at her, his good-natured caution giving way to genuine irritation, however mild. "I don't know what the Droyne thought it was when they made it, or what purpose they put it to," he said. "No one does knows that kind of thing, about almost anything that the Droyne left behind when they pounded themselves into dust. Those so-called 'black globes,' for example—they drink meson fire like ale and they make great ship defenses, but no one thinks that's what they were originally intended to do. It's just the use their lucky new owners have found for them." He had owned a black globe once; rather, it had fallen into his possession for a too-short period of time, and impressed him mightily with its utility.

Redling wiggled his fingers again. "I don't know what this thing is, either; I just know what it does, and that's override most security systems." Without looking, working on touch alone, he folded quilted packing wrap around a triangular fragment of pseudoceramic and put the pottery shard back where he had found it. "Now, I know you want to know what's in these crates. Are you going to help me search them, or are you going to stand there and chatter like a tree-weasel with a belly full of bad floogle berries?"

Dawn helped. With speed and precision that very nearly matched Redling's own, she examined the cargo module's contents. The two of them didn't talk much as they worked, falling fast into a steady rhythm of unwrap, examine, rewrap, and replace. There was plenty to work with, too; it took the two of them nearly three hours to work their way through all six of the cargo modules.

"Nothing but junk," Dawn said, as Redling used the override to reseal the last case. Nothing that either of them had seen seemed to possess any functionality or even aesthetic virtue, beyond simple antiquity.

Of course, they saw with human eyes and human standards. They Guy-troy might feel differently.

"Nothing that we can tell is anything but junk," Redling corrected her, even though he agreed tentatively with her assessment. He stripped the override off his hand and waited for it to power down and fold itself shut again. "This particular toy languished for years on a junk shop shelf, dusty and forgotten, until someone figured out what it did, and realized it was still operational." He laughed. "Drog knows what they built, but the Droyne built well."

"It would come in handy for Customs work."

"For all I know, the Droyne used it to open canned rations," Redling said. "I would like to know how it works, though. Too bad that taking it apart to find out doesn't seem like a very good idea."

"May I see it?" Dawn reached for the device.

Redling shook his head and pulled back from her extended hand. "Sorry," he said. "No touch. I went to a lot of trouble to get it, and I'm not willing to risk losing it." He stowed the override in his belt-pouch and zipped the pouch shut.

There was some truth to his words. In other circumstances, from someone else, he might have allowed a casual inspection, but Dawn's conduct had raised more questions than he could answer. Her actions during the search had been assured and confident, enough so that he was certain she had completed some formal training in the discipline. Then there was the matter of her apparent surveillance of the Guy-troy. That was part of the reason he had allowed her to help him, to gather more input on her capabilities.

Why would an engineer need such skills? More importantly, where had she gained them?

It was increasingly apparent that there was more to Dawn F'Ral than met the eye. The question now was, how much?

"There's more to you than meets the eye," Dawn said, a cool, appraising look in her eyes as she gazed at him. "I wonder how much."

"Huh?" A grunt of surprise was the only response that the genuinely startled Redling could muster. Her words were similar enough to his thoughts that he suddenly felt a mild twinge of concern. He'd heard about telepaths, psionic eavesdroppers, even if he'd never actually met one.

Or, at least, he didn't think he had.

"I thought the Guy-troy had you in his pocket," she said. "I thought he had you bought and paid for. I figured he had something to do with our little encounter the other night."

Redling wasn't sure what to say to that.

"But this," Dawn said, gesturing at the six resealed cargo modules, "this isn't the work of someone whose been bought." She paused. "At least, not bought completely."

"I think you'd better explain yourself," Redling said, suddenly tense, suddenly very concerned that she was going to explain him, too. "Yourself, and what you mean."

How much did she know?

He shifted his stance slightly, rocking back on the balls of his feet and tensing the muscles of his legs and arms, readying himself to move quickly if the time came.

The movement was slight, but not so slight that Dawn didn't notice—another indicator that she had undergone some type of special training. "Cool your jets," she said crisply. "We're not going to fight, unless you've got your heart set on it."

Redling wasn't sure he could take her word for it. The woman was smaller than he was, but size wasn't everything, and he had no idea what special tools or weapons of her own she might carry. She didn't appear to pose any immediate threat, but he had seen similar situations turn ugly, fast.

"What's your problem with me?" he asked. "And with Ku-Ril-La?"

"None with you," she responded, "unless you count the Guy-troy."

"That's not an answer."

"It's as much of an answer as I can give you. I don't like the Controlled; I never have."

"That's twice now you've used that term. Explain it."

Dawn didn't reply.

"And the last time we had this chat, you said that Ku-Ril-La was the first you'd met of the Guy-troy."

This time, Dawn nodded. "He was," she said. "Only, I met him before I met you."

Redling abruptly realized that the woman's references to the Controlled were now singular, not plural.

Dawn took a deep breath and continued, "He was on the *Waltzing Spider*."

Redling blinked. That made a certain amount of sense; the *Waltzing Spider* was a luxury liner, a vessel far more appropriate to someone of Ku-Ril-La's wealth and prominence. He had seen the ship's name on Dawn's papers, but hadn't reviewed those of Ku-Ril-La, thanks to the unusual nature of his negotiations with the birdman. "I think you'd better explain yourself," he said.

"Not much to explain," the engineer said, shrugging. "He was on the *Spider*. You spend a lot of time chatting with him; haven't you ever even taken a moment to ask how he got to Farworld?"

Redling hadn't, he suddenly realized. The issue simply hadn't arisen. Of course, there had been other, more urgent matters on his mind at the time.

"What's your complaint against him, then?" he asked.

Dawn laughed, a good, solid laugh that seemed to come from deep inside her. "What do you think? Are you looking for some deep, dark secret that links the two of us?" She laughed again. "The truth's easier. He's a rude jerk with too much money and too much power. He thinks he can buy his way through all of creation. I spent too much time hustling drinks on Star Street to put myself through school to have much patience with men like that, no matter what the species." She made a wry expression. "Sometimes pit sloths have wings," she said.

"I haven't had any problem with him," Redling said, though he had to admit to himself that the Guytroy had a tendency toward condescension.

"Yeah, well, you're at the top of the pecking order here," Dawn said. "You may not have money, at least by his standards, but you have authority. He showed the *Spider's* captain professional courtesy, too."

Dawn's responses to his questions during her original interview drifted up now from Redling's memory. "He's the passenger who caused trouble with the captain?" he asked.

"Trouble with the—?" Dawn looked genuinely puzzled, then laughed again, as if remembering. "Oh, Drog, no!" she said. "That was a cute little financial analyst with roving hands and good taste in brandy. We got caught—"

Redling grinned.

Dawn blushed. The sudden flush of color softened the strong lines of her face and made her look somehow less imposing. "Never mind that," she said. "The captain cancelled my papers and put me off the ship, and I went looking for work. I found you." She shook her head. "I didn't know that I'd found Ku-Ril-La, too, until that afternoon in 'port court."

"Quite a coincidence," Redling said, feeling himself relax, and seeing Dawn relax, too. "The two of you, off the same ship, together again on a different one."

Dawn shrugged again. She rubbed her neck, as if to massage a soreness. "Coincidences happen," she said. "That's what the word means, Drog-nab it. I don't know what prompted the birdman to leave the *Spider*, but once he did, he had the same limited slate of options I did." She paused. "Farworld's not exactly a high-traffic stopover, you'll recall."

That was true. Redling remembered all too well how many supplicants had been eager to leave Farworld on the *Gateway*, and how desperate some of those individuals had been. He wouldn't have gone there himself, if not for the happenstance that had lead the real Redling to leave his starship there.

"I wasn't too happy to see Ku-Ril-La board the *Gateway*," she continued. "But that's life, and I can take the stones where they fall. I figured if I kept out of his way, things would go better. I don't know why I bother; he probably wouldn't even remember me. He didn't say anything about it in the courtroom, anyway. To be on the safe side, I spend most of my free time in my cabin."

"That's funny; so does he," Redling said. "Probably for different reasons. But why were you on his tail at the restaurant?"

"He was—that was—you think I was—following—" Dawn sputtered. She laughed again, more loudly this time. "Oh, that's good, that's rare, that's hot. I might as well ask why you were there. That line about pit sloth wasn't much of an explanation."

"You owe the pleasure of my presence entirely to the poor gambling skills and unseemly ambition of young Helicron Daas, and to the easily aroused ire of intemperate centaurs," Redling said. He gave her a brief summary of what had happened. "Now that I've answered your question, answer mine. Why were you there?"

"I don't have to answer that." Dawn looked annoyed.

"Maybe my next engineer will be more cooperative." He said the words lightly, but not so lightly that they weren't a threat.

"Good luck finding one before launch," Dawn said. Her voice held equal amounts of confidence and caution. "This isn't Farworld. It's not a buyer's market. More ships than staff here."

"I'm waiting."

"And I'd file a grievance with the Guild. There's a Registry Hall here."

Redling waited some more.

She looked at him again, and fidgeted a bit. "Oh, Drog," she said softly. "I was—um—lonely. I'd been on the ship a long time, and I'd been cooped in my cabin, and I was lonely."

Redling didn't say anything.

"I'd been weeks on a starship smaller than some ground cars, breathing the same canned air and seeing the same faces. You're nice enough—you're all nice enough, but I wanted something more than that. The last thing I wanted was to go out drinking with my crewmates, even though that's what I ended up doing." She hesitated. "I wanted an evening on the town, and dancing and companionship and maybe more." She blushed again, at such an appropriate point in her discourse that Redling was fairly sure the coloration was deliberate. "I was lonely," Dawn concluded.

Redling relaxed a bit, as the worst of his suspicions subsided. Despite the elaborate artifice of its telling, Dawn's was a reasonably believable story.

Even if he didn't happen to believe all of it.

He nodded, gestured again at the cargo modules. "I'm trusting you to keep our little inspection secret," he said.

Dawn laughed. "Who would I tell?" she asked. "And why? We spend three hours digging through pottery shards and knickknacks; who wants to hear about that?"

"And I'd keep close lips about the override, too, if I were you."

She nodded, but this time, she made no comment. They both knew that the device was a treasure.

Redling glanced at the time display on his wrist com. "It's still about seven hours until launch," he said. "Use some of that time to make sure all the rest of the cargo is secure."

"That's not my watch," Dawn said.

"It is now," Redling answered. He spoke in a distracted tone of voice, most of his mind occupied with other thoughts. Whoever, whatever Dawn really was, she had already proven herself too competent and too clever to be left to her own devices. It might be a good idea to keep her a bit busier on the next leg of the journey.

Dawn nodded. "Fair enough," she said. "Let the others know I might be a little bit late getting to the bridge, though. There's a lot of cargo to check."

"I'll see if I can get you some help," Redling lied cheerfully, and then excused himself. There was plenty for him to do, too as they prepared for launch.

And plenty to think about, as well.

Draen was a big world that hung in an eccentric orbit around a two-star system; one of its two suns was a blue-white giant, with a companion star that was little more than a dead husk, the collapsed matter remnant of a long-dead star. The arrangement was an unusual one, and difficult to account for using traditional astrophysics, but it had some remarkable ramifications. The dead star was smaller than the live one. Its orbit was such that it eclipsed its companion regularly, and on occasion, came close enough to make the blue-white sun's outer layers churn and roil, affecting the bigger star's output. Seasons on Draen tended to fluctuate wildly in length and intensity, and the planetary system was a rippling storm system of gravitic eddies and currents.

It was a clear and sunny day on Draen's surface when the *Gateway* lifted off, but it was storming in space.

"How long until we Jump?" Redling asked. Six hours had passed since takeoff, and he was bored.

Space travel for him was a means to an end, a way to get from world to world, and nothing more. Travelling as a ship's captain gave him more to think about than did travelling as a passenger, but only a little bit more.

"At least twenty hours," Helicron responded. His brow was wrinkled with concentration and he looked rather more mature than usual as he worked the controls at his station. He had set his dodecahedral lucky piece on the console before him, and he glanced at it as he spoke, as if for inspiration. "The dead sun is at its closest transit right now, and it's generating a fourth-order gravity harmonic. Folks on Draen can't feel it, but our drive is more sensitive. It's going to take us a while to get clear."

"He's right," Dawn confirmed. "We Jump now, or anytime soon, and we come back Drog only knows where or if."

Redling nodded. The news neither pleased nor surprised him. He didn't know much about the workings of the Jump Drive, but he knew that it was in some ways a very sensitive beast. He also knew only too well the hazards of making a Jump under any but the best possible circumstances.

Still—

"Twenty standard hours is a long time," he said. He hated waiting. "Is there any way we can trim it back a little?"

Helicron shook his head, but said nothing. He glanced in the general direction of the engineering station and the woman who sat behind it.

"No," Dawn said crisply. "In fact, based on these numbers, I'd say we should wait a bit longer—twenty-three or twenty-four."

"I wasn't aware that your expertise extended to Jump navigation," Redling said mildly. "Pretty impressive, considering you're still short of full cert."

"Not expertise; familiarity, maybe. I need to know a bit about it to do my job and I've been—"

"She's been helping me review my calculations," Helicron interrupted. He sounded both embarrassed and pleased. "She's really good. If she says it's twenty-four, it's twenty-four."

"Oh." Redling didn't know enough to say anything in response to that, so he changed the subject. "Pikk? Security status?"

"Looks clean to me," Thyller rumbled from the gunnery station. "I don't expect any trouble in-system. Draen's built up, and the local vicinity is pretty heavily patrolled. Not much chance of an attack here."

Redling nodded again. That made sense. Piracy was a fact of interstellar life, but it was a fact that became more prevalent along the less-travelled space lanes. Draen's system was too busy for most pirates' tastes. "Do you want to shut down, then?"

"No." Pikk spoke without moving, or taking his sleepy-looking eyes from the proximity scanner. "We're still in normal space."

"But you said—"

"Not much chance; not no chance. I'll stay at my station until first Jump."

"Twenty hours is a long time."

"Twenty-four is longer." An obstinate note entered the big man's voice. "I'll stay."

Redling looked at the others. "How about you two?" he asked. "Any reason you shouldn't take a break?"

"I'll take first watch," Dawn volunteered. "Get it out of the way, then I'll come back when we're ready to Jump."

"Makes sense. Helicron?"

"I've got three more geodesics I want to model and map, then I can close out the subroutine and put the nav on auto," the younger man said. "Should take an hour, then I'll break. I can take second watch."

"You'll need to be here at Jump."

All three crew members looked at him with something like condescension, and he knew why. They were the technical experts, the people whose lives were intertwined deeply with the workings of the *Gateway*, and that commonality bound them together in a way that his authority could not. His current role gave him obedience, but not fraternity.

"Okay," he said, smiling. "I'll get out of your way and let you do your jobs. Watch change at—" he looked at his com and named a time. "In the meantime, I'll make the rounds. Let me know about any status changes."

The only responses he got were a few mumbled affirmatives, and then even they were gone as the bridge exit slid shut behind him.

Other than crew, the *Gateway* had space for six passengers and currently carried five. Four travelled Middle, paying moderate fare for moderately sized and moderately comfortable accommodations. The current contingent included a data engineer bound for Mariposa by way of Hawkin's World; two couriers serving combines somewhat less impressive than the Kaal; and a reserved Vilani gentleman who had declined to tell

Redling his business, but who had an excellent hand-shake. Redling had personally interviewed each before taking them on board, and he was reasonably satisfied with them as passengers. The data engineer laughed at too many of his jokes, the couriers were by turns smug and paranoid, and the Vilani kept almost completely to himself, but those drawbacks were small ones.

Now, Redling visited each of the passenger cabins, tapped on their hatch covers, and exchanged pleas-antries with the occupants. Were the accommodations to their liking? So far, yes, but the food could be better. Had the crew been helpful (at least to the appropriate level)? Sure, but kid with the die was always looking for a gaming partner. Were there any questions regard-ing the *Gateway*'s itinerary? No, but everyone hoped there would be no more unscheduled stops. Redling made the courtesy partly because they fit his role as captain, and partly because they gave him something to do while Dawn and the others labored over the com-mand station controls. There weren't many com-plaints—most travellers knew what they were getting when they booked passage on a Far Trader—and Redling fielded them all as best he could. He answered queries and gave assurances to one Middle passenger at a time before moving on to the next.

Ku-Ril-La was a different nest of tree-weasels, how-ever.

For the *Gateway*'s lone High passenger, someone had enabled his cabin's intercom, so that the Guy-troy could respond to Redling's knock without opening the door.

"Enter, Redling," the familiar voice said from the recessed speaker, even as the hatch locked clicked open.

"How did you know it was me?" Redling asked, entering.

The Guy-troy's stateroom was large enough to hold a few bits of utilitarian furniture, in addition to the folding bed that Redling knew was behind one wall. Ku-Ril-La was seated now in a chair purchased especially for him, at a combination desk and worktable that had been among the *Gateway*'s factory-issue accoutrements. He looked up from a book-reader as Redling entered, and the movement made the leathery folds of his wings rustle. "The cadence of your footsteps," the Guy-troy said, "and the timing of your visit. I've noticed that such calls are traditional among your kind."

The second part of Ku-Ril-La's response came as no surprise to Redling, but the first did. Apparently, the Guy-troy had hearing that was exceptionally keen, at least by human standards. Redling mentally filed the datum away for future reference.

There was a guest chair in the stateroom. Ku-Ril-La gestured with one talon, and Redling flowed into the battered piece of furniture. "Twenty-plus hours to Jump," he said. "We'll make up for it later, though."

"I assume Draen's two-sun system is the reason for the delay," the Guy-troy said.

"You assume correctly," responded Redling, who was fast tiring of other people knowing more than he did, no matter how arcane the subject.

"It was the same in my youth," Ku-Ril-La said. "Strange. So many years have passed since I was last here, and so little has changed."

"The sign of a mature culture and technology, I'm told."

Ku-Ril-La emitted a very human sounding snort and

drummed his talons on the chair arms so hard that
chips flew. "Mature? Hardly. Maturity comes with discipline and order, and the Imperium has neither. Your
people have built an empire, and then made of it a
playground."

Redling wasn't sure how to respond to that. He was
willing to grant that the Imperium was still, in many
ways, a raw and adventurous place—but he didn't
agree that such was an undesirable situation. "Personally, I'm not very fond of rules," he said. He grinned.
"Others disagree, I'm sure."

"A preference based on your heredity," Ku-Ril-La
said. "My ancestors flew in flocks, with one leader and
secure positions for all." He flexed his wings, unfold-
ing them only to half their span; even so, they seemed
to fill the stateroom. "We fly still, you know, in the
right gravity and the proper air. We are not prisoners of
the soil." He closed his wings. "Your people, however,
descend from social primates, with an incompletely
developed hierarchy—"

His words trailed off and he fell silent. One claw
pressed the book-reader's on/off switch, and waited for
its screen to go dark before speaking again.

"I err," Ku-Ril-La said, "and, perhaps, I offend."

"No, no, not at all," Redling said, surprised by the
sense of melancholy that had suddenly suffused the
cramped cabin.

Ku-Ril-La shrugged, a movement he had never
before made in Redling's presence. Was it a new addition to his repertoire? Redling couldn't be sure, but it
made the winged man look surprisingly human, at least
for the moment.

"No. You have paid me the courtesy of a visit, and

I have rewarded you with a lecture." Ku-Ril-La paused.
"I enjoy seeing new worlds, but I do not particularly
enjoy space travel, Redling. I do not like being sealed
inside a metal box and hidden so completely from the
sky."

"I can understand that," Redling said.

"Can you? Can you know what it means to such as
I, to know that an infinitude of open space awaits
beyond a few layers of steel and alloy?"

"Well, in about twenty hours, there won't be anything outside the *Gateway*'s hull, not even nothing."

"Eh?" The Guy-troy paused. "Oh. Jump Space; of
course. The space that is not space." He paused again.
"Your words do not give me comfort."

"So now I've offended," Redling said. He grinned
some more. "That means we're even."

"Mmph. Yes, I suppose we are," the Guy-troy said.
He thought a moment, and seemed to relax. "Did you
see to my associate's cargo?"

"All stowed and secure, waiting to land on
Carstairs."

"Did you inspect it?"

"Of course not," Redling lied cheerfully. "Your
word is good with me. Besides, you're exempt from
any rule you're likely to break."

"After a fashion, though that exemption carries a
price," Ku-Ril-La said.

"Most do."

"And I'm not certain my immunity extends to my
associates, in any case. Starport Court on Carstairs
may well be less easily cowed than that on a low nest
like Farworld."

Redling blinked as the implications of the comment

sank in. "You were running a bluff," he said slowly. "You risked my life and my ship on a bluff."

"Bluff? No landscape was involved."

"Same word, different meaning. Young Helicron can provide details. You claimed powers that were not yours."

Ku-Ril-La shrugged again. "They are mine," he said, "but they are also argued, from time to time, especially extended to cover someone else under my wing. I had no certainty that the judge would allow you to leave Farworld under my protection. Fortunately, the complexity of the jurisdictional question exceeded her limited reasoning abilities, and she allowed herself to be swayed by long words that she did not fully understand." Redling looked at the Guytroy for a long moment and said nothing.

"Does this news offend you anew?" Ku-Ril-La finally asked.

Redling laughed, and his laughter grew louder as he thought of Sascha and Chim Blork, and the frustrated expression on Judge Crondor's tired face. For the first time in his recent memory, he laughed long, loud, and hard, and when the guffaws finally faded he had to wipe tears from his eyes.

"Offended?" he asked. "Oh, no, no, no. Impressed is the word." He laughed again, more softly this time. "Oh, this was worth the price of a High passage, and worth more besides. I knew there was something about you that I liked, Ku-Ril-La, and you've just proven me right."

The *Gateway*'s staterooms were small, but the ship's crew cabins qualified as such only under a generous definition of the word. There were reasons for the disparity, as there are for most.

Every cubic centimeter on a starship is a cubic centimeter that costs a considerable investment in energy—energy to launch up from a planetary surface, energy to push through normal space, energy to transfer into the nonrelativistic wonderland of Jump Space, and still more energy to reverse all three processes.

To the owner of a starship, *energy* is just another word for *money*. Every bit of space in a starship that doesn't earn a profit (such as, this trip, the *Gateway*'s unused passenger stateroom) generates a loss instead. This mindset tends to encourage a certain degree of thriftiness among ship designers, one with especially noticeable impact on a utilitarian craft like the *Gateway*.

A Far Trader's passenger cabins are relatively large, and so are cargo holds, because they make money. Crew's quarters aren't, because they don't. A captain's quarters is scarcely larger than a secure public communications booth; a crewmember's tends to be smaller—sometimes, quite a bit smaller.

Forces other than brute economics shape design principles, of course. Style and aesthetics don't count for much, but ergonomics and morale do. Necessity—the need to make the best possible use of all available space—is the mother of some remarkably ingenious designs that wring every last bit of utility and comfort from the cramped cabins. Morale, on the other hand, demands that ship personnel—at least, human personnel—be assured of a reasonable degree of security and privacy.

A member of the K'Kree will go mad when given solitude. A human can go mad when denied it. When that same human is on a starship, surrounded by the close company of only a few faces, faces that all too quickly become all too familiar, the need for privacy can become especially great.

To that end, the crew cabins on a Far Trader have locking hatches, keyed to the thumbprints of their assigned occupants. The hatches aren't particularly heavy ones, and the locks aren't especially sophisticated, but both are quite adequate to ensure that the occupant can detect any intrusion, even one by the ship's captain.

Unless, of course, the ship's captain happens to wear an override hand unit, crafted by the long-dead Droyne.

Redling tapped the index finger of his right hand against the lock to the hatch cover he stood before. This time, it took only one touch; the catch mechanism clicked and released, allowing the hatch cover to swing out on recessed hinges. Redling pulled it shut behind him as he stepped into the confines of Dawn F'Ral's "private, secure" cabin.

Once, when he had been wearing another face and using another name, certain business endeavors of Redling's had gone suddenly, spectacularly bad. He had taken refuge then in the monasteries of Nephlim, a backward planet occupied largely by anti technologists who had embraced an aggressively austere style of living. Dawn's cabin on the *Gateway* was smaller even than his monkish cell on Nephlim had been, and only slightly more decorated.

It was the twin of several others on the craft. Four steel walls bounded a rectangular bit of plastic flooring about as long as Redling was tall. The wall opposite the hatch was a structural support, adorned only with a minimalist holoscreen that could display entertainment files. Panels in the wall to his left hid a folding cot; more panels on the right wall masked a closet and storage space. He started there, opening each drawer, lifting out it the contents, and then replacing them after careful inspection.

Like most spacers, Dawn travelled light. Mostly, Redling found about what he had expected—clothing, toiletries, papers, and a very few keepsakes, most of which, Redling figured, would fit comfortably into the single duffel and valise that rested in the tiny closet.

His engineer apparently owned two of the jumpsuits she wore onboard (three, counting the one she presumably wore now), and two more casual outfits, with a small selection of versatile accessories. Her vanity case held a good assortment of makeup, cosmetic contact lenses, and grooming aids, along with unsurprising over-the-counter medications. A zippered portfolio yielded a dozen certification forms that Redling had already reviewed, and the study disks that would enable Dawn to earn more. Another small case, this one padded, held a half-dozen pieces of jewelry. There was nothing that Redling's educated eye found particularly desirable, but nothing that qualified as trash, either. Redling assessed their value at levels entirely appropriate to a woman of Dawn's apparent means. He tucked the glistening bits of metal and precious stones back in their home and turned his attention to the duffel and valise.

The duffel held only air, but the valise proved a bit more disconcerting. The first surprise was the lock—it was a good one, better than the one that held the door, and good enough that Redling had to tap it twice for the override to engage. The incongruity of the lock faded in significance when compared to what it secured, however.

Pistols: one laser and one projectile, with matching energy cells and ammunition stowed below them. Knives: steel-bladed, ceramic, and plastic, a half-dozen assorted sizes and shapes with concealed carry-sheaths, clipped to storage boards that folded out for easy access. Electronic equipment: tiny surveillance units and recorders, and a miniature fuel-cell arrangement to trickle-charge them. Money: two thick sheaves of bearer bonds that were good at any Kaal-backed bank, which meant that they were good almost anywhere.

Redling locked the case again and put it away. It seemed lighter than its contents suggested, and he wondered if its structure hid some kind of gravity compensation device.

Why shouldn't it? It was similar to his personal weapons case in nearly every other respect. Only the lack of fake IDs made the match incomplete. Despite that shortcoming, whoever Dawn F'Ral really was—assuming for the moment that was really her name—she certainly came well equipped. With equipment like this, a properly trained individual could do an significant amount of damage in a very short time.

Certainly, Redling knew that he could.

He had to assume that "Dawn" could, too.

Redling's face wore a thoughtful expression as he clicked the closet door shut. Everything was precisely back in place; he knew how to search for clues without leaving any. He pressed one ear to the hatch cover's cool surface, listening for footfalls in the corridor outside, and then he left his engineer's quarters.

He had hoped the search would yield some answers; instead, it had only generated more questions.

Ones that seemed far more urgent.

CHAPTER SIX

The gravity currents sweeping invisibly through Draen's planetary system proved more problematic than either Dawn or Helicron had anticipated. The wait until first Jump stretched from twenty standard hours all the way to twenty-seven before the faint but familiar sensation coursed through the ship and its occupants, and the *Gateway* dropped once more into Jump Space.

"About time," Redling said softly, and almost immediately wished he hadn't.

Even as spoke, Pikk Thyller was disengaging himself from the gunnery station. Wordlessly, the big man peeled off the wireless headset that linked him to the ship's defense systems. It was a flexible web of sensors and pickups that conformed itself to the shape of his skull. Now, as Thyller emerged from behind the headset's tinted visor, all could easily see the signs of fatigue on the big man's square features. Dark shadows pooled beneath his eyes, and his typical reserved expression had eroded enough to reveal something much more human, more vulnerable beneath.

Amazingly, Thyller had remained at the cramped gunnery station continuously for the entire twenty-seven hours, Redling abruptly realized. The big man had been so silent and unmoving that he had faded into the background, and Redling had very nearly forgotten his presence.

Now freed of his duties, Thyller stood and stretched.

As he did, the stiffened joints of his body popped in rapid sequence, sounding for all the worlds like bones breaking or like shots being fired. The staccato barrage was loud enough to cut easily through the background chatter and hum of the bridge area.

"Tired," the big man said. He massaged his thick neck with blunt fingers, but seemed reluctant to expend the energy it took to say anything more. "Back later." He trudged toward the bridge exit. The cramped space suddenly seemed more spacious as he left it.

Redling watched Thyller go, quietly astonished by the feat of endurance that had just come to an end.

"He never took a break, either," Helicron said, in something like awe. He had his lucky die in one hand and was fidgeting with it again, rolling the multisided bit of colored plastic between his fingers, then casting it on his console's work surface. He looked at the characters the gaming piece displayed, nodded as if seeing what he expected, and then rolled it again. He looked tired, too, but Redling knew that the young man's fatigue had considerably less justification. "I don't know how he did it, I've only been back on duty for four hours," Helicron continued, "and I'm already beat."

"That's because you spend most of your energy playing games, or thinking about them," Dawn said tartly. Ever since their encounter in the restaurant on Draen, she had displayed an inconsistent impatience with Helicron. Redling had been doubly surprised to learn of her sessions helping the younger man with his studies—both in view of her deteriorating relationship with the youngster, and also that she even had the requisite knowledge.

"Didn't you notice?" Dawn continued. "Thyller

scarcely moved a muscle the entire time he was in that chair. He was conserving himself. That's discipline." Her admiration was evident.

Redling disagreed. "That's overkill," he said. "His choice, but still overkill." He had taken more than one long watch himself, in settings rather spectacularly less hospitable than the *Gateway*'s bridge, and he knew how difficult they could be. Pikk Thyller's accomplishment impressed him more than the fact that he had accomplished it unnecessarily. "Draen's a secure port; Pikk could have taken a break."

"It's discipline," Dawn repeated, but in a milder tone of voice this time, as if seeking to avoid a confrontation. "He came up through the Imperial Marines, and they make it a point of honor not to leave their posts while there services are still—or might be—required."

Neither Redling nor Helicron had anything to say to that.

"Besides, he was right," Dawn continued. She was looking at her control monitor, tapping a key now and then, and closing out her part in the initial Jump. Recalibrating the complex engine circuitry would come later, but there were preparatory steps for her to take now. "Just because a sector is heavily patrolled doesn't make it immune. Security can't be everywhere. There were two major incidents in-system a year ago, involving merchant liners, even if they weren't widely reported."

"How did you hear about them, then?" Redling drawled lazily. He asked the question less to elicit a response than to amuse himself. The mystery surrounding his lone female crew member was troublesome, but it did have the advantage of offering the opportunity for entertainment. He liked listening to

Dawn's glib explanations to his occasional question. Games like Spindledrift and Choskey bored him, but he had always been able to derive some enjoyment from a brisk round of tree-weasel and floogle rat.

"Heard about it on the *Spider*," Dawn answered promptly. "The *Spider* and one of the merchants were chartered by the same combine. Captain Steevrosafool had some tales to tell."

Redling grinned. Dawn hadn't disappointed, so he decided to press the issue. "I'm surprised he took the time to chat with you. You two were less than close, last I heard." He said the words in a carefully casual tone of voice, taking caution not to let his suspicions give color to them.

Dawn didn't rise to that bait, either. "He wasn't speaking specifically to me," she said. "We were in Jump, he was drunk and at dinner, and he thought we were all as bored as he was."

Her account was pretty believable, actually. There simply wasn't much for most members of a ship's crew to do while the craft was in Jump Space, especially on a heavily staffed starship, and alcoholism was not exactly uncommon among the higher ranks.

Luxury liners like the *Spider* were both big and profitable enough so that a captain could get away with besotted behavior, at least for a while. Ships that size could also support elaborate dining halls, where the tradition of dining at the captain's table still held sway.

"Pirate incidents in heavily trafficked zones aren't exactly publicized," Dawn continued, "but word gets around," She paused. "It has to."

Redling nodded. "The only thing that moves faster

than a ship in Jump Space is gossip on the floogle vine." The floogle was a widespread, fruit-bearing vine used in many different popular dishes.

"Most people like to talk. It's something to do," Dawn said sourly. "Travel can be so monotonous."

"You've picked the wrong profession to pursue if you really feel that way."

"There's plenty to do onboard," Helicron said eagerly. He rolled his die yet again. It clicked as it bounced against the projecting switches and control buttons of his workstation. "If you're a gamester, I've got Spindledrift and Kimble, and Choskey, and multilevel Spa'am." He seemed ready to rattle off some more names, but fell silent as Redling shot him a pointed glance.

There was a reason for that. Words spoken earlier by a passenger drifted up from Redling's memory, a comment the data engineer had made about the ship's youngest crew member's unrelenting search for gaming partners. That, and his recollection of a frantic chase through the alleys of Draen reminded Redling that a certain shipboard situation still needed solving. He strolled over to the navigation workstation, and his long fingers easily caught Helicron's rolling die in mid-tumble.

"You've got gaming equipment on board, do you?" Redling asked, gazing at the single die. "You and I should have a bit of a get-together, then."

The younger man looked up at him. "You told me before you don't gamble," he said cautiously.

"I don't," Redling said, "usually."

Helicron didn't seem to have a response to that, other than an apprehensive expression.

"Oh, don't worry," Redling continued, clapping a

hand on his shoulder, gently enough to signify cama-
raderie, but forcefully enough to signal command, too.
"It'll be fun."

He didn't say for whom.

Two hours later, very obviously nervous and even more
obviously unhappy, Helicron Daas rolled his dice
again. This time, his hand held the full complement of
Spindledrift pieces—two dodecahedral dice and a cubi-
cal one. The three bits of dense plastic rattled and rolled
across the surface of the Spindledrift board. Two landed on black squares and one lay athwart the single
available green space.

Helicron sighed, drew a card—blank to the human
eye—from the appropriate stack, and slid it into the
board slot nearest him. Within the Spindledrift unit,
sensors read the card and chattered to one another, and
then the colorful markings on the board surface traded
places.

The spaces that the dice rested on—all of them—
were red now.

Helicron smiled and breathed a sigh of relief. The
smile that spread across his face made him look his
youthful age once more, which was a change. He had
spent much of the last two hours looking old beyond
his years.

"Now, there's a Full Narkle," Redling said, genuinely happy. He scooped up the three dice. "Very nice.
Looks like a winner to me."

Helicron smiled some more. "Some folks have the
touch," he said.

Redling rolled the dice, then drew a card and
entered it, performing all three actions so swiftly that

they seemed to flow together into one. Almost as swiftly, the Spindledrift board redrew its boundaries yet again.

This time, the squares where the dice had fallen were green, purple, and gray.

Helicron's face, however, was the color of sloth's milk.

"Yes, some people do," Redling said. "Double Narkle, game and set!" He was delighted but not surprised, and manfully resisted the temptation to chortle as he examined the values that the gaming board's liquid crystal display revealed. One string of numbers was the round's score, expressed in points. The other was a tally of winnings, expressed in credits. Both numbers were in Redling's favor, and quite high, at least by most people's standards.

As Redling watched, the numbers in his columns grew higher.

"Another round?" the man who claimed to be Navis Redling asked. He and his subordinate were seated in a multipurpose space that served thrice per ship-day as the dining area for those passengers who chose not to take their meals in their staterooms. Right now, however, its function was less clear.

Helicron was clearly laboring under the impression that it was a temporary gambling den. Certainly, he had been told as much by his superior.

Redling knew that it was a classroom, and that he was the teacher.

"That's not—that's not possible," Helicron said softly, managing to pack an entire life's worth of anxiety and doubt into a few tentative words, spoken in a youthful voice. He smiled nervously, apparently trying to soften the implication of his words.

Redling, for his part, chose to take a different tack. He was extremely skilled at freighting a single syllable with an inordinate amount of menace, and he used that skill now.

"Oh?" he said softly.

He didn't smile.

"I—that board—it—" Helicron said. His lips, pale now, trembled and turned downward, and he fell silent.

"Might something be wrong with the board?" Redling asked. His voice was a silken purr now. "You have reason to believe that it malfunctions? I had noticed some eccentricities in play. Oddities in the odds, shall we say."

Helicron didn't say anything.

"But it's your board," Redling mused. The younger man had been very eager to retrieve it from his cabin two hours earlier, when Redling had proposed playing a few games, "just to take the edge off and to keep you from pestering the passengers too terribly much."

"If there's something wrong with it, it's your responsibility," Redling continued.

"No, no, it's a good board, it's been calibrated," Helicron said nervously. He touched the brass-colored certification seal fused to one corner of the Spindledrift board. "See?"

"I was meaning to ask you about that, Helicron. A properly certified board isn't cheap, and it seems to me that one would be almost impossible to come across in a slither pit like Farworld."

"My mother gave it to me. It belonged to my father," Helicron said doggedly. "He left it behind when he—"

"Your father?" Redling composed his face in a quizzical expression. "The dear departed professional gamester who looms so large in feted memory?"

Doggedness gave way to defensiveness, and Helicron balled his hands into fists, though he did not raise them. "Don't say he's dead! No one knows if he's dead!"

"The word *departed* has more than one meaning," Redling observed mildly. "But a professional gamester like your absent antecedent would certainly know how to tickle a board." He made a show of studying the numbered seal. "This is a very old cert stamp," he said.

"You know how to tickle, too. You said so."

"Oh, Helicron, oh, oh, oh," Redling said, making each syllable more ominous than the one before. "Just because you've had a run of bad luck, that's no reason to suggest that your captain—your *superior*—would stoop so low as to cheat his subordinates." He did not smile as he spoke, or allow any mockery to enter his voice; he knew full well that Helicron was implying precisely that.

One secret of *being* dangerous lay in knowing when to *sound* dangerous, Redling knew. He also knew himself sufficiently well to recognize that he was very dangerous, indeed.

"No! No, I didn't mean anything like that!" Helicron was a paler shade of milk now.

Redling continued as if the younger man had not spoken. "Because if you are, and if you'd rather not stay in my service, we can divert to a mining colony—"

"No, no, I know you would never cheat."

"Good," Redling said, well pleased by the words, even though he knew precisely the contrary. He grinned so broadly that his handsome features positively radiated cheer and good will once more. He scooped up the dice. "Another round?"

"No." Helicron shook his head. "No. I—I don't feel like playing anymore."

Redling gazed levelly at him. His silence was eloquent.

"It's not that, no," Helicron repeated his denial to Redling's unvoiced question.

"What is it then?" Redling paused. He tapped one long finger on the Spindledrift board's surface. "I really must insist you provide a reason."

The younger man fidgeted, looking even more youthful than his years. "Can't play. I'm broke," he finally said. "You've cleaned me out."

"Really? Now, that's a shame." Redling extended the hand that held the dice, and opened it. "I thought you had done well on Draen. Certainly, a half-dozen centaurs were in awe of your gaming skills."

Helicron stared longingly at the three chunks of plastic that rested in Redling's extended hand. "I did," he said, "and since, too, but you've cleaned me out." He paused. "Even my reserves."

"Ah." Redling paused a moment, pretending to think. "I've got it!" he said cheerfully, smiling even more broadly than before. "I don't know why I didn't think of it before! There's no problem!"

"There isn't?"

"We can play for your wages!"

"My wages!?"

"Of course, of course." Redling said a value. "You've got that much coming to you, maybe a bit more, for the rest of the trip. We can play for quite a while against a credit-clutch that size. That's not including your meal allowance, of course. We'll keep that separate."

"But—my wages—I—"

"And maybe beyond." Redling composed his face in a mask of paternal sincerity. "I want you to know that your credit's as good with me as your credits are."

"But."

"No, no, no; no objections. I insist on giving you a chance to win back your reserve," Redling said. The humor and good will left his voice for a moment, and the dangerous quality returned. "You really must take the dice and play some more. I wouldn't want to think you don't trust me."

Helicron took the dice. He rolled them, then drew a card and inserted it.

"Say!" Redling said, reading the board. "Good toss! A Double Narkle of your own! Maybe your luck has turned."

Then Redling took up the dice again, and proved his words wrong.

"Helicron told me you had quite a run of luck on the board yesterday," Dawn F'Ral said to Navis Redling. They were both seated in the bridge cabin, the only two current occupants of the cramped space that was the *Gateway's* control center. Redling was more than an hour into his watch shift, which meant that Dawn was well out of hers, but she showed no signs of leaving. That didn't particularly surprise Redling. On duty, a crew member could read displays, look for problems, and sound alarms, should the need arise. Off duty, a crew member could occupy his or her idle hours by choosing between—

Very little, actually, especially during the night's smallest hours, when the galley closed and everyone else was asleep. There were disks to read or watch and little else.

The *Gateway*'s official schedule reflected typical human circadian rhythms—the ship's clocks demarcated twenty-two standard hours, grouped in two equal blocks further designated as night and day. The latter labels were entirely arbitrary; not only was the *Gateway* nowhere near any planetary surface or star that could define such a division, but there were no worlds or suns in Jump Space to do that job.

The *Gateway*'s sixth passenger was boredom, and that unwanted companion spent a great deal of time with the crew.

"Helicron tells me you taught him a bit about Spindledrift yesterday," Dawn said. For once, her words seemed to carry no hidden meaning. "Most captains wouldn't treat a crewman like that."

"I'm not most captains," Redling said. He flipped a switch and accessed a data log, then began reviewing the characters that filled his screen. He didn't have much idea of what most of them meant, but he wanted to look as captainlike as possible. "And what way?"

"You cleaned him out."

"He wanted to play; we played."

"He doesn't have a credit to his name now. Come Plimbo, he won't even be able to afford shore accommodations."

"Maybe he can earn a bit by volunteering for extra duty before then," Redling said. He had a few jobs in mind that the younger man could accomplish easily enough, even though they didn't fall within his job description. He hadn't told Helicron about them yet. "Inventory the dining utensils or polish the deck plates or reline the septic system, scut work like that. I seem to have a bit extra in my operating budget at the moment."

"That extra being the wages that he works so hard to earn whenever he sits at his station."

"Feeling sorry for the lad? I thought you and he were less than chummy these days."

"So he's naïve and he can be a jerk. That doesn't mean he shouldn't get paid for his work." She paused. "He's a good kid."

Redling took his gaze from the display screen and shifted it to Dawn's thoughtful features instead. "He's a good kid who was fleecing the passengers," he said, "or trying to. I had complaints, and I had to do something about them."

"You could have simply told him."

Redling shook his head. "No. I tried that, over dinner, back on Draen. Remember our little get-together? Besides, if he wasn't going to listen to six drunken centaurs with knives and clubs, he wasn't going to listen to me, either. He's read a dozen text disks on how to win at gaming, and nothing I could say was going to convince him that the 'latest techniques' he knows are hopelessly out of date." Redling paused. "Port players like to see their money up front. The kid can't play if he can't pay, and he can't pay if he doesn't have any money. I had a problem, and I solved it." He smiled tightly.

"Did you cheat to do it?"

Redling waited a long moment before answering. "I didn't cheat," he said mildly, forcing back the same wave of irritation he had felt when Helicron made a comment similar to Dawn's. "I played according to Helicron's rules," he continued. "I didn't do anything that he didn't do, or didn't try."

"That's not much of an answer."

"It's the only one you're going to get."

Plimbo was densely populated, a highly urbanized world with more than a thousand years of history to its society—enough years that the original colony had matured to a nation, then split, and split again. Now, more than a dozen nations squabbled incessantly over their portions of the planet's main land masses. Though Plimbo in theory was an integral part of the Imperium, with a duly appointed Imperial Governor, the reality was that it behaved more like a planet in the pre-star-flight stage of development. The separate states all pledged fealty to the greater interstellar authority—the Imperium—but various ethnic and political factions contended for dominance on a planetary level. The situation was a direct result of three key factors—an established, industrialized society, a diminishing frontier, and a succession of weak Imperial Governors who commanded great power but only rarely wielded it effectively.

In short, Plimbo tended to be an adventurous place.

"We're inside the outermost surveillance perimeter," a remarkably subdued and nearly penniless Helicron Daas said, "and we're making our closest approach to any civilian navigation beacon."

"Can you raise the Starport Authority yet?"

Helicron shook his head. "Haven't tried. We're too far out, and even if we could, transmission lag would make communications difficult."

"Plimbo's governments have traditionally believed that distant borders make good neighbors," Dawn said. "At least, on an intersystem level."

Redling shrugged. "They might be right. I've been to worlds where seeing the smoke from a neighbor's cooking fire means it's time to move."

"What worlds were those?"

"None you're likely to have heard of," Redling said easily, but he was annoyed. In recent days, Dawn had become steadily more inquisitive, and correspondingly less discreet as she probed. Instead of actually answering her question, he asked one of his own. "How long before we're close enough for an update download?"

While drafting the *Gateway*'s itinerary, Tithe had bought data files on most of the ship's various destinations, providing input on local politics, economy, geography, etc. Tithe being Tithe, however, those files had not been the very best available. They were incomplete and sketchy. Moreover, the limitations of interstellar communications meant that they were already outdated, even before being loaded into the *Gateway*'s computer. Regimes might have raised themselves and fallen again since the time-date stamp on the data file. Most starport authorities provided detailed data dumps to bring visiting starships up to date.

"Doing that now, Captain." Helicron had become a bit more observant of on-board protocol of late, and displayed the desperate courtesy of the impoverished. "The nav beacons serve as com relays, too." He looked at his display, nodded. "Twenty minutes to completion, out of forty-two."

"Forty-two minutes?" A typical flash download took less than a third that long. "What in Drog's name are they sending us? Their entire census reports?"

"There are many factions on Plimbo," Dawn said. "Countries, political parties, religious sects, ethnic enclaves. There's a lot to detail. Plus, there's usually at least one war going on somewhere."

Redling thought about that for a moment. "How do they feel about visitors?"

"They love them," Helicron said eagerly, before Dawn could respond. "Everyone on Plimbo loves anyone who's from anywhere else!"

"I find that hard to believe."

"No, no, really! I've heard about this place! It's a tourist's paradise! Bars, bawdy houses, casinos," Helicron's face fell fleetingly as he mentioned a pleasure that was no longer a realistic option for him, then rose again as he continued. "They—"

"There's some truth to what he says, actually," Dawn interrupted. "Plimbo's economy relies heavily on interstellar commerce for export, and the culture as a whole is old enough to have created some pretty interesting tourist sites." Her voice took on a sweet note, too faint to be noticed by any but Redling's practiced ear. "I'm surprised you don't know more about the place."

"Oh?" With speed that had been enhanced by recent practice, Redling reviewed his cache of purchased memories and found no matches. Neither of him had ever been to Plimbo before. "Why would that surprise you? This track is new to me."

Dawn closed out the Jump control panel and turned in her chair to face him. "Plimbo's famous," she said. "At least, to commercial spacing personnel. The locals all love off-Plimbo credits even more than they hate each other. The whole place is just one big Star Street.

Or so the story goes." She sounded almost challenging now, but not quite.

"I've heard that about other places," Redling said. "Even been to some of them. In my experience, it's never that simple."

Helicron had the disappointed look of a child given the wrong toy, but Dawn merely looked skeptical.

"Tell us more," she said.

Redling opened his mouth to reply, only to be cut off by another voice, a rumbling growl, that voiced a single word.

"Noisy," Pikk Thyller rumbled.

Redling, Helicron, and Dawn all blinked as they heard the single word. It was the first time in any of their experience that Thyller, while on duty, had joined in a conversation, at least during approach or departure. Typically, he remained utterly silent, unless asked a specific question.

"Noisy here or noisy on Plimbo?" Redling asked patiently. He had to wonder that had prompted the comment.

"Too many brawls," the gunnery officer continued. He still wore his headset and his voice had a faraway quality to it. Thyller was obviously still focusing closely on the job at hand, and Redling was surprised that he had even noticed the words spoken around him, much less made a response.

"Um, yes," Redling said, genuinely stunned that someone of Thyller's size and combat skills would adjudge any place as having too many brawls. He glanced in Dawn's direction again.

She was still gazing at him steadily, as if in expectation.

"Waiting for something, Dawn?" He knew what she was waiting for—his answer to her seemingly casual question. Redling was a facile liar and his mind now filled with explanations for his lack of Plimbo expertise—half a dozen different rationales, all of them perfectly reasonable. He pushed them aside. The answer to Dawn's question didn't matter, but the question itself did.

The question, and the fact that Dawn had asked it, and the fact that she expected him to answer her inquiry. It certainly had been no mere conversational gambit.

He turned in his chair and looked in her direction. "Waiting for something?" he repeated. He thought about the weapons he had found in her quarters.

Who was Dawn F'Ral, really? And was it time to consider getting rid of her?

She looked back at him, and an inconsequential second stretched into several awkward ones and then began to congeal.

A computer chirped.

"Done!" Helicron said cheerfully. He pushed some more keys. "Who wants to read the download?"

His words were enough to break the tension of the moment, and gave Dawn a chance to look away. "I'll take it," she said, "patch it through to me."

Redling watched her as she began to review the data, and shrugged.

There would be time for that storm to break later.

As the *Gateway* approached Plimbo's atmosphere, Redling's bridge monitor provided a better look at the planet than all the files and file updates in creation could hope to. From a distance it looked like many other human-hospitable worlds—a dappled orb set against a darker sky, with a film of atmosphere and clouds incompletely obscuring its surface. The files Redling had reviewed stated that only forty-seven percent of the planetary surface was covered with water, which sounded about right; even to his naked, eye, Plimbo was more green and brown than blue, more land than sea. That suggested the planet had an overall greater density than most in its class, which explained its paired attributes of Terra-normal gravity and sub-Terra size. He had no doubt that whichever explorer had stumbled onto the place some ten centuries before had been delighted with his or her discovery; it must have been a beautiful place.

It wasn't now.

Even from low orbit, even with the limited resolution of the *Gateway*'s hull cameras, Redling could see the scars of war. The main land mass, a vaguely oval continent that stretched across the equatorial boundaries, was marked with overlapping dark rings that were easily recognizable as weathered blast craters. A small piece of land, bridged by an isthmus to the larger one, was mostly a dull brown, only slightly fringed with a halo of green—a sure indicator of long-term defoliant bombardments, with the poisons' work only slowly being undone by the cleansing sea. Even the northern ice cap, instead of being the expected pristine white, was punctuated by a black crescent that stretched across most of its width. The mark of a weather bomb? A biological weapon gone wrong? The wreckage of some large-scale cataclysm? Redling couldn't be sure, and he wasn't sure that he wanted to know.

He didn't mind a necessary killing now and then, but he cared little for war.

"Current meteorological and environmental stats coming in now, on the 'port frequencies," Helicron said. "Clear and cool at the primary starport. Low humidity, some sunspot activity. High Chryssling factor."

Redling thought of something. "Background radiation?" he asked.

"Low-Normal," Helicron said. "Why?"

"Is that our reading or theirs?" The *Gateway's* hull carried various sensors, long-range and immediate proximity, and Redling remembered spending more than a few credits on their recalibration while docked on Draen. One function of the equipment was to scan planetary surfaces, though that capacity was typically reserved for worlds less developed than Plimbo.

Helicron pushed some buttons, looked at another screen, then made a puzzled sound. "That's a surprise," he said. "How long is our stayover?"

"Four standard days," Redling said. He wondered where the younger man would spend it. "Why?"

"We should be okay for four, but if these readings are correct, the ambient radiation isn't Low-Normal— it's High-Normal, verging on pure High in some sectors. Not a hazard, but—"

"But a lie, " Redling said softly. "Or just a bit of misdirection?" He had no doubt that, if confronted on the issue, starport administrators would claim to have made an honest mistake.

"That's if we're right and they're wrong," Helicron muttered. He seemed to have invested a lot of himself in the idea that Plimbo was a spacer's paradise.

Redling glanced at Dawn. She had been in charge of equipment overhaul.

"We're right; they're wrong," she said crisply. "I haggled a good price out of the best technicians available, and had a Guild officer certify their work."

Redling thought about that for a moment.

"So? It's only a few rad-units extra. Why did you ask in the first place?" Helicron wanted to know. "What's the significance?"

The *Gateway* had moved a half-circuit of its orbital track now, travelling far enough along toward Plimbo's night side that the battered planet's third continent lay within range of the hull cameras. That continent lay half in day, half in night, and Redling could see the narrow slice of shadowed land beyond dusk's boundary. The camera image was good enough that he could see the rough outlines of upthrust mountains.

He could see the pale glow of ionizing radiation, too, recorded by the hull sensors and integrated into the viewscreen image by the *Gateway*'s imaging system.

"The significance is, at some point, our hosts have had an atomic war," Redling said slowly. "That might explain their passion for interstellar commerce, if enough of their agricultural base has been affected."

"Atomic weapons? Planetside?" Helicron spoke with the shock of the naïve.

"It's not a big deal in and of itself; a lot of people on a lot of worlds have made that mistake. But they didn't mention it in their data pack, and they don't seem interested in giving visitors any hint of the situation. The local commercial authorities don't want to discourage long stays."

"And what does that mean?"

"It means, watch your backside," Dawn interrupted. "What you said before was right. They love the off-world credit more than they hate each other, but—"

Redling finished the thought, not entirely pleased at how clearly Dawn had anticipated him. He said, "They love the off-Plimbo credit more than they love the off-worlder, too."

Plimbo's primary starport was a reasonably modern facility, with multiple-redundancy navigation systems, several different ground service providers, and automated clearance procedures. It should have been a comfortable place to land and do business, and it would have been, if not for the off-putting presence of a seventy-meter concussion crater in the center of the blast apron.

"What the Drog happened there?" Dawn asked. She gestured through a terminal window at the pit, and at the repair crews working to undo it. Men wearing utilitarian uniforms were using power tools to shore up the pit's walls, while another man used a backhoe to scoop debris from its bottom. A cement mixer waited nearby, presumably filled with the appropriate construction materials.

"Did some poor spacer have a blocked rocket tube?" Redling asked, knowing that the explanation had to be something different. He examined the pit in some detail when it had first shown on the *Gateway*'s surveillance screen, and he knew that an accident such as he had described could not account for it.

A shaped explosive charge could, though.

"Precisely. Very perceptive of you," Omar Tredlib

said. He was a balding, pudgy man who looked uncomfortably like a less-developed version of Tithe. The biggest difference, other than sheer mass, was that he wore a pair of external vision-corrective lenses, held before his watery eyes by heavy, black plastic frames. Tredlib worked in the liaison office at the Plimbo starport, serving in two roles that Redling regarded as incompatible, if not quite opposed to one another. Apparently, the pudgy man was both a Customs official and a representative of the local Commerce Council. "Last week it was, yes," Tredlib continued.

"I saw a tube blast on Galeg once," Redling said. He was sure that the other man was lying, and found in the lie the curious reassurance that came from consistency.

It seemed as if everyone else he had spoken to or met during this trip had lied to him. Why should the starport official be any different?

"Saw it happen, but from a great distance," he continued. "If that's what happened here, I'm surprised your terminal is still standing."

Tredlib shrugged. "We were very fortunate," he said. "The vessel was very low on fuel, so the damage was quite limited." He reviewed some forms that Redling had tendered to him, then set them down on his desk. "Everything's in order. Signed, countersigned, and registered—that's good. Allow me to be the first to welcome you to Plimbo," he continued. "Now, if I can be any help as you pursue business opportunities here—"

"We'll certainly let you know," Redling interjected smoothly. "Right now, my main concern is making delivery of a few thousand gallons of stasis-sealed beer that we took aboard on Farworld. I've got some people to call. Can you tell me where I can find a public com registry?"

"Easier than that," Tredlib responded. He handed each of his two visitors a standard-size data chip. "Just insert these in your com units. They're directories, current and complete."

Redling and Dawn complied, slipping the cardlike devices into the appropriate slots on their wrist communicators. They clicked up easily, and the devices chirped as they concluded accepting the data.

"Here," Tredlib said. He handed Redling another seven chips. "These should cover the others in your party. Just return them when you leave. Drop them in any postal pickup box."

"Expensive?" Redling said.

Tredlib laughed. "Not expensive, just useless—at least, anywhere else," he said, "and except as a souvenir. They're read-only."

Dawn nodded. She had keyed something into her wrist unit, and the little device now displayed a list of call options in response. "Smooth," she said. "Very considerate. More places should do this."

"We're a hospitable planet. That's why we don't impose duties—import or export—and why we expedite clearances," Tredlib said. "We're a busy world, however. Three more freighters have landed since the *Gateway* and I really must see to their needs. You'll have to excuse me." He handed the sheaf of documents back to Redling. "Please, don't hesitate to com me, should you need anything. My name is priority-flagged on the directory chips, of course."

"Of course."

"If I can be of any help, if you need anything at all—" Tredlib, continued, even as he ushered them to the door.

* * *

"D'ya need anything? Ya need a place to stay, a place to eat, a place to stay and eat, someone to do that with?" The words came in a hectic flow from the ground-car shuttle driver. She was a middle-aged woman with heavily muscled arms that looked stronger than most men's legs. Right now, she was using that strength to spin the ground-car's steering wheel on its axis as she guided the vehicle along a traffic-choked boulevard. Plimbo was apparently a very busy place, indeed. "'Cause if you do, I can help," she continued.

"That won't be necessary," Redling said, keeping the irritation from his voice only with a deliberate effort. Typically, he found even sporadic obsequiousness annoying rather than reassuring, and the driver's eagerly ingratiating behavior was a good match for nearly every other conversation he had endured since reaching Plimbo. Even the space traffic controllers in the observation tower had done their share of fawning as they guided the *Gateway* to its assigned landing slip.

Right now, he was seated in the rear of the big ground-car, with Dawn, Helicron and Pikk Thyller, Catra having elected to remain on the *Gateway*. The *Gateway*'s four crew members had elected to ride the shuttle to Star Street while the passengers saw to their own transportation.

"I'm sure we can fend for ourselves," Dawn said.

"Sure, I'm sure you can," the woman said. She had told them her name was Rolth. She had lips the color of dried blood, and they scarcely moved as she spoke. "It's just, no one knows a planet like a native, and I been here all my life. No short-timer, me."

"Maybe you can tell me something, then," Redling asked casually. "That big piece of emptiness, out on the blast apron—what caused that?"

"Buncha dims with too much time on their hands, you ask me. Some kind of demonstration, or statement, or something. Local politics. There's a cashiered Marines general—Chilhoub—in the 'port pokey, and the people who work for him don't want him there. Admin was supposed to ship him back to the Core Worlds last week, for trial. Some of his boys tried to keep that from happening, managed to delay the launch. Cracked the transport's hull, good. They got it in a repair bay now. Word on the street is, at least a week before it's go again."

"Ah." Redling glanced at Dawn and felt oddly gratified as the handsome woman nodded at him in acknowledgment. After the visit to Tredlib's office, he had mentioned his skepticism regarding the crater's alleged origins.

"Tell me, Rolth," he continued, "why did no one in Starport Administration want to talk about it? Something like that's hard to cover up."

"Ah, I dunno," the heavyset driver responded. She snapped the wheel to the left, and then the right again as a cargo truck tried to pass. "They don't like anyone else talking about it, either. That kind of stuff, bad for Plimbo's rep, they say. Bad for the tourist trade, bad for business, bad for something. That's the party line. Doesn't make much sense to me. You're here, right? You're not going to turn around and leave, just because someone divoted the launch pad."

"That's right," Dawn said. "We're not going anywhere except Star Street, or whatever you call it here."

It was a moment before Rolth responded. She had opened a window and stretched her tree-trunk neck through the opening, the better to exchange business commentary with her fellow drivers. Now, she quit screaming curses at the other vehicles and rejoined the interior conversation.

"Hey, I know Star Street like I know my own face," she said eagerly. It wasn't exactly news; she had said words to that effect at least ten times since taking on her passengers. "You want to know where to bunk, or eat, or play, I can help you find the best place."

"Play?" Helicron said, his first words in some distance. "Gaming is legal here?" He sounded wistful.

"Legal? Hah," Rolth snorted. "This is Plimbo, kid! Gaming for money's not just legal, it's almost mandatory!"

"Not for you it isn't," Redling murmured in Helicron's direction. Shortly after entering the system, he had pressed upon the younger man an opportunity to try his luck at Choskey, and then allowed the navigator to win back a small portion of his wages, enough to enjoy himself discreetly, but no more than that. He reminded Helicron, "You're going to behave, remember?"

Helicron nodded for Redling's benefit, but almost immediately changed the nod to a headshake when the driver spoke again.

"So, you wanna ride to the casino?" Rolth asked. "You do, I can take you there."

"No," Helicron said sadly. "Not now, no I don't."

"You change your mind, you let me know," Rolth said eagerly. She reached back, over the back of her seat, and extended one huge, open hand towards her passengers. It held ten or so of the now-familiar directory chips. "Take a chip, all of you! My name's priority-tagged. Just key my code, and I'll take you where you want to go!"

Helicron took four of the proffered items and distributed them among his fellows. Redling took one, but only reluctantly; his belt pouch already bulged with twins of the little data chips, far more than he could ever use. Nearly every encounter in the terminal's confines, no matter how brief, had ended with the emphatic offer of a directory card. What had begun as a considerate gesture on the part of Plimbo's bureaucracy was fast becoming an annoying one on the part of its citizenry. Despite that, he still felt the need to at least feign politeness, so he accepted the gift.

"So now, Rolth," he said, settling back in his seat as the highway rolled by. "You seem to be a well-informed sort."

Rolth nodded in agreement. "I know enough to get by," she averred, "and a basket more, besides."

"Tell me a bit about the local political situation."

"Situation? Hah!" Rolth snorted again. "That's a nice word for it!"

For the remainder of the drive, she regaled her passengers with a spirited recounting of the who, where, what, and why of Plimbo politics, a bewildering farrago of names, dates, and terms that ran easily into one another.

Yes, there had been a nuclear war, but more than a hundred years before; the mutation rate was way down lately, and nobody worried much about eating fish anymore.

No, General Chilhoub was not an especially popular figure hereabouts, not since he had tried to wrest control of Plimbo from the Imperial Governor, but he did have his followers, and they tended to be on the impassioned side.

Sure, Plimbo in general and Plimbo City—the starport's host city—were hospitable to travellers, but wise ones were careful where they went, nonetheless. Rolth followed this last bit of advice with a long list of neighborhoods, quarters, and divisions that were "safe, but not as safe as they could be."

By the time she had finished presenting her account of local society, even Helicron looked less than eager to sample the pleasures of the planet that billed itself as "one big Star Street."

It was Pikk Thyller who closed the conversation, as the shuttle parked in front of the hotel Rolth recommended, and the four members of the *Gateway*'s crew stepped out.

"Told you," the big man said. "Noisy."

For a change, it was the other three who remained silent.

CHAPTER SEVEN

Like war, like sport, like romance, like life itself, interstellar travel is mostly an exercise in patience. In Jump Space, a ship's crew has essentially nothing to do, other than prepare meals and perform minor maintenance. In normal space, there are the added joys of readings and measurements to make, but little else to occupy an idle mind. Only passengers in Low berths—the cryogenic capsules of which the *Gateway* now had none—were immune to boredom. Such empty monotony demands diversionary interruption, and such diversion was the secondary purpose of every stop the Far Trader made along its itinerary.

Redling's ship really didn't have very much business on Plimbo, certainly not enough to justify a four-day stopover. The ship's freighting deals and booked passages were all easily concluded within twelve hours of planetfall. It took scarcely as long as that to replenish the ship's diminished stores. Except for a few odds and ends, the remaining days were to be filled with rest and recreation for crew and passenger alike. That, and a bit of half-hearted effort on Redling's part to perpetuate his cover story by seeking new business.

His desultory, even minimalist, efforts yielded fruit with astonishing ease. As Rolth had promised, the Plimboners were very much a commerce-oriented people. Their rich tradition of internecine warfare had badly damaged Plimbo's industrial and agricultural base, and almost grotesquely stimulated that part of the environment that served offworlders. Plimbo was a free port, with no duties or pass-through charges, and an ideal stopover point for shipments between less tolerant worlds. The end result was that there were many shipments of many sizes and goods available, bound for locations in every direction. Redling had but to name a destination before he was besieged by offers and consignments. The few remaining merchants and fabricators were especially eager to have their goods taken offplanet.

Some of those consignments fit very neatly indeed with the *Gateway*'s logged itinerary. Almost as swiftly as the consignments in the cargo holds made their way to their new owners on Plimbo, those spaces were filled again with goods bound for other worlds, and bringing very competitive rates. Redling was pleased, in a distracted sort of way, but he really didn't care. He was more concerned with what the ship already carried.

Not to mention who.

"What do you know about the Guy-troy?" Dawn F'ral asked Redling.

It was the second day of the stopover. The two of them were in front of the counter in a diner adjacent to the Plimbo Registry Hall, where the four members of the *Gateway*'s complement had gone to file forms and itineraries required by local law. Now, Redling and Dawn were waiting for Helicron Daas and Pikk Thyller to conclude their respective businesses there, which involved a few rounds of computer-based testing and scoring. To kill the time, Dawn was working her way though some kind of gooey pastry and a cup of java, an aromatic brew that acted as a mild, non-euphoric stimulant. Redling, for his part, had ordered a piece of fish and was getting tired of waiting for it. A mug of java sat cooling at his elbow.

"You've asked me that before," he said. "Are you using the word as plural or singular this time?"

Dawn gave him a reluctant smile, as if acknowledging some small triumph. "Plural," she said, taking a sip of her java. "The race, not the individual."

"Same answer, then—big fellows, wings, social but cliquish, successful in business, as a general rule. At least, the unsuccessful ones stay at home and don't travel much. Ku-Ril-La says there are about a thousand of his folk here on Plimbo, most of them here in Plimbo City, most of them in the same district. He's staying with relatives, I think."

"And all of them working for the Kaal."

"You don't know that."

"Yes, I do," Dawn said, nodding. "No Guy-troy young—"

"Hatchlings," Redling interrupted, correcting her reflexively, using the term that Ku-Ril-La had used more than once. He took a taste of his own java and wondered fleetingly if he had been spending too much time with the winged man.

"No hatchlings onplanet, then," Dawn continued easily. "That's remarkable, in and of itself, I think. You get enough of any species together in one place, it's not a question of whether they'll reproduce, but a question of how many times they'll do it. 'Enough' is a lot lower than a thousand, too. I would expect a good-sized second generation by now."

Redling shrugged. There wasn't much he could say to that. "You've been doing some research on the subject," he said.

"Not here. Not the kind of research you've been doing, anyway." Dawn smiled, a sweetly calculating expression that made her features suddenly, impossibly, resemble those of the blue-skinned dancer and assertive businesswoman, Sascha Blork, left many parsecs behind.

The diner chef was an Aslan with a tawny mane and dappled fur. He stepped out from behind the grill now and presented Redling with a plate of steamed fish, attractively arrayed on a bed of floogle shoots. The food smelled good, but Redling ignored it, much to the chef's apparent consternation.

"Explain," Redling said flatly to Dawn.

"Explain?"

"Explain your comment, and yourself," he said. "You're hiding something, and I'm getting tired of your games. What makes you think I'm so interested in the Guy-troy?"

"That part's easy," Dawn said. All humor fled her sea-green eyes now, and she spoke crisply and professionally as she continued, but she nonetheless had the air of a gamer playing her trump. "You spent three hours in the Registry Hall library yesterday. Each and every file you accessed had at least some tangential relationship to the Controlled."

Her words stunned Redling, having such an impact that he didn't even comment on her third use of the unfamiliar term for the Guy-troy. His cover identity's Guild membership carried privileges, and he had been trying to learn a bit more about his passenger and his business, perhaps egged on by Dawn's manifest interest. She was right, and the implications her words carried were considerable.

From somewhere inside her tunic, she drew a sheet of plastic film, covered with filenames, and set it on the counter. "I think that indicates some kind of interest," she continued.

"I think it indicates a little bit too much interest on your part in my business," Redling said slowly. For once, he was very nearly at a loss for words. The real Navis Redling's purchased memories were screaming at him now, warning of a fundamental breach of Guild regulations, rules that even a low-class trader such as his namesake respected. In their own way, the words that Dawn had spoken so calmly were more disturbing than the discoveries or observations that Redling had made earlier regarding her. A captain's research trail was his private business, and knowing it could give a rival an almost immeasurable tactical advantage. No one was supposed to be privy to that kind of information, at least not without a warrant.

What justification could Dawn muster for a search warrant? And how could she have gotten one issued so quickly?

"How the Flarge did you access my data account?" he demanded, some corner of his mind pleased by the realization that his anger was both justified and in character.

Despite his overriding sense of irritation, he was sincere in his curiosity. His engineer had accomplished something he had tried more than once, and never successfully. Knowing how to access a ship captain's data account would make many kinds of operations much easier.

"You have your tricks," Dawn said, looking Sascha-esque again, "I have mine."

"You can play them somewhere else," Redling said, "and on someone else. This isn't Farworld, or even Draen. It's not a seller's market for qualified personnel. I can replace you easily enough."

"You can, but you don't want to," Dawn responded. "You don't want me where you can't see me, and you certainly don't want a disgruntled ex-shipmate having a bit of a chat with Helicron or Pikk Thyller. They might get ideas, ones you wouldn't like."

That was true, Redling supposed, but something else was true, too.

"If you've learned anything at all about me, you know I don't respond well to threats," he said, "no matter how gently they're phrased."

Dawn nodded. "That's why we're having this conversation here, in a public place," she said. "And notice that I've made no threats, at least not yet. I've simply pointed out some facts."

Redling paused silently for a moment, part of him tracking the men and women who came and went from the diner's various tables and booths. The place they were in catered to the starship crowd. Its current clientele was made up mostly of ship personnel and Guild members, precisely the type of individuals who could bear the absolute most damaging witness against him.

The whole idea behind taking the Redling identity had been to lower his profile, not to make it more prominent. His façade was not particularly fragile, but nor was it invulnerable.

"Good point," he said making himself suddenly cheerful, his appraisal of Dawn F'Ral rising another notch. She certainly wasn't in his league, but she was showing great promise. It was always nice to find someone who knew what he or she was doing, even when that someone was on the other side, as he had already decided Dawn was. "Got any more?"

"Not a point of argument, but one of information," Dawn said. "I know you searched my quarters."

That was a surprise, too. Chief among the Droyne override's many advantages was its absolute transparency to all security systems in Redling's experience. He had popped safe doors and top-level security bins with it, and never left a trace of his passage. Some unknowable secret embodied in its incomprehensible (to humans) technology prevented the gadget from leaving any trace of its use.

"Now, what makes you think that?" Redling said. He composed his features in a mask of studied nonchalance, and then tasted his fish. It was delicious, so he nodded in acknowledgement to the still-hovering cook and lifted another forkful to his mouth.

"Process of elimination." Dawn had finished eating her pastry now, and was nursing the dregs of her java. "Someone other than me had been there. I can tell when a lock's been doctored, and this one hadn't been. The only guy I know who can do such things without leaving a trace is you, and that trick glove of yours. There can't be two of those floating around."

"If there was no trace, what make you think anyone intruded?"

She looked at him, disdain evident on her face. "Please. Just because you have a high-tech solution to a problem doesn't mean you should turn you back on low-tech options. When I went on duty, there was a hair stretched across the closet panel and across each storage drawer, right where they meet their frames.

When I came back, each hair had fallen to the floor. One, I could credit to chance—but not all."

Redling nearly winced at his own oversight, but managed to stifle the expression before it reached his face. He had checked for a scanner or other surveillance device, but not something as simple as a hair.

There was some irony to the situation, he knew. He had a long-held preference using tools that he understood completely, whenever possible; now, he had outfoxed himself by relying too heavily on a device with workings that no one understood. That failing would be cause for amusement, did it not present such possibilities for disaster.

A single misstep, no matter how minor, could ruin an entire campaign. It was a lesson he had learned more than once, and did not relish learning again.

"Now, why would you feel the need to do that?" he asked.

"Why would you feel the need to conceal the fact that you searched my quarters? As ship captain, you've got the pass-codes; Guild regs let you look where you want, provided that you have just cause. The only advantage to Droyne device is that you would leave— or thought you would leave—no trace of your tour." Dawn paused. "Why do you feel the need to be so secretive, Captain?"

"I could ask you the same." He thought about the portable arsenal he had found in her closet, but said nothing. Technically speaking, he still had not said anything to confirm that the intruder in Dawn's quarters had been him.

He had to wonder how many of those weapons she wore now, however.

Dawn shook her head, making her short reddish hair ripple like fronds in a sea current. "You can ask, but not with any justification. I allow that I've been discreet and private, but not secretive. I've asked my questions directly, rather than trying to pry them out on my own." She grinned, crookedly this time, and expression that he found suddenly quite attractive. "I haven't slipped into *your* cabin unasked, for example," Dawn continued.

The woman really had remarkable control over her features and comportment, Redling realized. She was either a born actress, or a well-trained one—and she certainly had the manipulative bent to make good use of her skills.

He would have to allow for both factors in the future.

"There's the little matter of reviewing my data log." He was still curious as to how she had done that. "I have to assume you asked some other questions, too."

The thought suddenly struck him that Plimbo was a heavily trafficked world, and the Registry Hall, in turn, was highly trafficked by spacers. If any of them were familiar with the ways of the real Navis Redling, and had responded to probing questions from Dawn—

"Only after you searched my quarters and began prying into my business," Dawn said. "Mine, and the Guy-troy's. I did it as much to make a point as to learn anything. I can match you, Captain, measure for measure, if you choose to make it necessary." She spoke softly, but her voice held a note of steel.

Redling recalled Dawn's and his clandestine search of the consignment Ku-Ril-La had arranged. She had been very effective then, in a support mode. He suspected now that she would do equally well in opposition.

"We need to talk," he said. "And this isn't the place to do it."

She nodded. "Maybe not, but it should be somewhere similar—someplace public, at least until we work out some things."

"What do you suggest?"

"We've both got things to do today. I'll meet you in front of the Registry Hall at dinner time." She grinned again. "We keep eating so many meals together, Captain, the others will start to talk."

"Not if they know what's good for them," Redling responded.

"That's the problem," Dawn said bleakly, all sense of feint-and-parry gone from her voice. "Most people don't. They know what they want, and they might—might—know what they need, but they almost never know what's good for them."

"You sound like someone who would like to make that decision yourself."

"No. Just like someone who understands the way the universe works." An attendant had refilled her mug, and she drained it with a single gulp, then gestured to indicate two figures coming closer.

"Oh, look," she said. "Here come the boys." She waved.

Helicron and Pikk were edging their way between close-set diner tables, working toward the counter seats where Redling and Dawn sat. Helicon looked very pleased with himself—as was his typical wont—but the bigger man looked even more dour and glum than usual.

Spending time with Helicron could wear a fellow down, Redling knew full well.

"We can continue this at another time," Dawn said.

Redling nodded. "Dinner it is, then. We'll decide where, then." He smiled, the expression coming to his face with surprising ease.

The situation concerned him, but he had a certain fondness for challenges.

"I passed!" Helicron said cheerfully as he settled onto the stool next to Dawn's. "Top percentile!" He was holding his Universal ID and handed it to Dawn, who smiled, nodded, and passed it to Redling for review.

"Very nice," Redling said, noting the new certification indicated on the device's glistening screen. Helicron was now fully accredited to perform interstellar navigation duties in high-matter density regions, such as a nebular cloud. It was a certification that made him much more employable to luxury lines. "You collect a few more certs, and you'll be overqualified for our little tub."

"Think that's the idea," Pikk Thyller said. He had remained standing, and his blunt features wore an impassive expression. Even so, he dominated the quartet for the moment, his sheer bulk dwarfing the other crew members who were seated.

"It's all thanks to Dawn," Helicron said, looking even more boyish that usual, which was saying a lot. "She helped me study."

"I had no idea you two were spending so much time together," Redling drawled.

"It was something to do," Dawn said, clearly irritated by the tone in Redling's voice. "There's a lot of boredom on a ship the size of the *Gateway*."

"What about you, Pikk?" Redling asked, turning to face the big man. "Any new qualifications? Any reason I should up your rates before the next Jump?"

The dusky giant shook his head. "None worth mentioning. Ran into someone I knew from the Marines, though," he said. "Busy tonight." It was very nearly as many words as he had ever been heard to speak in one stretch.

"Are you guys gaming? Are you going to go gaming? Does your friend like Spindledrift?" That was Helicron again, so excited that he was positively fidgeting. "I'm always ready for a few rounds of Spindledrift."

Redling looked at him. "You have money for gaming?" he asked, genuinely surprised.

"Not much; a little more than a hundred credits. I rebudgeted." Helicron looked suddenly defensive.

"Where did you get a hundred extra credits?" Redling purred. While playing Choskey on the *Gateway*, he had been careful to let the younger man win precisely enough to pay for a room in reasonable inn, and to eat fairly well. The kid simply shouldn't have had any money left over for gambling.

"Rolth helped me with that," Helicron said warily. "I talked with her after she dropped us off at the inn. She gave me some pointers on Plimbo living."

"Such as?"

"The Registry Hall here has dormitory space, nothing fancy, but clean. It's intended for distressed travellers, but not restricted to them. I can bunk there."

"That leaves meals. Or does the dorm have a kitchen, too?" Redling asked. Helicron's words did not please him. Redling didn't want to have to go looking for the younger man in the morning, and he particularly didn't want to go looking for a new navigator before launch time. Despite his earlier words to Dawn, he didn't feel much like conducting another round of employment interviews.

"No, but Rolth helped me with that, too," Helicron said. "She gave me a list of places where I can eat cheap, not like this tourist trap."

The Aslan cook, who had come closer to pick up an empty plate, growled something that Redling couldn't quite hear. Then he moved on without offering to take orders from the newcomers.

"That's nice. Just where are these economical eateries? In the bad part of town?"

"Oh, no, no, no, there is no bad part of Plimbo City, Rolth says."

"There's always a bad part of town."

"Sure, they aren't all as nice as this district, but why pay for frills when you can invest the money, instead?"

"Invest," Redling said flatly. "In Spindledrift." Under other circumstances, the idea might have been amusing, but he was irritated to see that his earlier efforts to bring the younger man under control had been wasted.

"This really isn't a good idea," Dawn said, interrupting. "You don't want to trust the first person you meet on a new planet, especially not one with a background as interesting as Plimbo's."

"First Rolth, now Dawn. You're good at getting the ladies to look out for you, Helicron," Redling said to Helicron, smirking.

Dawn shot him an glance, her green eyes bright with fury that she somehow managed to keep from her voice. "You command a fair amount of attention yourself, Captain."

Redling's smirk changed to something else.

"No, no, it's nothing like that," Helicron said hastily. He shook his head. "Rolth is just being hospitable."

"Oh, yes," Redling said. He knew that he was losing control of the situation, but he felt he had to make one last try. "Hospitable, and earning a commission."

"Commission?"

Redling nodded. "Think about it. Think how many fares Rolth and her shuttle business take in each day, how many of those data chips she hands out to them. She's a businesswoman, Helicron. She steers fares and earns commissions. And that's if you're lucky."

"Lucky?"

"Lucky, as in lucky enough to find someone who is and who does precisely what she claims. Rolth takes you to a few dives, shows you some sights, you wake up in the morning with a sore head and an empty wallet. If she's lying, though, the payoff becomes a lot worse. You don't wake up at all, or you wake up in chains, on a planet with air you can't breath and with duties you won't like." That last was the least likely of the possibilities that Redling listed, but it had been known to happen.

Moreover, he knew the people who had made it happen.

"You're staying at the inn she recommended," Helicron said, trying hard to make his words sound like an accusation and failing miserably. He had his lucky die out now and was fingering it nervously.

"A hotel's a hotel," Redling said, exhibiting a degree of patience he did not feel. "It doesn't matter if Rolth gets one-tenth of every credit I spend here. You're talking about a different nest of weasels altogether. And if you get caught cheating—"

"I can take care of myself," Helicron said stiffly. "And it's not really cheating. Anyone who plays Spindledrift must know that some Narkles are tickled."

"I know a half-dozen centaurs on Draen who seemed quite aghast at the very notion."

Helicron looked stubborn, and sounded that way, too. "I accounted for myself well enough in that," he said, demonstrating a combination of ingratitude and foolishness that Redling found breathtaking.

Dawn laughed softly at that one, an under-the-breath chuckle that reached Redling's ears easily and did a bit to defuse the tension of the moment.

"I was there for at least part of that, remember?" she said. "The only thing you accounted for was an obscene amount of house beer."

Helicron flinched, but he made no other response.

Redling shrugged. What had begun as a casual chat was in danger of becoming a heated confrontation, and he wanted no more of it. His authority—any captain's authority—over his shipmates was limited onplanet, and what Helicron did during his leisure time was his business. Redling only hoped that he wouldn't have to interview replacements for Helicron; almost despite himself, he had managed to develop some affection for the kid.

Besides, better the nuisance you knew than the one that you didn't.

"Do what you want," he said, "but watch your backside. I won't be prowling the streets of Plimbo City tonight." He glanced in Dawn's direction.

"I have other business to attend," he concluded.

* * *

Redling's "other business" scarcely qualified as business at all, at least in regards to the *Gateway*. After the other three had departed, he returned to the Guild library and spent another three hours choosing and reviewing data. He took care this time to diversify his requests enough to mask the focus of his true interests.

His researches the previous day had been into Guytroy in general and their Plimbo enclave in particular. Those studies had been the product (primarily) of casual curiosity, prompted by Dawn's earlier comments and by his lengthy shipboard conversations with Ku-Ril-La. The search hadn't yielded very much information that he found useful or even interesting—only generalities regarding the race's culture and a remarkably sketchy outline of their history. He supposed that a Core World library would have more specific data, but his curiosity was not enough to justify making the trip.

Today's researches, once stripped of their smokescreen of obscuring queries, were quite different, and unique to his personal needs.

Redling, in his real identity, was a member of a reasonably exclusive if loose-knit fraternity, the kind of informal brotherhood that comes into being any time that enough men and women of similar interests rose from the ranks of society. In this case, those interests were crime, thefts and ransoms, and confidence games executed on a scale that reached beyond most normal folk's wildest dreams. Redling was a professional criminal, with a heavy emphasis on both words, who specialized in high-credit crimes of a diverse nature. Since embarking on his career path, he had encountered countless outlaws of lesser skill and smaller vision, but only a scattered handful of whom had raised themselves to his level of expertise and ambition. Some members of that handful operated in identities as variegated as his own; others used only a single name and relied on other measures to keep one step ahead of the forces of so-called order.

There was the Gab Tuzzle, the Vilani data pirate who had brought an entire colonial system to its knees by overriding the local navigation network and sending commercial convoys into the waiting arms of pirate bands. There was Taen Daezter, whose face Redling had never seen, but might as well have signed the theft ten years ago of twenty thousand megacredits in untapped fire-crystals from the "absolutely secure" stasis vault in the capital of Mariposa. There was the enigmatic Black Hunter, the terror of the Outer Reaches and the venomous mastermind of a coordinated series of pirate attacks that had brought the Chan-Tez shipping line to its figurative knees. There was Alesha Aal-Koth, a willowy wisp of a woman, sweet and innocent-looking, who commanded seven percent of the interstellar drug trade, specializing in exotic variants of Eurphorinol, including one that had been the real Navis Redling's downfall.

Their numbers were fewer than fifty, all told, and membership in that exalted rank was determined more by the skill and the scale of their endeavors, rather than by their absolute success. Some of his fellows had earned Redling's enmity, some had earned his friendship, but all had his respect. Whenever possible, on whatever world he found himself, he always looked for signs of their passing, or of the presence of their agents. Farworld's data management assets had been rudimentary, to say the least, and Draen's had not been much better. Plimbo, however, was another story.

This was a busy enough world that the Registry Hall's databanks might hold some clues or hints, gleaned from trip reports, published accounts, and even rumors from other travellers who had placed them on file there. By its very nature, such information could be neither as current nor as reliable as that gathered within a single system, but that was one of the limitations that the universe had chosen to impose on communications, and Redling saw no practical way to challenge it. Now, he continued his researches, careful to mask them by matching each sincere inquiry with several spurious ones.

The most reliable clues, and the easiest ones to find, all involved money. He looked for the credit value of recent jobs, then among them for the skill and panache he associated with his equals.

A payroll's worth of bearer bonds disappeared from a secure holding facility on Mongro only to resurface a year later, two systems away. Before that financial audit trail could be followed to its source, the bonds had been cashed and the money converted to untraceable assets. That might have been the work of Alesha's organization; she had branched out in recent years to dabble a bit in such operations.

A freighter heavy with Droyne artifacts—functional Droyne artifacts—had made planetfall on Hydrox, only for the crew to find its holds filled with fragments of worthless space-rock instead. That sounded like the work of a man named Haalon, originally of Carstair's World, but now of parts unknown. Haalon was a skilled master of misdirection, counterfeiting, and fraud. If the switch had been Haalon's work, Redling would have loved dearly to know the details of the operation—but he suspected he was unlikely ever to learn.

Twenty prototype fusion reactors belonging to the Kaal Combine, specially engineered to work in high-gravity environments, had been hijacked in midshipment. They had been on their way to a testing satellite orbiting the dead star companion of Draen's sun. The brigands storming the Kaal craft had claimed to work for the Black Hunter, but Redling found that doubtful, at least in light of the available accounts. The Hunter used piracy less for material or technological gain, and more as a tool for social change, subscribing as he did to a version of crypto-monarchism that struck Redling as particularly crack-brained. (He and the Hunter had argued that particular issue more than once.)

A renegade Colonial Governor had looted his territory's treasury and used the moneys to fund the purchase of a private pleasure satellite, forming the basis for a vice ring that served three interstellar systems. Someone with considerable financial expertise had put that deal together, providing an armed escort and arranging with other entrepreneurs to construct the artificial world that was now the governor's home; in return, that satellite served as a clearing house for data pirates from all three systems—Gab Tuzzle included. Redling had to wonder who that someone was. Had it been a familiar presence or a new player? There was no way for him to know, based on the available information assets.

He spent much of midday in the library, reviewing files and committing their contents to his excellent memory. Only when absolutely necessary did he copy specific entries into his com unit for storage, and even then, he did so reluctantly. Finally, he signed off from the computer terminal and stood, then rubbed his aching eyes.

A Guild attendant hovered nearby, apparently waiting for the use of the unit. She was an elderly woman, presumably retired from the space trade, but her eyes were bright and she had a friendly smile as Redling approached her.

"Can you help me with a question?" Redling said.

"I can try, but if it's about search criteria—"

He shook his head. "Nothing as technical as that," he said. "I've been to many Guild halls in my day, and not everyone does everything the same way. I'm still feeling my way around this operation."

"Oh, my, yes. I've been on staff for seven years now, since I had a stroke and lost my nav certs. I know this place inside and out."

"If I wanted to review the log of files another researcher had accessed—"

The old woman stiffened, and her demeanor abruptly went from helpful to inhospitable. Anger painted white spots on her cheeks. "Without a duly executed warrant, that would be a gross violation of protocol and regulations," she said sharply. "You can get a letter of reprimand for even suggesting it."

The warning was sincere, but constituted a very nearly empty threat, nonetheless. Written communiqués were hard-pressed to keep up with a free-travelling spacer.

"They'll even put a data flag on your Universal ID," the woman continued.

That threat carried a bit more muscle, since a spac-

er relied on his Universal to carry records of his certifications and résumé.

"And even if you ask, it can't be done. They've got
a secure data lock on the log files." She paused. "If
that's the way they do things on other worlds—"

Redling grinned, and shook his head at the attendant, who was still gazing at him suspiciously. "No,
no, not at all," he said. "And I was hoping that would
be your response. It reassures me enormously to know
that my privacy is secure against unauthorized access."

Of course, that raised again the issue of how an
ordinary engineer with a résumé as uninteresting as
Dawn F'Ral's had managed to accomplish the so-called
impossible.

As a whole, Plimbo City was nothing special, though
the popular assessment of it as "one big Star Street"
proved reasonably accurate. A good-sized metropolis,
most of it was divided into zones and subzones by a
grid of numbered streets (east to west) and color designated avenues (north to south) that Redling found emi-
nently reasonable. The Registry Hall was at the corner
of Dark Blue and Sixteenth, the best restaurants ran
along Light Blue between Fifth and Tenth, and the Kaal
Combine's offices were in a handsome, twelve-story
structure. Redling sat at a lunch counter on the other
side of Green from that structure now, nursing a cup of
java. He nodded in approval at the way the midday sun
shone on the metal and tile mosaic that finished the
building's façade. His wanderings had taken him there
primarily by chance, but he suspected that his subcon-
scious had done a bit of prompting along the way.

He had been thinking about goods of value, after

all, and about Ku-Ril-La, and the Kaal Combine was where the two overlapped rather emphatically.

"Impressive establishment," he said to the counterman.

"Thanks," came the reply. "We try."

"That's not quite what I mean," Redling said. He gestured at his cup and waited for a refill. "I meant, the establishment across the street."

"I know what you meant," the counterman said. He was approximately the same height as Redling, and wore white utilitarian garb—apparently a uniform—with the name COLIN stenciled on the shirt pocket. "You've been staring at that place for twenty minutes."

"Really? No wonder my java had gone cold." At least some percentage of the surprise he voiced was genuine. He was unaccustomed to losing track of time, or to letting his interests be divined so easily—but these were special circumstances.

He had spent much of the afternoon trying to learn a bit more about Plimbo City's denizens. So far, he had failed miserably, which was not unprecedented but was certainly anomalous in his experience.

The problem was that more people wanted to sell than wanted to talk, at least about the topics that interested him. Moreover, no one had anything he particularly wanted to buy, licit or illicit. The *Gateway* had discharged the cargo bound for here and had taken on new consignments bound for other worlds. He had eaten and drunk well, had no desire for souvenirs, and was reasonably confident in his own ability to find companionship and excitement. That left only useful information, something he constantly wanted and that he was hard-pressed to find today. Gossip was hard to gather when someone was trying to sell you a fourth-interest in a spider bush farm.

The desire for knowledge was what had brought him to the lunch counter, not any thirst that could be quenched by java, and that was what he knew would take him to Plimbo City's taverns and bawdy houses after the sun set.

"Tell me, the place across the street," he said. "I recognize the name the mosaic spells out. The Kaal Combine owns it?"

Colin laughed. "What don't they own? Biggest off-world investor on Plimbo."

"You get much business from them?"

"Only indirectly. We don't cater to the Guy-troy palate, but we get a lot of carryover from folks doing business with them," the counterman said. "And that's a lot. They're the biggest single offworld commercial concern with permanent offices on the planet."

"You don't seem very busy today," Redling said. He glanced around the restaurant. He was the only customer in the place, other than a young couple seated in one corner booth. The uneaten remains of their meals lay cold and congealing on the plates before them, but neither patron seemed to notice. The young man was whispering urgently to the slightly older woman, apparently pursuing negotiations of his own as eagerly as anyone else on the planet.

Colin shrugged. "Happens every once in a while," he said. "I think they've got company calling from off-planet."

Offplanet. That might mean Ku-Ril-La. The winged man had said nothing about calling on his company's offices, but it seemed reasonably likely. "You think?" he asked. "Not know?"

Colin nodded. "Think," he said. "Anything those folks do, they keep under a tight lid," he said. "Whatever's going on, it came up fast. Three of my regulars, salesmen and data-couriers, came in complaining that their appointments had been cancelled without notice. That's happened before, usually for an inspection or grand tour."

"You seem to know a lot about the Guy-troy," Redling said.

"No. Not much. You work a joint like this, you pick up a little bit about your neighbors, but nobody really knows much about those folks."

"Have you ever heard the name Ku-Ril-La?"

Colin made a negative sound. "Sounds like one of theirs, though," he said. "The *Ku*," he pronounced it a bit differently than had Redling, "is an honorific of some sort, not hereditary. It's related to the Kaal." He dragged the last out, in a rattling exhalation that sounded odd coming from human lips.

He was right, Redling knew. That much, at least, his researches had taught him. *Kaal* was a less-formal derivative of the *Ku* honorific, which apparently (according to his sources) was an honorific that the Guy-troy did not so much bestow as claim. When a member of that race reached a certain level of accomplishment, he added the *Ku* prefix to his name, without any formal procedure or certification of accomplishment. Redling had his doubts about such a system, but it seemed to work for the Guy-troy.

No one else in the Kaal's directory, or at least in the publicly distributed version of it, bore the title.

"Like I said, you seem to know a lot," Redling said.

"And like I said, it's really not very much, just what

I can pick up from the clientele. The Guy-troy, they're a cliquish bunch. They first opened that office about ten years ago, just before I opened up. In the old days, they came here once in a while. Now that there's enough of them, though, they can support their own restaurants and entertainment. I haven't seen one come through these doors in at least seven years."

That fit in well with what Redling knew, too. Draen had apparently hosted a less mature or simply less numerous Guy-troy enclave, leading to the use of private dining rooms in establishments with a more heterogeneous clientele. He remembered how surprised he had been to see Ku-Ril-La and his fellows in the restaurant there—and how surprised Dawn F'Ral had been that he had caught her following the Guy-troy.

Because that was what she had been doing—there was no longer any room for doubt. Whatever Dawn's agenda was, whatever her name really was, she knew entirely too much about the Guy-troy in general and Ku-Ril-La in particular to be what she claimed. That raised a number of possibilities, one of which Redling found quite tantalizing.

What if she were a competitor, or working for one?

The thought had crossed his mind, more than once, as he pursued his researches in the Guild library. She could be an operative for the Black Hunter, or Gab Tuzzle, or even Alesha—all three had claimed territories in this part of the galaxy for their operations. She had the kind of skills that would make her useful to any of them, and she certainly had the tools. Redling thought back to the portable arsenal he had found in her cabin earlier, the case filled with weapons and tools that had reminded him so much of his own. They simply didn't seem to be the sort that any conventional law-enforcement officer would carry; they didn't have the look of government issue, and had been too obviously chosen by someone with an eye for quality, and not much concern for expense.

They were tools he might have chosen.

"I can't really blame them," Colin continued. "Not with all the trouble Chilhoub's antixenoes are making these days."

It wasn't the first time that Redling had heard the general's name that day, but it was the first time he heard it spoken by someone who was willing to tell him more—at least, with some prompting.

"Sure, no problem," Colin said. He folded the bill that Redling had handed him and tucked it in the pocket that bore his name. "Lotta folks are embarrassed by him, and they should be. The guy almost made it to the head of the Commerce Council, for Drog's sake."

On another world, Redling knew, that achievement might not have been as impressive. His experience at the starport, however, had shown him that the Commerce Council had woven itself rather thoroughly into the warp and woof of Plimbo culture, and wielded considerable power. This was the first he had heard of Chilhoub's connection to that august body, however.

"About twenty, twenty-five years ago—standard years, not local—the Core Worlds Ruling Council got tired of hearing reports of local squabbles, especially since Plimbo is on one of the main commerce routes. Right after the nuke war, they sent Chilhoub and some of his bully boys here to lower some uprisings, as it were." Colin paused. "That was before my time. I've only been on Plimbo about twelve years. I'm from Mraz, originally."

That explained Colin's relative volubility regarding Plimbo current events, Redling realized. The counterman was working from the viewpoint of an outsider. All Redling said aloud however, was, "Been there."

Colin nodded and continued. "Anyhow, word is, Chilhoub found a lot of opportunities here and decided he liked the place. He's been a force in local politics ever since, a big player in the antinonhuman movement." Colin spoke more softly now, after a glance a the still-occupied corner booth. "Lot of xenophobes onplanet."

"That doesn't make sense. The entire economy relies on offworld credits."

"Yeah, but Chilhoub's crowd would prefer that they be human credits. You should have seen the protest when the Kaal Combine opened its offices. Doesn't make any sense to me. I worry about the color of money, and not about the color of the hand holding it, or how many fingers it has."

"Most money doesn't have fingers," Redling drawled.

It took Colin a moment to understand Redling's point, and when he did, he scowled before continuing. "Anyhow, about two years ago, the Ruling Council got word of what was going on, and called Chilhoub home. He didn't want to go, and his people have been fighting his extradition ever since. You saw that big crater out at the starport?"

Redling nodded. "They told me a tube blew."

"You talked to Tredlib, then," Colin said, and continued as he saw Redling nod. "He's a real jerk. You want to do business with someone, you need to have some trust, I say. You don't lie to him the first time he asks a question."

"I always wait until the fourth or fifth query."

This time, Colin nodded. "Yeah, that's the way. Don't believe anything Tredlib tells you. In fact, believe the opposite, and you'll do okay, especially on the subject of Chilhoub. Flarge, I don't even think they've officially announced his arrest, even though everyone knows about it."

"How come I've been having such a hard time finding out anything about anyone?"

"Commerce Council," Colin said. "They've got a finger in every pot, and they do everything they can to keep the bad stuff from making the media. Even nonmember operators toe the line."

"Thanks," Redling said, meaning it. "You've been very helpful."

"Yeah, well, we offworlders got to stick together."

That was when Redling's wrist com buzzed.

"...in a daring daylight raid earlier today," the neutral voice said, nearly an hour later. *"The kidnap victim was a member of the Guy-troy, believed to be a newcomer to Plimbo. The City Watch has not yet identified the party in question, and the Kaal Combine has declined to comment on the situation. However, Customs authorities have confirmed processing an Imperium Diplomat—"*

Redling thumbed the PAUSE key, freezing the image and soundtrack. "I imagine the esteemed Tredlib will have the skin of whoever issued that confirmation," he said sourly.

"I'll tell you about that later," Dawn said. "Just watch the rest of it." They were seated in her room at the inn, watching a mass transmission she had recorded earlier in the day and relayed now to a larger display screen.

Redling released the PAUSE key.

"*—all media outlets have received copies of the same recorded statement, issued by individuals claiming to represent the Human Plimbo, Human Now movement, a radical coalition with ties to controversial political activist General Daxam Chilhoub.*"

The image on the screen changed to what looked like a computer-generated image created by averaging together characteristics of all human races and ethnicities. Neither dark-skinned nor light, neither male nor female, the face had an anonymity that went light-years beyond the announcer's studied neutrality. When the image spoke, it was similarly characterless, devoid of emotion, accent, racial, or gender characteristics.

"*This is a command to the loyal denizens of Plimbo, and a warning to the inhuman scum who would take your world from you. Even as the traitorous, fallacious government of this planet seeks to banish a true hero of the people, it seeks to embrace an enemy of the race.*

"*We, the free forces of Human Plimbo, Human Now have countermanded that decision.*"

The image on the screen melted, flowed, then coalesced again as the familiar, avianoid features of Ku-Ril-La. It was impossible even for Redling's practiced eye to read any expression on the Guy-troy's face.

"*We are merciful in our justice, however,*" the synthesized voice continued, as the Guy-troy faded from the screen and the averaged face appeared again. *"Return to us our leader, the esteemed General Daxam Chilhoub, and we will return the mongrel outworlder to your custody. Failure to do so will leave us no alternative but to execute him, for crimes against the human race. You have seven standard hours to decide."*

The newscaster returned to the screen now, and said nothing of any real use. Redling waited until the man had moved on to another story—some kind of financial scandal—and turned off the com in disgust.

"That's more coverage than I would have expected the locals to allow," he said.

"They aren't allowing it now," Dawn responded. "That aired precisely once. It was sheer, dumb luck I was logging transmissions on my wrist unit."

Redling doubted that, but he didn't say so. When he had received Dawn's call at the lunch counter, he had expected a reminder about their dinner and promised conversation. The news about Ku-Ril-La had been a shock, and still took some getting used to.

"That transmission was this morning," Dawn said. "I've spent most of the time since fielding calls from the local authorities." She made an unpleasant sound and wrinkled her nose. "They're not very good."

"Why didn't they let me know immediately?" Redling asked. "For that matter, why didn't *you* let me know immediately?"

"There wasn't time. The City Watch scooped me up near the Registry Hall and pestered me with questions about Ku-Ril-La, who he was and how he came to be here. Not a very competent crowd, actually. I kept referring them to you, but they wouldn't let me place any calls until an hour ago."

Redling doubted that very much, but let it pass. He thought a moment. "What about the others?" he asked.

"Others?"

"Helicron. Pikk. The passengers, for that matter. Do any of them know?"

Dawn shrugged. "Only if they happened to be watching the newscast the one time it was made," she said. "My experience is, most Plimboners don't like to give bad news to visitors." She paused. "And, our differences aside, this is very bad news. Ku-Ril-La is a very wealthy individual, and his organizations wields an immense amount of power. If they want to, they can make enormous trouble for us. For that matter, the locals won't be eager to issue launch authorization until and unless they think the situation is under control."

"I'm quite aware of that," Redling said.

"So, what are we going to do?"

Redling thought for a long moment. "We're not going to dinner, that's for certain," he finally said. "I'd better get back to my own place. I've got some calls to make."

"But—"

If Dawn said anything more, Redling didn't hear it. The door had already slid shut behind him.

CHAPTER EIGHT

Every port city on every world has a warehouse district, no matter what kind of port the city supports—air, water, or space. That had been a consistent experience in all of Redling's lives, and Plimbo provided no exception to test the rule.

Specifically, Plimbo City played host to a sprawling district of warehouses, storage facilities, and tank farms that lay to the south of the bustling metropolis. Defined by broad thoroughfares and narrow alleys, it was a ragged, rambling maze of structures that ranged from the shabby to the slightly-less-than-sleekly modernistic. Even without researching the matter, Redling was reasonably certain that the sector he explored now represented the very oldest part of Plimbo City, perhaps even the site of the original colony. That was the typical growth pattern followed by most new settlements: an evolutionary track that led from strictly utilitarian facilities and structures to more diverse, more "civilized" ones.

Whatever its specific history, the warehouse district was obviously very old, and the address that he had been given lay in the very oldest, most decayed and dilapidated part of the district. His specific goal was a two-story, brick-and-timber structure set back a few meters from the street, apparently a small consignment house rather than a bulk storage facility. From a nearby alley's darkened mouth, perhaps thirty meters distant, Redling studied the place carefully through a pair of folding binoculars. It had taken him a while to reach this vantage point, more than two hours of careful reconnoitering through the surrounding zones and sub-zones, with frequent pauses to gather information and strategic intelligence.

As he made his way through alleys and side streets, he had encountered no one, although that was due more to his own skills than to any lack of opportunity. Four times, he had spotted armed sentries stationed in windows and alleys, obviously the eyes and ears of the gang that had taken Ku-Ril-La. He had chosen to leave all four undisturbed and unknowing, lest they miss the assigned check-in times that Redling would have assigned in an operation of his own. The first sighting, he had taken as confirmation that he was on the correct trail; the second through fourth, he took as evidence that General Chilhoub's people didn't know much about how to run an efficient kidnapping. Certainly, their sentries were woefully lacking in the appropriate skills. Putting one where he could be spotted, even by someone as observant as Redling, was forgivable, but four—

Five, actually, the fifth being the green-haired Vilani man he gazed at now. The man leaned against a utility pole, squarely in front of the building that bore the address that Redling had been given. The guard made no effort that Redling could see to conceal himself, or even to be discreet. The Vilani was lean and lanky, dressed casually, and he had raised his wrist com unit to his lips to whisper something into it. Redling couldn't hear him clearly, but whatever the alleged sentry was saying, he was certain that it wasn't official business. The tone and the cadence of the Vilani's whispered words were wrong for that, and the expression on his youthful face was a lazy smile, not the anticipatory awareness or studied reserve that would have been appropriate to a man in his role. His lazy grin marked him as an amateur.

Redling didn't care much for amateurs, especially not amateurs trying to work an operation that demanded professionalism. If he had been in the business of kidnapping a multimillionaire businessman—and he had been, more than once—the green-haired kid who stood before him would not have lasted a second in his service.

He was wearing a pair of image-intensifying contact lenses, so the pale light cast by Plimbo's three moons was enough to illuminate the Vilani and the place behind him with daylight clarity. Redling looked past the pathetically ineffective lookout and studied the structure behind him. Whatever the place was, it hadn't been used for any legitimate purpose in some little time. The remains of municipal authority seals clung to the entrance and lower-floor windows; the upper-story windows had been boarded over.

Even though he could not see one from his vantage point, he felt reasonably certain that the structure had another entrance. While working his way closer to the place, he had passed several similar buildings; each had featured two entrances into a ground-floor receiving area, and this one looked likely to follow the same design. That was good, and suggested possibilities, depending on which door the kidnappers were using. Moving silently, Redling slipped deeper into his alley and then out the other end, and worked his way back toward the target building, but from another approach this time. In seconds, he was well inside what the kidnappers no doubt thought was their surveillance perimeter, and approached the safe house.

His guess had been right; a second doorway, old and dirty, faced a bank of unused recycling receptacles. Above it was a transom ventilator inlet that looked precisely right for Redling's purposes, so he decided to address that first. It took less than a minute of silent effort to peel back a section of the vent's cover and reveal darker darkness beyond.

Strapped to Redling's left leg was the very small but highly specialized toolkit from the bottom section of his weapons case. He had spent some years and no little expense assembling its contents. Now, he reached into it and withdrew a small, wheeled device, not much larger than his hand and with contours that vaguely matched those of common rodentoid vermin. The resemblance wasn't close enough to deceive, but it would pass muster for a brief glimpse, and the thing could move fast enough to make more than a fleeting glimpse unlikely. Redling thumbed a switch on the robot rat's belly, then set the gadget inside the building's open duct. Almost immediately, it was lost to sight.

Redling looked at the time readout on his wrist com, and waited.

Ten seconds passed, then twenty, and then the dark expanse of the com screen came to life. A silent image filled it, only moderately well resolved, but good enough for his purposes. In it, Redling could see three men—two standing, one seated.

He had been told that Chilhoub's right hand, and the probable architect of the abduction, was a man named Kiggle. He wondered now if any of the men he saw had that name.

More to the point, he could see Ku-Ril-La, seated in a chair too small for him, and obviously not happy to be there. The Guy-troy's wings were folded tight against his body—restrained?—and his head was bowed.

Years before, an electronics expert heavily in Redling's debt had constructed the robot rat to his design, adding a few improvements of his own as he went. The device was a remote surveillance camera, packed with enough reasoning power in its logic circuits to seek out situations that met Redling's rather specialized interests and report its findings. Right now, it was parked near a ceiling vent inside the storage facility and relaying what it saw to Redling's specially modified com unit.

Redling nodded, pleased by the revealed data . He didn't much like such devices, but he could certainly recognize their utility. So much for the ventilator; now it was time to turn his attentions to the door.

He had donned the Droyne override before leaving his hotel room. In the hours since, it had conformed itself so precisely to his hand that it felt like a second skin as he tapped one finger on the door lockplate. He pressed his palm against the scarred plastic panel and pushed gently, testing it.

The door remained closed.

Redling blinked in surprised, then tried the override glove another time. The door remained immobile.

That made no sense at all, and it was hard to reconcile with what else he had seen. The door's lock was nothing special, a simple deadbolt affair with an electronic keying system; there was simply no way that it could be proof against the unique tool that Redling wore, which had opened vault doors with ease. Unless, of course—

He opened the small toolkit again and took out another, more prosaic piece of equipment, a small magnetic probe that he had found useful for tracing wiring and support members. A flexible lead connected it to an imaging display, similar to the one on his com unit. Kneeling, Redling silently drew the probe's tip along the door's frame, not touching the plastic but coming close enough to disturb the film that clung to its surface. As he worked, he paid close attention to the images the device's display presented. They weren't of particularly high resolution, but they were good enough to show him what he needed to see: a series of metal spikes driven into the door's other side, and biting deep into its frame.

That explained why the Droyne device hadn't worked. By some quirk of the override's workings, the portal fell outside its parameters. Technically, the door wasn't locked, wasn't even a functioning door anymore. At some point, someone had sealed this side of the storage by nailing it shut.

Who? Had the kidnappers done it, or a municipal authority, or the place's owner? The thick layer of dirt suggested that the work was not of recent vintage. Redling supposed it was even conceivable that the people inside didn't know about the situation, given their general level of apparent inexpertise. He certainly couldn't count on that theory being correct—but even so, the sealed door promised to make things easier.

Redling stowed the probe away again, then glanced at his com unit. No change inside, as far as he could tell. The com screen was a good one, but the tiny camera feeding it had its limitations. Ku-Ril-La was still lashed to a chair at the end of the room farthest from the main entrance, but still reasonably distant from the sealed door. His perimeter stroll had told him that those were the only two ways in or out of the room quickly, but a curtained alcove to the camera's left suggested an adjoining space of some sort—presumably a toilet or a rest area. Redling noted it, but didn't spend any time wondering what—or who—waited behind the rippling, flimsy barrier; there simply wasn't enough information available from which to draw a conclusion.

Besides, he had enough mental work to do with the remainder of the image.

One of the three men inside was seated by front door at a small table. He was playing some sort of card game—maybe solo Choskey. Apparently he was an indoor counterpart of the outside sentries, which meant he probably wouldn't offer much trouble. Redling couldn't see whether he was armed, but had to assume he was. The other two stood near the seated, bound Guy-troy, obviously standing guard over the captive. Redling studied them carefully, gleaning as much data as he could from the low-resolution picture.

One of the standing pair leaned against the wall, as unmoving as a statue, something long and dark hanging at his side—a weapon of some sort, presumably. At least, the man's stance and body language said it probably was. The image resolution wasn't sharp enough to be certain. That wasn't the case with the other guard, however. The other, bigger man paced impatiently. His course carried him in and out of the camera's field of view and yielded to the Redling's eye a fairly clear, if sporadic, view of the weapon he carried. It was a long gun, almost certainly a laser, and Redling disagreed with the choice for two reasons. Long guns in general were hard to use effectively in a confined space, and lasers in genral were easy to use, but hard to use well. The two weaknesses tended to reinforce one another.

Redling was a practiced professional, and he preferred projectile weapons. They were a bit harder to use, but less likely to fail.

That didn't mean he had no use for electronics in general, of course.

Another belt pouch yielded three remote grenades, flat little ovoid objects about the size of a directory card and much heavier than they looked. Redling armed one and gummed it to the door, using a blob of adhesive plastic that set and hardened immediately, forming a secure bond with the dusty panel. He clipped the other two grenades to his tunic in case he needed them later, then walked silently back the way he came. The stretch of cracked concrete was still quiet and still unattended, and the stroll, no matter how brief, gave him a moment to assess the situation.

Things were looking up. One against four in a clearly defined space didn't constitute favorable odds, but they weren't bad ones, either, especially considering the caliber of men and weapon he expected to encounter. Certainly, he had dealt with much more dangerous situations, albeit only rarely on his own initiative. Even now, some assistance would have been welcome—but experience had taught him that the wrong sort of backup in the sort of situation that confronted him now could cause more problems than no backup at all.

The problem was, he knew no one on Plimbo he could trust, at least not with his life, not even among his crew.

Certainly not among his crew.

The green-haired Vilani guard was still whispering sweet nothings into his wrist com unit as Redling rounded the corner, but the conversation was obviously nearing an end. A full minute passed before the lovestruck sentry whispered a final few crooning syllables, then pressed his communicator's DISCONNECT key. He looked skyward and smiled, the angle of his face and the brightness of the moons working together to show Redling that the sentry's lips were green, too—another dye job. The Vilani man laughed softly, a pleased sound that suggested both satisfaction and anticipation. He drew a pipe from his belt and brought it to his lips.

Redling stepped closer.

The sentry drew on his pipe. It lit itself, and the surrounding night air filled with the scent of burning herbs. The Vilani breathed deeply, thus committing another significant security risk. Redling could see a grim humor in the situation. Bad enough the alleged sentry had violated the com silence that any sane schemer would impose; now, he was announcing his presence to anyone in the vicinity with a nose. He could scarcely do a worse job of being discreet.

Tonight's target was definitely in the wrong business.

Redling decided it was time to put a halt to that situation.

Rippling shadows flowed along the contours of Redling's body as he silently approached the smoking man. The fingers of Redling's right hand flexed and bent, then straightened again as he readied himself to strike. His left hand opened, and he released a bit of gravel he had found near the sealed door. It fell, and as it hit the walkway, it made a clicking, rattling sound not unlike one of Helicron's dice.

Startled by the unexpected sound, the Vilani dropped his pipe, making a louder clatter that drowned out the one made by Redling's pebbles. The sentry's other hand clutched and drew a pistol—commendably, it was a projectile weapon—and raised it now, thumbing back the hammer even as he spun in Redling's direction.

He moved fast, but not fast enough and much too late.

Redling dropped down and his right hand came up. His long, elegant fingers were locked in rigid alignment, and their tips glistened like teeth on a saw. He used them like a saw, too, moving his hand in a tight, swift arc that intersected the sentry's throat just below his chin. The keen blades glued to Redling's fingertips, the same four bits of alloy he had used to threaten Tithe two planets ago, found scarcely more resistance than air might offer as they penetrated Vilani skin and muscle and cartilage, before continuing on the path that Redling had set for them. The sentry went rigid, then limp, and his red blood was black in the moonlight as Redling dodged the arterial spray he had released.

The sentry was dead now, even if he didn't realize it yet. In a very real sense, he had been dead since first coming to Redling's attention.

The Vilani made a choking, gasping sound, a gurgling rasp that he tried, but failed, to shape into words. Redling watched impassively as the sentry fell back against the utility pole and leaned heavily against it, seeking some measure of physical support in his last moments of life. The fingers of his gun hand opened, releasing his pistol. Almost instinctively, Redling's noted the movement, and he kicked at the gun in mid-drop, so that the plummeting weapon fell silently on a patch of scrub instead of clattering to the synth-stone walkway. At the same time, he clamped one hand across the sentry's mouth, to block the choking noises, and held it there until the other man went completely limp. Gently, Redling lowered the body to the ground. There was no need for noise just yet.

Noise would come later.

Now, Redling blinked three times in rapid succession to reset his night vision contact lenses to their greatest definition, then knelt and began the task of searching the dead man. He worked quickly and efficiently, paying particular attention to the sentry's weapons belt and pouch. The effort proved fruitless; there was nothing unexceptional to find, only a Universal ID in the name of one Graaple Osclard, some notes in local currency, and a fistful of the directory chips that were almost omnipresent on Plimbo. Redling left them, but took the money and the ID.

Young Graaple certainly had no need for them anymore.

Midway through the search, Redling's keen ears heard a faint—very faint—rustling sound. It was the dead man's wrist com, set to vibrate instead of buzz, perhaps the deceased's only gesture toward professionalism. Right now, the device was registering an incoming call. Redling raised the dead man's arm and glanced at the com screen, then wasted a split second wondering who was at the other end of the transmission. Who was trying to contact the late sentry Graaple? Redling doubted very much that it was an assigned checkin. A girlfriend? A confederate?

It really didn't matter anymore, he supposed.

Nothing mattered to the dead.

He glanced at the sentry's relaxed face, at the dead man's slack features and blankly staring eyes. They were pale in the moonlight but still easily visible. Graaple looked less like a dead man than a dead boy, Redling realized, but the observation carried with it no particular freight of regrets or compassion. Redling had seen enough death in his life to realize that it came to everyone, sooner or later, but he also knew that it was never too early to make a wrong decision. For whatever reason, the deceased Vilani had chosen to run with predators. That run had been down a short path, but it had been a path of his choosing. If Graaple Osclard had wanted to live, he should have selected a different vocation, or learned how to do his chosen one more effectively.

The communicator on the dead man's wrist throbbed again, more forcefully this time. Whoever was sending was persistent, which was only appropriate, given the circumstances. He or she would have to wait a long time for an answer.

Redling released Graaple's hand and let it fall limply to the ground. He had to get back to work. If the call was from one of the other three men still waiting inside the storage facility....

Redling headed back towards Ku-Ril-La's makeshift prison. He walked briskly, taking long, loping strides that covered the distance quickly. As he did, he drew from its holster the pistol that Milos Grogan of Mariposa had given him, snapped its cylinder open and verified its load. Then he took a moment to adjust the spring-sheath that held his Ambernassian dagger close to his left forearm.

Three steps back from the main door, he glanced again at his wrist com unit's screen. The situation inside the consignment house showed no sign of change, so Redling thumbed back the hammer on his pistol, raised it, and used his left index finger to press the appropriate key on his com.

Now was the time for noise.

The grenade that Redling had glued to the far door exploded in instant response, lighting the night briefly and filling it with a muffled thunder. He had set the explosive for a low-yield blast, loud enough to tear the door from its hinges and shake up the building's occupants, but low enough that the sound of the blast would be swallowed up by the surrounding blocks of the warehouse district. As the last of the concussion faded, he heard angry shouts from within the suddenly sundered prison.

"Who is it?"

"What the Drog?"

"Some kind of—"

Redling waited one second, then two, then three, and grinned as the locked door before him swung open.

Amateurs were so predictable.

Smoke and chaos spilled from the open door and then a figure stumbled through it. The trigger on Redling's pistol drew back, carrying his trigger finger with it, and the gun roared. A ten-millimeter alloy slug leapt from the gun's muzzle and found a new home in the head of a man whom Redling recognized as the one who had been playing cards a minute or two before.

The man framed in the open doorway fell silent, and then just fell.

Redling darted forward, taking a deep breath as he moved. These were the moments that would count the most, and they passed with an elastic slowness that lent each split second a crystal clarity. He bounded over the dead man in the doorway and charged into the room beyond, dropping to the floor and rolling, unmindful of debris shards and stinging smoke, except insofar as the impact they had on his ability to aim and shoot.

That impact was not very great.

"What? Who?"

"Get him, Flarge it! Kill him!"

Two human voices now, which meant (probably) that no one else waited inside. He heard nothing from the Guy-troy, which could mean anything or everything, but Redling wasn't making any guesses at the moment.

The men inside the facility were at least slightly better at their work than Graaple Osclard had been, even if Redling didn't care much for their taste in weaponry. Certainly, they were quick to respond to his sudden intrusion. Laser fire cut through the smoke and noise, moving at precisely the speed of light, but not moving in a path that intersected Redling's tumbling trajectory. He bounced and rolled, hugging the floor, holding his arms close to his body as he dodged the energy bursts that missed him and found the concrete of the floor instead. The slab beneath bubbled and cracked, but offered more resistance to the searing beams than Redling's flesh possibly could.

Not that he saw any reason to put that comparison to the test.

Redling's last tumble took him into the curtained alcove he had noticed earlier. One of his guesses proved correct: the area held an unmade bed. Behind the drape now, he was in relative darkness, not completely hidden but at least obscured, and the curtain barrier was thin enough that he could see the shadowed forms beyond it. One of them, the larger, came closer now, raised something and trained it in Redling's direction. Red fire tore through the drape and burned into the unmade bed.

Redling returned the favor. He didn't raise his pistol, but kept it close to his body and fired once, twice, directing its fire with the ease of long practice. The bigger of the two remaining men staggered as the heavy rounds caught him squarely in the chest, then he fell back, but did not fall.

"Haw!" the man laughed. "Show you! I'll show you!" He raised his laser rifle again. It cut and seared though the drapery, and the last of the frail barrier fell, giving Redling his first good look at the man who was so eagerly trying to kill him. The glimpse, however brief, answered two questions—why the big man wasn't dead, and why he had paced so incessantly before, not that Redling had particularly wondered about the latter point.

The big guy was wearing flex armor, a torso piece that conformed so closely to his body that the medium-resolution rat-camera hadn't shown it clearly. Personally, Redling didn't like flex, though he was willing to use the stuff when necessary or appropriate—it limited the mobility that was so vital to his combat style. Moreover, it was damnably uncomfortable, especially for a man in a seated position, which probably explained why the big man had spent so much time on his feet. Even so, Redling had to acknowledge that it did its job, and was doing it now.

It stopped bullets.

The big man had rocked back after absorbing the energy of Redling's two shots, but he had recovered now. He roared a curse in a language that Redling had never heard before, remarkable in itself, and raised his laser rifle again. Nothing in sight offered much promise of providing effective cover, so Redling ducked and rolled some more, firing his own pistol even as the laser beam stabbed at him again. This time, the big man's aim was better, even if not quite good enough—the laser burst found Redling's hair, and neatly sliced a lock from his dark mane.

Redling's aim, however, improved not a whit—but his choice of targets did. His shot caught the big man neatly in the throat, punched through the soft tissue it found there, and then continued in an upward trajectory and buried itself in the ceiling.

The rifleman made a strangled noise, remarkably similar to Graaple Osclard's final, futile verbalizations, but he did not fall. Liquid redness gushed from his holed throat, but, incredibly, he remained standing and struggled to train his rifle on Redling once more.

At another time, Redling might have pondered the gunman's remarkable vitality. Now, however, a more appropriate course of action seemed to be to shoot him a fourth time, trying the head this time. With gratifying promptness, the big man fell, and hit the floor with a satisfying *thump!*

By then, Redling had already turned his attention to the other side of the room, where Ku-Ril-La should have been waiting. He was; so was someone else, who was already in Redling's sights.

The third gunman.

"Drop it now!" Both Redling and the gunman roared the words simultaneously, but Redling was reasonably certain that only he found any humor, however faint, in the coincidence. Of course, the other man could probably find some solace in the fact that he had the tactical advantage.

"Drop the gun!" the last surviving captor shrieked, speaking solo this time. He was a stocky fellow with a high-pitched voice, and his features were enough like Graaple's to mark him as the dead man's brother. Right now, the presumed member of the Osclard clan stood behind the seated Ku-Ril-La, with one arm drawn tightly across the birdman's throat. Apparently, he had lost his rifle during the shock and confusion, but he had a laser pistol now, and its muzzle was pressed against Ku-Ril-La's head at the approximate point where a man's temple would be. Redling had no doubt that a shot fired there would find the Guy-troy's brain without stopping to ask directions.

Ku-Ril-La stared at Redling with wide eyes. Whatever emotions they showed were unreadable.

"No need to speak so loudly, chum," Redling said. Without taking his eyes from the Vilani's, he spoke to Ku-Ril-La, instead. "Have they hurt you? Can you walk?"

Ku-Ril-La's head shook, then nodded. Neither motion occupied more than a fraction of a percentage of a degree of arc, but neither was lost to Redling's peripheral vision.

"Drop the gun," the gunman repeated, "or I drop

the Guy-troy!" The volume of his voice was greatly reduced, but not the tension.

Redling shook his head. Most people in such circumstances would be rigid with tension, confused with contradicting fight-or-flight signals, buffeted by the biochemical demands of their nervous systems. Redling, however, felt utterly calm now, awash in a wave of tranquility that swept through him without dulling his razor-keen senses or blunting his sense of anticipation. With two men down, only one adversary remained, and he had never known himself to fail against a single adversary.

"That's not how it's done," Redling said, still in a crouch. "Believe me, I have plenty of experience in this sort of thing." He paused. "The way we do it, is, you put down your gun and release my friend, and I let you walk out of here." That was a lie, of course, but one that was expected, considering the circumstances. "I didn't go to all the trouble of killing your sentry and killing your partner," he continued, "just so that I could let you take over the entire show. Be reasonable." He spoke with utter confidence, but not overconfidence; he had long since learned that any even odds were actually odds in favor of a man with his skills.

"Killing—?" The surviving gunman said, but this time, his voice was a whisper. "Graaple?" "Dead," Redling said. He grinned and nodded, twisting the verbal knife a bit more. "Smoking will do that to you, I'm sorry to say."

The Osclard brother made a noise halfway between a swallow and a moan, the tentative birth cries of a sob, but he didn't move. "Drop the gun," he said doggedly. "Drop the gun now."

He tightened his grip on Ku-Ril-La's neck and the Guy-troy made a strangled noise, too—but his was literal, and mechanical in origin, rather than emotional.

Redling shrugged. "If you say so," he said, still utterly calm. The war was essentially won now, even if its loser didn't realize it. Redling leaned forward a degree or two, lowered his pistol to the cracked and scarred floor. The gun was still hot from being fired and his hand felt cool as he released it.

"Now, back, back," the gunman said. "Move back, away from it."

Redling dropped back a step or two, but no further. Several things happened then, in such close sequence that they blurred together, even in the distorted, elongated time of Redling's adrenaline-charged senses.

Ku-Ril-La's dark eyes blinked, their nictitating membranes sliding across their dark surface and then retreating again.

The arm that Osclard had coiled so tightly around the winged man's neck released slightly, and a rattling gasp sounded as the captive took a desperate breath.

Ku-Ril-La blinked again.

Redling continued to smile. He tensed the muscles of his left forearm, releasing the sheath's spring. Instantly, the hidden dagger's hilt filled his hand.

Osclard said something, something that was guttural and harsh, and barely recognizable as words. Then he took his weapon's muzzle away from Ku-Ril-La's temple and began bringing it to bear on Redling.

"Graaple was my brother," the gunman said, confirming Redling's suspicions, and making it almost certain that one of the other two men had been the ringleader. The Osclards didn't seem to possess the brains to run anything, even an operation as poor as this one.

Redling nodded. "I rather thought as much," he said affably. "You both suffered from a similar lack of looks and brains." He purred the words. "I guess that means you're not Kiggle." Osclard hissed in fury and tightened his trigger finger.

Redling's left hand, at about eye-level now, twitched.

Osclard made another noise and then fell, dead. His gun fell, too, and bounced and rattled as it came to a rest on the floor beside him.

Ku-Ril-La took a deep, shuddering breath and spoke. "Very adroitly done," he said. "I was unaware that your species was capable of such swiftness."

"I can't speak for the rest of my species," Redling said, "but I sure am." He stepped to the winged man's side, examined his bonds. They were made of tangler tape, the type civilian authorities used to bind criminal suspects, narrow ribbons of steel-tough plastic that fused together when activated. They were activated now.

"There are others," Ku-Ril-La said. "Besides the sentry."

"I counted another four," Redling said. "More lookouts, all within three subzones. Strictly amateur." He knelt, drew his dagger from Osclard's eye, and began using it on the tangler tape holding Ku-Ril-La to his chair. The ribbons offered only minimal resistance to the narrow blade. "We can get past them, easily enough. I've got a ground-car."

"More than that," the Guy-troy continued. "Two more. They went for food."

"Amateurs," Redling repeated. "If I were running

this show, no one would come or go except to run money. There would be enough food and weapons on hand to make it unnecessary and I sure as Flarge would find a more secure site than this." He paused, thinking. "I wouldn't allow anyone to use their coms, either. And I'd cut the fingers off the first man I found smoking on duty."

"Your expertise and tactical savvy impress me," Ku-Ril-La said. "But we are still outnumbered."

"Four to two, six to two," Redling said. "With this caliber of help, it doesn't make much difference. We'll manage. The other sentries don't worry me; I could have dealt with them before, but thought they might miss a checkin time. That's not an issue now." The strips of plastic fell away. "Can you walk?"

Ku-Ril-La stood, unfurled his wings, closed them again. He flexed the long muscles of his legs, then nodded. "They took care not to injure me," he said. "In that, at least, they were wise. The Kaal is unforgiving."

Redling cleaned his dagger and returned it to its sheath. "So am I," he said calmly. He glanced to one side, and then picked up one of the dead men's laser rifles.

"What are you doing?" Ku-Ril-La asked.

By way of answer, Redling fired the rifle. A lance of red fire stabbed forth, blasting an overhead ventilator grille from its frame, amid a shower of debris. A moment after that, Redling's remote control robot rat dropped from the sundered ceiling and into his extended hand. He stowed in his toolkit and then turned to Ku-Ril-La.

Ku-Ril-La didn't say anything, but his interest was evident.

"It's a long story," Redling said, rather than waste time on an explanation. He offered the winged man the laser rifle. "Do you want a weapon?"

"Do you think it wise that I take one?"

"Not wise or unwise; just unnecessary."

Ku-Ril-La nodded. "A synonym for unwise. I bow to your insight."

"I'm glad someone does. Let's go."

It had taken Redling more than two hours of careful reconnoitering to find his way through the warren of alleys and streets that was Plimbo City's warehouse district to the place where Ku-Ril-La was held. He had worked his way past the occasional brightly lit open space or sleepy-eyed sentinel, scuttled though alleys and passageways until he found his quarry. The knowledge he had gained along the way served him well now. It took him much less than half that long to find his way back out again, even slowed by the less-fleet feet of his companion. Along the way, in the stretches that Redling knew were at least reasonably unattended, the two spoke in soft whispers.

"How did you learn of where they were holding me?" Ku-Ril-La asked.

"The capture made the media, at least until someone who had an eye on public relations—and who doesn't, around here?—got it downplayed. A local got me some more details."

"You found someone you could trust so quickly?"

Redling shrugged. "It's a knack," he said. "I've been in the business for a while. And *trust* is too strong a word."

"What business is that? Piloting a starship?" From a human throat, the tone in the Guy-troy's voice would have sounded mocking. "I was unaware that the career engendered such skills."

Redling declined to answer, at least directly. "I had to spend a bit of your money for that," he continued. "I'm not in this for my health, and the *Gateway*'s profit margin is slim enough as it is." He named a figure.

"For that amount, you should have been able to hire some assistance."

Redling shook his head. "Generally speaking, I work better by myself," he said. He looked at the worn features of his companion. "It takes more than money to buy loyalty," he said, "and much more than money to buy talent. Ninety-nine times out of a hundred, I'm better off working by myself than with someone I don't know." He grinned as the two of them turned another corner. "Besides, I didn't need anyone at my back for a job this easy."

"Easy." Ku-Ril-La paused in midstride and massaged one wrist, where the tangler tape had bitten deeply into his skin and left an angry discoloration. "You define some words more interestingly than others, Redling," he said. "What of the local? Weren't you concerned that he would sell word of your interest to the other side?"

"She, actually," Redling said, "and it's still a matter of trust."

"Someone you knew?"

"Someone I met. Our shuttle driver from the starport. She seemed well-connected, and I persuaded her to tell me what I needed to know. She gave me a name, Kiggle, and a few bits of data. After that, it was just a matter of finding the right people and shaking the details loose. That's a knack, too."

"You were willing to trust your life—my life—to a woman you've known only since planetfall?"

"No," Redling said. He shook his head. "I trust the cuffs I bound her with, though. She's not talking to anyone until I let her." He grinned, but didn't mention a welcome second result of his interrogation of the big-armed shuttle driver.

With Rolth cuffed in her own quarters, Helicron wasn't likely to go anyhwere tonight.

Ku-Ril-La's talons twisted and flexed. Had there been an appropriate hard surface for them to strike, the gesture would have been accompanied by the clattering noise that Redling had come to recognize as representing amusement.

"You define some terms quite interestingly, indeed," Ku-Ril-La said, then changed the subject. "Why did you come for me?"

"No one else was going to."

"Untrue. The local authorities would, and so would representatives of the Kaal."

"Incorrect. The local powers that be don't want to do anything but get Chilhoub offplanet, and your friends in the Kaal—well, let's say that merchants don't like to part with money, and they don't like to part with their lives. If they were going to send someone after you, they weren't going to do it quickly. If they had delayed even another three days, Chilhoub would be offplanet and you'd lose your value. If you were going to be gotten, someone had to get you quickly," Redling said.

"That doesn't answer my question. Why did you come?"

Redling paused in his tracks before answering. They

were near the boundary of the warehouse district now, less than a subzone from where he had left his borrowed ground car. "I came because I promised you that you would complete your tour," he said. "That was our deal."

"And you did this alone, because of a promise?"

"I didn't know anyone qualified to help," Redling said, though Dawn's face drifted briefly through his mind. "And I work better alone, anyway," he continued, speaking very softly. He raised one hand, gesturing for silence. "Now, hush."

Something was wrong.

A dozen yards of poorly lit synth-stone sidewalk stretched between Redling and his vehicle. This had been where he sighted the first sentry, a dark-skinned woman stationed in a second-story window. Getting past her on the way in hadn't been particularly difficult, but he had expected a bit more of a challenge on the return route, especially considering he was accompanied by someone who lacked his own practiced grace.

He couldn't see her there now.

Why not?

Redling blinked his to reset his contact lenses, and took a second look. The window, little more than a patch of blackness to the naked eye, suddenly sprang into sharp relief.

He was right; the dark-skinned woman wasn't there.

Ku-Ril-La looked at him questioningly. Redling lay one hand on the Guy-troy's shoulder and guided the winged man to a convenient alcove that he had spotted earlier, then gestured for him to stay there.

Something was definitely wrong—or had, at least, changed, which amounted to the same thing.

Redling flattened himself against a convenient warehouse wall, and then began to inch his way along the short distance of battered sidewalk that stretched ahead of him. Several alley mouths and recessed doorways punctuated the route that lay before him, all of them sufficiently deep that he could not see what they held from where he had left Ku-Ril-La. He had to pass them all before reaching his escape vehicle. Any of them could hold the woman sentry, or reinforcements.

Now, he thought about the other two kidnappers that the Guy-troy had told him about, the pair who had gone for food. Counting them, as many as three gunmen waited for him in the shadows—enough to pose a challenge, especially if they were expecting him and he had to look out for the safety of a companion. His right hand already held his pistol; now, he tensed his left forearm muscles and let the Ambernassian slide into his hand once more.

He hadn't come this far only to leave the board so late in the game.

The first alley he passed was empty, and so was the second. Redling kept moving, flattening his trim from as much as he could, hugging the shadows to avoid presenting a target. He seemed to walk on the sidewalk less than he slipped and slid along the wall's rough surface. The first recessed doorway was empty, so he let himself slither into it and out again, and kept moving forward. He strained his augmented eyes and his excellent hearing to their utmost, searching for any clue and hint that someone was waiting—

That was when he smelled something, something that was oddly out of place against the backdrop of dirt and oil and industrial odors.

Redling paused in his tracks again, and stood motionless. He flared his nostrils and took a careful, shallow breath, just deep enough to draw aroma-charged air across his olfactory nerves. He closed his eyes for a dangerous moment, and setting aside sight so that he could concentrate instead on what his oldest sense had found.

Cooked meat. Vegetables, maybe floogle shoots. Java. He reviewed the aromas and drew the only conclusion that seemed reasonable.

Someone's food run had proven successful.

He took another, deeper breath, then moistened his lips. They dried and cooled more quickly on the left side than on the right, giving him a directional fix on the wind-born aromas. They came from his right, probably from the next passageway that separated two buildings.

He felt the familiar sense of utter calm sweep over him again, as it had so many times before.

Moving so slowly that he scarcely seemed to move at all, Redling edged forward, noiselessly passing through one boundary of shadow to another, until his leading fingers found the edge of the alley's mouth.

The smells were stronger now—but strangely, not reinforced by the sounds of eating, or by any sounds at all.

He could hear nothing from the alley but silence.

Stealth was suddenly joined by speed as Redling dropped to one knee and threw himself into the target alley, moving even more swiftly than he had earlier, when storming the kidnappers' sanctuary. He came in fast and low, pistol cocked and knife poised to throw as he rounded the corner and readied himself for battle again.

There was none.

The twin sensations of surprise and confusion, relative strangers in Redling's adventurous life, swept through him as he took in what waited in the alley. He saw the scene before him with razor-keen clarity—the spilled plastic trays of food, the dark pools of java from toppled, now empty cups, and unused utensils and napkins. Nearby, a laser rifle leaned against the alley wall.

Of the most interest to Redling however, at least at the moment, were the three forms, silent and unmoving, that littered the alley floor.

Redling sheathed his knife but not his gun as he stepped closer and took stock of the situation. Two men and one woman lay in a single, tangled heap. The woman he recognized as the sentry who had previously occupied a certain nearby, second-story window, but the men were strangers to him. Judging from the evidence, however, they were more members of Chilhoub's loyalist band, apparently the pair who had been sent out for food.

All three were quite dead.

It wasn't hard to figure out what had happed, at least approximately. The two foragers had returned, met with the lone sentry, and presented her with her share of provisions. The impromptu meal that followed had been their last.

Redling wondered who had done the job. It had been someone—perhaps several someones—who was at least reasonably competent. Certainly, he, she, or they were more skilled than the amateurs he had encountered thus far this evening. There were no signs of struggle, only of surprise—the dropped food, the spilled drinks—and one man's pistols were still holstered. The woman's laser rifle might have been dropped from a marksman's stance, but Redling thought that unlikely; it hadn't even been cycled for discharge. More likely, she had set it aside to eat. At any rate, none of the weapons had been fired.

He stepped closer, pressed the back of one hand to the underside of the dark woman's jaw. She was still warm. Only minutes had passed since her death. Gently, he brushed aside the disheveled tresses that had fallen across her face. For the second time tonight, dead eyes stared up at him. They didn't interest him, however.

What he saw in them did.

The pupils of the dead woman's eyes were contracted to their absolute minimum, forming tiny pinpoints that were scarcely discernable against the field of her irises. That didn't make much sense, given the circumstances—the alley was dark, the woman wasn't wearing lenses like Redling's, and even if she had been, eyes tended to dilate upon death, not contract. Somehow, someone had drugged her. The food was a possibility, but another cause seemed more likely.

He continued examining her carefully, reasonably sure what he would find somewhere on her cooling body. In seconds, he had proven proved himself correct, as his carefully searching fingers found a dart, tiny and unfletched. It was so needle-sharp and had been cast with such force that more than half its length was buried in the dead woman's throat.

Redling recognized the ammunition, had even used it himself, once or twice. Pneumatic dart pistols with poison loads were very popular in some circles, even though they were not his weapon of choice. To his way of thinking, their chief advantages—near-total silence and the lack of laser-flash—were outweighed by their shortage of penetrating power. Even heavy clothing could block the little darts. In the hands of the right user, and in the right circumstances, however, they were deadly.

Certainly, they had been so tonight.

Redling had no doubt that he would find similar missiles embedded in the two dead men, but he didn't bother to look for them. Other issues were on his mind at the moment, demanding enough attention that he was dangerously close to being distracted.

He had seen a pneumo-gun recently, and under unexpected circumstances. He wondered if that gun was the one that had done this job. He was still thinking about that when a noise drew his attention, the sound a foot would make on an alley floor—specifically, a foot other than his own.

Redling's knife was still in his left hand as he began to turn; his left was filled with the revolver's grip before he had completed the turn.

"We must be away," Ku-Ril-La said urgently. If he saw the grim tableau, he made no comment. "Others are on their way."

"Oh?" Redling asked, annoyed that the Guy-troy had disobeyed his instructions to stay where he was.

Ku-Ril-La nodded. "Your ears are good," the Guy-troy said, "but mine are better. Listen closely now."

Redling listened. Now that he had been alerted, he could hear the sirens, too, the familiar wail that law enforcers used to advertise their presence with such annoying consistency.

"You're right," he said, and then followed it with two other familiar words. "Thank you. Let's go."

Staying where they were meant answering questions, and his interest at the moment lay more in asking them, instead.

CHAPTER NINE

Unfortunately, nearly everyone else in Plimbo City seemed to feel the same way, and most were pretty emphatic about it.

The first question came from Rolth. She asked it as she sat on the edge of the bed in the hotel room that Redling had rented under an assumed name and used as a meeting place after calling her. Now, she rubbed the angry red marks on her wrists and glared even more angrily at him as she massaged the feeling back into her hands.

"What did you go and do that for?" she asked. Her brutish features were a study in truculence and hurt outrage. "Credits you promised—they were enough to keep my mouth shut." She paused, either for affect or to think. "Gonna pay me, right?" A worried expression crept across her face. "Because if you aren't—"

Redling, grinning lazily, nodded. He had stepped back immediately upon unlocking the handcuffs he had used to bind the shuttle driver and removing her gag. Now, he leaned against the doorframe, careful to keep some meters behind the burly woman's reach, motivated less by any fear of her than by a simple desire to avoid further physical conflict.

He had killed enough for one evening.

"Of course I'm going to pay. You'll get what's coming to you," he said. "I'm a man of my word, even if I never expect anyone else to be."

"Not a man," Rolth said sourly.

"Oh, I know that, my sweet," Redling continued. One hand drifted beneath the hanging folds of his tunic, flowing as smoothly as the ocean's currents, too smoothly for bone and muscle to move. His grin became a trifle less lazy and the still-visible hand seemed to tense slightly. "But I'm still going to take care of you."

Rolth didn't say anything, but watched carefully as Redling's hand disappeared, and then returned to view again.

"Huh," Rolth grunted, as she saw what her erstwhile captor held now, but the sound was one of pleasure. The look of anger faded from her features and a greedy smile took its place. "Now, that's more like it!" she said happily.

Redling nodded, an element of mockery in the acknowledgement, and before his head finished moving, he tossed the thick sheaf of bank notes in Rolth's direction. The bundle of money fell with a muffled thump on the rumpled bed, and Rolth snatched it up eagerly.

"Count it. You'll find that's twice the price we agreed on," Redling said. "Somewhat more than enough to pay for the information you gave me, I think you'll agee."

"Huh," Rolth said again. She was counting now, her thick fingers a blur of motion as they shuffled through the bills. Plimbo's economy relied heavily enough on offplanet money and casual transactions (many of them illegal) that the electronic currency system had never taken over completely. The wheels of Plimbo's commerce required the grease of graft, and that lubricant was best delivered in solid form.

"What's the extra for?" she asked, once she had confirmed that the extra was, indeed, present.

"Discretion," Redling said. "There are going to be a lot of people asking a lot questions in this weasel warren you call a city, and I'd really rather you not answer any of them for a bit."

"So now you trust me to keep my mouth shut?"

"I trust that you'll know better than to blab when you hear the news," Redling said.

"You found your birdman, huh? Where is he?"

Redling had remanded Ku-Ril-La into the protective custody of some reasonably competent-looking representatives of the Kaal Combine before returning to Rolth's temporary residence.

"Rolth, dearest, let's merely allow that I took certain actions, based on the data you gave me, actions that will make that data's source less than popular in certain quarters." He smiled. "You might want to avoid the family Osclard, or for example, or what's left of it."

Rolth didn't say anything.

"Keep an eye on the newscasts," Redling continued, "and an ear to the floogle vine. When—if—you hear about certain interesting developments in the warehouse district this evening, you might do well to bear in mind that I was the author of those events. I accomplished them on my own, dear Rolth, and they do not come near to testing the limits of my capabilities. That knowledge should be enough to make you want to keep your mouth sealed until I've departed for other parts." He grinned again. "That is, assuming you enjoy the exciting little section you've woven for yourself in life's rich tapestry. You want to close down the loom, cease your weaving, we can do that, too." All humor fled his voice as he continued. "We can take care of that right now, if you'd like."

"No, no, no," Rolth said. The money had already disappeared, stowed away somewhere on her person. "You can trust me."

"Not really, but I like to believe that I can trust your instinct for self-preservation," Redling said. He derived no great pleasure from making threats, but he didn't mind the process, either. It was just another skill to master. "The *Gateway* lifts just after sundown tomorrow," he continued. "I don't want to hear from or see you again before then. After that, do what you want and sing until your throat bleeds; I don't care."

Rolth nodded. "Can do that," she said. "Osclards, huh? They're a tough basket."

"Were."

"Were?" Rolth quoted, and then shook her head emphatically. "You can trust me. No hear, no see."

"And another word of advice—hands off the kid. For your own good."

Rolth looked at him, questioningly.

"Helicron Daas. I haven't spent this long taming the terror of the North Arm to have you tempt him back to his troublesome ways."

"'Terror of the Northern Arm'!?"

Redling nodded somberly. "Don't let his act fool you," he said, as seriously as he could manage. "That boy has evil in his genes. He's seen the inside of more prisons on more worlds than you'd believe. I keep him on a tight leash because of some promises I made his mother, but I can't answer for any actions he takes when he's out of my sight."

"Was just going to show him some gaming—"

"Gaming?" Redling made the word a sound of shocked dismay that nonetheless sounded remarkably sincere, even to his own ears. "You were going to take *Helicron Daas* gaming? Oh, Rolth, you should give me back that money now, and count yourself well ahead of the game, still. I've already more than paid you for your services by keeping you out of the monster's clutches."

"Monster? Clutches?" Rolth shook her head, puzzled. "He's just a kid, looking for a good time. You skroced that for him, but good."

"And you don't know how lucky you are that I did. You don't know what he means when he says that," Redling said. "The good citizens of Fingeroth still wake up screaming when they dream of what Helicron Daas called a 'good time'."

Rolth was obviously baffled.

"Now, be a good girl," Redling continued, "and stay here an hour or so, then be on your way. Just remember what I said, and what you shouldn't say." He paused. "*You* were going to show Helicron Daas a 'good time'," he quoted, and shook his head. "Helicron Daas."

He was still laughing as he left the room.

The next barrage of questions was less amusing, though scarcely harder to deal with. Representatives from the municipal constabulary and the Starport Authority were waiting in the lobby of his own hotel. One representative was familiar, but the other was not. The latter was a balding man named Teal, who was from the local police's Major Crimes Unit. The familiar face belonged to Tredlib, who, remarkably, had accompanied Teal on his impromptu visit, apparently to look out for the local economy's interests in any dealings with the Kaal or its people. At first, both claimed to be investigating Ku-Ril-La's abduction, and seeking details regarding the winged man's movements, preferences, and likely enemies. Redling received their interest as graciously as he could, and ushered them into his rented room, where all three men seated themselves.

Some seventy minutes into a remarkably unproductive conversation about Ku-Ril-La's comings and goings, things changed. Redling was spinning a few lies that would be hard to disprove but that amused him when Teal took a call on his personal com.

"Teal here," the pudgy man said. The com unit's tiny speaker said something that Redling couldn't quite overhear. Teal made a noise of agitated disbelief before asking for details, and then more sounds of increasing intensity before he broke the connection and looked thoughtfully in Redling's direction.

"Mind if I ask you how you spent your evening, Captain Redling?" he said.

"Oh, just the usual this and that," Redling said lightly. "Taking in the sights of lovely Plimbo City, making the acquaintance of your delightful citizenry, playing a rousing few rounds of Spindledrift." He smiled, the kind of grin that came easily whenever he faced a challenge as minimal as Teal seemed to offer.

He knew what questions were coming now. He knew them so well that he was tempted to ask them himself, but refrained, lest it spoil the effect.

"And did your wanderings take you to the warehouses, by any chance?"

Redling's features were a study in innocence as he responded. "The warehouse district? Hardly. I was looking for diversion, not exertion. I have quite enough business to keep me busy, thank you."

"Someone answering your description was seen, on foot, in the area a few hours ago."

"Many individuals are fortunate enough to answer to my description. It's not my looks that make me special."

"And while you were there, did you make the acquaintance of any individuals, or encounter any difficulties?" Teal's voice was a tired drone, but his eyes were bright and attentive as they gazed in Redling's direction.

"I'm afraid you misheard me," Redling said. "I haven't had the pleasure of touring your doubtless lovely warehouse district. Liftoff is tomorrow, dusk. If I have time, I'll certainly try, but I can't make any promises."

Teal shook his head, making the near-universal (for humans) signal of disagreement. "I can't promise you'll be going anywhere tomorrow, Captain Redling."

"But I'm fully loaded and I've reserved the launch window," Redling said, making himself sound indignant. "You can't detain me, just because one of my passengers can't make launch time!" He looked eagerly at Tredlib. "He can't do that, can he?" Redling asked plaintively to the Merchant Council functionary.

"You really can't, Inspector Teal," Tredlib said. "Once the fees have been paid—"

Teal grunted. He reached into a pocket and drew forth a piece of candy, slid it into this mouth, and began chewing doggedly. "I can and I will," he said, a strong odor of mint wafting from his lips as he spoke. "I've got two major crimes, and Captain Redling here just might be connected to both of them."

"Two?"

Teal nodded. "First, the birdman. Now, I've got four dead men on Black and Twelfth. Forensics is going over the scene now, but the scene has all the marks of some kind of holding pen. Given who the dead man are, they're probably connected to the other crime."

There were other casualties, the dead woman sentry and the two men, a few blocks distant, but Redling decided not to raise the issue. Instead, he said, "And you're associating me with these dreadful events?"

Teal looked at him somberly. "Your act doesn't fool me," he said. "I've seen your kind before."

Redling doubted that very much.

"You come here from offworld, and you think you're top of the list, just because we're hospitable," Teal continued. "But while you're doing business on Plimbo, you do it under Plimbo law, see?"

"I see," Redling said, pretending to be chastened. "What I don't see is how you link me to either of the events that my fellow subjects of Plimbonian jurisprudence have gotten themselves into."

Teal grunted. "Material witness on the Guy-troy case," he said. "And if you think I'm letting anyone in your party leave the planet before that one is solved, you can think again."

"But, Inspector," Tredlib said, "we can't let commerce be blocked—"

"By a petty thing like justice," Redling interrupted, concluding the sentence for him. "Your organization never has before, from what I've heard." The last was a general-purpose gibe, one that came easily after years of banter with officers less qualified than Teal would ever be.

Teal glared at him.

"And, besides, you said I was connected to both crimes," Redling said, doing his best to take charge of the conversation. "How?"

Teal shrugged. "Maybe it's just my gut," he said, "but—"

"I'd trust it then, if I were you," Redling interrupted again, speaking as earnestly as he could. "It's much too big to ignore."

Teal gave his glare a bit more practice, and then continued. "But there's more to you than what you say. I don't know what your story is, but you're more than just a tramp freighter captain. I can tell from the way you walk and the way you talk. I've seen and heard men like you before, and none of them worked for a living," Teal said. "At least, not how respectable folks define work."

Redling felt a degree of surprise. Teal's soft features hid unexpected depths.

"So now I've got a suspicious-seeming offworlder, who has too smart a mouth for someone being interrogated by the Major Crimes office," Teal continued. "I've got the head—the founder—of the Kaal Combine riding a tramp freighter he could buy with a minute's interest on his personal fortune. I've got four of Chilhoub's bully-boys dead under circumstances that have yet to be described to my satisfaction, and I've got a very dangerous man—"

"You say I'm dangerous," Redling said mildly. He was still a study in utter repose. "I prefer to think of myself as charming."

"A very dangerous man," Teal said doggedly, "whose passenger—patron?—has been abducted under circumstances that remain unclear, but the responsibility for which is claimed by representatives of General Chilhoub—"

"Sounds like a foodstuff. Domestic or imported?"

"Who, in turn, is responsible for many of the troubles we've seen in recent weeks, even before any meddling offworlders stuck their spoons in the pot."

"That's a remarkably convoluted sentence, Inspector, but it doesn't explain what you think is my role in this tawdry little production."

Redling still wore the weapons he had taken with him in the raid on Kiggle's hideaway, and he thought fleetingly of them now. He knew full well that they could connect him to the deaths of those four men, but he felt no pangs of worry. He rather doubted that their presence, or the presence of his weapons locker, would become an issue.

One way or another, the investigation would end before then.

"Three points define a plane," Teal said. "Still-missing dignitary, dead kidnappers, you. They fit together, somehow, and only one of them is where I can do anything with it—you. At the very least, you're a material witness, at worst—" He paused, then began to tick off the possibilities. "You could have something on Ku-Ril-La, or the Guy-troy could be fleeing some bit of nastiness, the news of which hasn't reached us here, yet."

Redling hadn't thought of that. The lag of communications over interstellar distances was such a constant factor in his life that he rarely focused on it.

Teal continued. "Chilhoub's boys could have gotten to you, or you could have sold your passenger. Either way, you could be in it together. We spent some time looking for you earlier, Redling, and we couldn't find you. Is there a reason for that? Were you meeting with someone?"

Redling didn't say anything, but only smiled.

"On the other, maybe Chilhoub's creatures took the Guy-troy, and you saw an opportunity, and took him back. The Kaal is a big player, with plenty of money to pay in ransom. Any thoughts on that, Redling?"

"Now, Inspector, I'm certain that Captain Redling has a perfectly reasonable explanation for why Ku-Ril-La had chosen his ship for his journeys," Tredlib said soothingly. "And as for the rest—"

"There is no 'rest,'" Redling said, enjoying himself again. Despite Teal's unexpected perspicacity, this was a role he had played many times before, and always found amusing. "I've half a mind to file a protest at the Registry Hall! Let's see how hospitable a reputation Plimbo has when this is all over!"

Tredlib looked remarkably upset.

"I'm a simple businessman," Redling continued, "trying to do a simple bit of business on a simple little world—"

Tredlib flushed angrily.

"Since arriving, I've nearly landed my vessel in a blast crater, I've had carrion birds try to make a feast of my navigator, and I've seen my star passenger vanish to parts unknown," Redling continued, feigning indignation. "Now, just because your own people can't vote with ballots instead of laser blasts, you're accusing *me* of—"

"No one's accusing you of anything!" Tredlib said, his small mind still obviously focused on Redling's threat to file a complaint.

"Speak for yourself, Tredlib," Teal said angrily.

"Four counts of murder!" Redling concluded. "Well, I won't stand for it!"

Then he stood, instantly towering over both of the seated men.

"There's really no need to become so excited," Tredlib said pleadingly, and rising, too. He looked desperately from Teal to Redling, and then back again. "I'm certain we can come to an accord on this."

"I'm not," Teal said.

Redling glanced at the still-seated, balding man, and felt some small fraction of his feigned anger become real, at least enough of it that he could feel genuinely irritated. The planetbound police inspector showed no signs of buying into Redling's act.

"Please be seated, Captain Redling," Teal said placidly. He was still chewing his candy, and a look of studied tranquility had flowed across his pudgy features. "You too, Tredlib. You aren't going anywhere. I have a dozen of my best men ringing this place."

Tredlib sat.

After a moment, Redling sat, too, less because he attached any particular importance to Teal's veiled threat—he didn't—but because he felt silly as the only man standing.

"I'd like permission to search your person and your quarters," Teal said.

"I'd like a lot more money than I have," Redling responded. "That doesn't mean I'm likely to get it, though."

Teal nodded. "About the response I expected," he said. He pressed a switch on his com unit and raised it. "I can have a warrant here in about thirty-five seconds," he continued, "with hard copy in as many minutes. You've got that much time to think it over." He pressed a key on the communicator.

"I don't need that much time," Redling said smoothly. "I've made my decision."

He didn't waste any mental energy wondering how he would get past Teal and his underlings. If that course of action proved necessary, it would offer no real challenge. Instead, he considered the best, fastest ways to reach the starport, and how he would secure the *Gateway* for launch. There would be lies to tell and bribes to pay, and there was the two-part issue of alerting his crew or finding a new one. Passengers weren't a major concern. He felt mild qualms only about leaving Ku-Ril-La stranded, but the Guy-troy could fend for himself and had no grounds for complaint, given all that Redling had done for him.

"Teal here," the pudgy man said briskly into his communicator. "I want—eh?"

Teal's words trailed off into annoyed silence as the com chattered at him, then he stood and took a few steps away from the other men.

"But," he said softly, and "you mean," and "no," and "who?" and then some muttered syllables that sounded less like words than like curses.

Teal glared at Redling as he clicked the communicator key and broke the connection. "You've got friends, Redling," he said, genuine tension and anger evident in his voice. He had the sound of a man who had been trumped in a game he was accustomed to winning.

"The Municipality of Plimbo City offers you its apologies for the inconvenience of this interview." Teal said the words in a bitter, sardonic tone that made it obvious that they conveyed a sentiment somewhat different from his own.

"Why, that's excellent! Excellent!" Tredlib said eagerly.

"Further, the Imperial Governor personally wishes you good speed on your journey, a wish that I most devoutly second." This time, the words were sincere, in a grudging fashion; Teal obviously wanted Redling off-planet, and soon.

"There's got to be more to it than that," Redling said easily. "What's the news?"

"Your passenger, Ku-Ril-La, turned up at the Kaal offices, having been released by his captors—released 'without explanation,' I'm told. Turns out he wasn't very happy to learn that members of his party had been detained during his time of duress."

The others had probably enjoyed similar interviews, Redling realized, or were doing so now.

"He probably wasn't too happy that your boys had let him get snatched in the first place."

Teal scowled. "My resources are limited," he said angrily. "Rich offworlders can afford their own babysitters."

"Surely there's more to the situation than that," Redling continued. He smiled, carefully not quite making it smirk. "Loose ends, and all that?"

"There are loose ends aplenty, but they're going to stay loose," Teal said. "Like I said before, you've got friends."

That was the second time he had used the plural,

Redling realized. He had to wonder if it were deliberate, and if someone other than Ku-Ril-La had closed some switches.

"Well, then, if you gentlemen are done with me—"

Teal shook his head. "Not just us," he said. "All of Plimbo. The sooner you're offplanet, the happier I'll be. The Chilhoub situation is giving me enough trouble without foreign *dignitaries*—" he stressed the word "—muddying the waters."

"We're scheduled to lift tomorrow evening."

Teal shook his head again. "You're scheduled to lift in seven hours," he said. "As of three minutes ago."

"First you say we can't go, then you say we must," Redling observed. "Not the best way to do business."

"Don't care. You've done your business by now, or at least all the business you're going to do. For the next seven hours, you'll enjoy the hospitality of the Plimbo Starport," Teal said. "Isn't that right, Tredlib?"

He made the question a command.

Looking up from his own communicator, the bespectacled starport functionary nodded, making the loose flesh of his neck and face quiver. "Apparently." He looked at Redling. "Captain, we have a very pleasant lounge area, reserved for visiting dignitaries. I would be honored if you would make it home for the next quarter day."

"The very nicest of prisons, eh?" Redling asked.

"It's not—"

"Call it what you want, Redling, it's where you're going, until you leave for good. You're tied up in this somehow, and I don't want you in my jurisdiction anymore—or again," Teal said. His thin lips were set in a resolute grimace and his right hand—probably his gun hand—had found its way into the side pocket of the long jacket that he wore.

That pocket had a large bulge in it, Redling noted, larger than Teal's hand could make alone.

"Tsk. I had heard that Plimbo was a hospitable place."

"We are, we are," Tredlib said eagerly. "You can tell your friends—"

"To stay off my world and out of my city, if they're anything like you," Teal interjected. "At best, you've brought trouble; at worst, you've made it."

Redling glanced at him. Unless Teal's exterior hid truly astonishing depths, he was certain that he could take the inspector in less than three seconds, no matter what weapon the other man had. Even so, that would simply make it necessary to take down Tredlib, too, and the twelve of Teal's "best men" waiting outside. None were likely to pose much of a challenge, but he didn't see any point in expending the effort, just so that he could spend another day on a world he didn't particularly like.

Redling didn't like being told what to do, but he didn't like wasting effort, either.

He nodded. "What about my crew and passengers?"

"We're rounding them up now. They'll meet you at the port, all except Ku-Ril-La." Teal made a sour face. "Seems the Guy-troy doesn't quite trust our local security element. He'll join you an hour before launch time."

"We'll need to ready the *Gateway* for launch."

"No," Teal said doggedly. "You'll 'need' to do nothing but watch three-dees, listen to music, read disks, and eat, or all or none of the above. Tredlib's people will see to your craft."

"Our honor, really, Captain. You'll get top-cut service."

"And at top-cut prices, too, I assume."

"No, no, no," Tredlib said, indignant. "All fees and charges come courtesy of the Plimbo City and the Imperial Governor."

"That means my budget, Redling," Teal said, smiling without humor. "Now gather your stuff and let's go."

"Certainly, but if you'll give me a moment to settle with the front desk and make some calls."

Teal shook his head, but Redling decided to let him keep it.

"So we get to have dinner, after all," Dawn F'Ral said.

"Only if you want to eat," Redling said sourly. He wasn't in the mood for the engineer's feint-and-parry approach to conversation, an approach that he enjoyed when it was his, but found remarkably annoying when he was on the receiving end. "I'm not sure I do."

There were in the starport's dignitary lounge, a cavernous hall that could have served a dozen times their number. A large three-dee projector occupied one corner of the space, and an elaborate auto-kitchen opened onto the area opposite it. Comfortable chairs and couches were scattered in between, along with gaming boards and reading stations. Redling was pacing through the spaces between the various furnishings, driven by an unaccustomed edginess, and Dawn sprawled comfortably on one of the overstuffed couches.

As holding cells went, it was a remarkably opulent

one, Redling had to grant, and his companion was making more use of its splendors than he was.

"Eating wasn't the part of dinner that concerned me," Dawn continued. She smiled, projecting once more the ersatz sweetness that Redling found so annoying.

He supposed that was why she used it.

"I was thinking more about conversation," Dawn said. "We were going to talk, remember?"

Redling shrugged. "You're going to have to wait for that little palaver," he said. "I wouldn't say anything here that I wouldn't want Teal to overhear, and that's just about everything I can imagine." The facility was shielded against civilian com traffic, but he was certain that any police surveillance tools functioned quite well.

"He is good, isn't he?" The note of respect in Dawn's voice sounded genuine.

"That might not be the word I would use," Redling responded. "He's certainly perceptive, though."

"More than that, I think. He's a good man doing a hard job. Ever consider how hard law enforcement must be on a world with open borders? Especially with Tredlib, or someone like him, tripping your every step."

"You two had a chance to chat, I gather?"

Dawn nodded. "He showed up a bit after you disappeared. I've been here ever since."

Redling rather doubted that. Still fresh in his memory was the tiny dart he had found in the dead sentry's throat, the dart that would have fit comfortably in the pneumo-gun he had found in Dawn's effects.

"Did he have Tredlib in tow?" he asked.

"No, he was working alone, then. I guess I didn't rank Tredlib's presence," Dawn said. "But where did you get to, anyway? You missed Helicron's little tantrum."

Redling sat opposite her and thought for a long moment before answering the question. "I'd made some contacts during the day," he said carefully. "I wanted to see if I could find out more about what had happened to Ku-Ril-La."

"And did you?"

"Not really," Redling said. "And what's this about a tantrum?"

Dawn laughed, an easy sound of amusement that seemed quite sincere. "His guide never showed," she said. "He had shined his boots and cashed his notes, and Rolth stood him up." She laughed again. "He was quite crestfallen."

That last wasn't unexpected, but good news nonetheless; the kid had needed some deflating. Aloud, he said, "Too bad, I suppose. I wonder what happened to Rolth."

"And I wonder who those 'contacts' of yours were," Dawn said merrily, merry enough that Redling wondered yet again how much more she knew than she said.

"Did you calm him down?" he asked.

"Tried too. He stormed off, looking for fun on his own."

That wasn't good.

"You let him do that?" Redling said, with genuine irritation. He glanced at his com unit's time readout. "We're supposed to leave in less than five hours, thanks to our gracious hosts, and we're short half the crew."

Dawn grinned. "Don't look at me," she said. "I'm sure that Teal's boys will round them up fast enough." She gestured at her own com unit, then pressed a tab on its gleaming surface. The directory chip popped free and she showed it to him. "Remember these?" she asked.

Redling nodded. "I've had—and disposed of—at least seventy since touchdown."

"I did some research on them. Most are junk," Dawn said, "not worth the slot space they occupy."

"But," Redling prompted.

"But," Dawn agreed. "A certain number are 'live.' Depending on how they're configured, and on the com's capabilities, they access the unit's ID code and transmit a 'here I am' signal. Anyone who knows how to listen for it, can. Some of them can monitor calls, I think, but no one has confirmed that for me." Her smile widened. "The locals love offworlders, Redling. They love us so much that they watch our every move, when they can get away with it."

"Who's listening? Starport Authority or the police?"

"As far as I can tell, anyone and everyone. The chips that Rolth gave us had the homing element, and if a small-time operator like her can afford them, a lot other folks must, too."

Redling nodded. It made sense, though he hadn't considered the possibility. The tracking capability also went a long way toward explaining why Plimbo's passport procedures were so casual. Aliens—legal or illegal—were all registered automatically.

They just didn't know it.

"That raises an interesting question, though," Dawn continued. "During my interview with Teal, he was very curious as to your whereabouts, maybe because you're the *Gateway*'s captain."

"Or maybe because of something you said."

"Maybe," Dawn agreed. "It seems to me, if he was that curious, your chip wasn't doing its job."

Redling thought about that for a moment. The most likely explanation was that his own, custom-built communicator had an internal architecture that was incompatible with the chips' needs and capabilities. On the other hand—

"Maybe it was," he said slowly. He opened his own com and removed its directory chip. It was the one that Tredlib had given him. He squeezed it, hard. It broke between his strong fingers with a satisfying *snap!* He knew that the action was pointless now, too little and too late, but he found it satisfying, nonetheless.

Dawn looked at him, her curiosity obvious.

"A lot of people know more than they're telling," Redling said sourly. "It seems to be a popular pastime."

"You play that game, too."

"But it's not as much fun when everyone else plays, too," Redling responded. "Teal might not be as perceptive as I thought. He might just have been better informed."

A corner of Redling's mind concerned itself with the possibilities. How much could the chips tell about their bearers? How much could an analyst deduce from the sounds that the com received, and what would a man like Teal do with the resulting knowledge?

How much of Teal's act had been an act?

What, precisely, had been the content of that first call he had taken, back in Redling's room?

Would Teal allow an outsider to resolve a major crime, feign rage about the situation, and then seek to punish him for it? It occurred to Redling that he had almost certainly solved more than one problem for the candy-chewing inspector. He had rescued a captive, and eliminated several members of a particularly troublesome political faction, and he had done it without involving anyone else. If Teal were of a sufficiently duplicitous nature, he could actually allow an offworlder to perform those services for him, and then feign ignorance when the job was done. After the fact, the inspector would doubtless want to contain the troublesome newcomer—Redling—or dispose of him.

Or banish him.

Fall guys were always handy.

It didn't matter, Redling realized. No matter what Teal knew or didn't know, the end result was the same—a hurried "goodbye" to Plimbo, and an earlier-than-expected arrival in their next port of call.

Suddenly, Redling wished desperately that this entire trip were behind him. The unknown dangers of the Red Nebula were becoming more and more inviting.

"What do you mean by that?" Dawn asked. She tapped her fingers on the couch arm, making a rattling click not unlike Ku-Ril-La's laugher equivalent. "Informed instead of perceptive?"

"Nothing," Redling said. "Never mind."

Dawn's only response was to shrug eloquently.

An awkward moment of silence passed, then another, then—

"Nice nails," Redling said, having noticed something that had previously escaped his attention.

"Hmmm?" Dawn glanced at her fingers, at the rainbow-hued crescents that tipped them. Their curved points glistened with an eerie, rippling radiance that shifted and flowed like something liquid. "These?" she said. "I wanted to look nice for our little get-together."

"No," Redling said. "Not the cosmetic effect; the offensive capability." He pointed at the polished wood of the couch's arm, where a few casual strikes from Dawn's fingers had gouged a deep scar. "I hope that aspect wasn't meant for me, too," he said.

"Maybe it was, maybe it wasn't. A girl's got to be careful," Dawn said. She presented the back of her hand to him so that he could see all five nails clearly. "So you like them?" she asked. "It's a biochemical treatment of the nail beds, not cheap. The horn in the nails binds with iron, magnesium, and other metals in the body. The only drawback is that you need a diamond file to shape and form them. The things never break, though, and they're permanent—which is more than you can say about those plastic-alloy jobs you're wearing."

"Good point," Redling said, concealing his surprise. One of the key charms of his little finger-blades was that they were essentially invisible to the human eye. "Mine are less painful when someone decides to remove them, though," he continued. "To take yours off, they'd have to take the fingers, too. That's why I don't like surgical implants in general."

"No one gets the opportunity to try," Dawn said primly.

"No one?"

She shook her head.

"There's an exception to every rule," Redling said calmly.

"Is that a threat? I don't receive threats well."

"It was just an observation," Redling said. He was sincere, too. Despite her proven capacity to annoy and confound, there was something about Dawn he liked.

Maybe it was nothing more complex than the fact that she seemed to know what she was doing, even if he didn't.

He was going to have to rectify that situation, and soon.

The lounge's door slid open, admitting familiar voices, and then the men who spoke them.

"Hey? Are we under arrest?" Helicron Daas sounded querulous and annoyed as he stumbled into the lounge area. "Because if we are, I want to know why, and I want to see my—"

"Hello, Captain," Pikk Thyller's rumbling voice interrupted.

The *Gateway*'s navigator and gunner entered the lounge area in rapid sequence.

"Captain!" Helicron said happily. "You're here!"

Redling nodded. "And so are you," he said patiently.

Helicron looked around, puzzled, and then grinned. "Why, yes, yes I am!" he said, pronouncing the words with exaggerated precision.

He was obviously drunk again.

Dawn looked at Thyller. "I suppose it's too much to hope that you kept an eye on him," she said.

The big man shook his head, then settled into the largest empty chair. "Told you. Had my own plans."

"Nope! You all think I'm just a lap weasel, but I slipped the leash, I did!" Helicron announced proudly. He looked around for an empty place to sit, of which there were many. Apparently confounded by the broad range of choices, he stumbled tipsily from one piece of furniture to another, before finding one to his liking— specifically, the couch where Dawn already sat. Grinning drunkenly, he plopped himself down.

Dawn got up and changed her seat without comment.

Helicron looked disappointed, but his grin did not fade as he turned to face Redling instead. "Good news, Cap'n," he said. "You were wrong!"

"It wouldn't be the first time," Redling responded, "especially lately."

Helicron nodded. "Oh, tha's okay," he slurred. "'S good news, not bad." He opened his wallet and pulled out a thick sheaf of credit notes, all high denominations and all drawn on major banking syndicates.

Redling blinked. It was a fair bit of change, at least by the standards of his borrowed identity.

Helicron beamed. "Not finished yet," he said, and began emptying his pockets and storage pouches of more money. By the time he was done, the low table before him was heaped high with bills.

"Very nice," Redling said, speaking sincerely again. "Did you rob a bank?"

Helicron shook his head. "No, no, no," he said. "Just changed my luck." He winked. "Tried some of your Choskey gambits." He leaned close. "Didn't need Rolth. Found a game on my own! An' no one else knew floogle about the game!" He laughed uproariously, then settled back in the couch.

"You won that much money? In only one evening?" That was Dawn, her disbelief evident.

Helicron nodded, closing his eyes. "Gonna like this planet," the younger man said drowsily.

"Too bad we're leaving in a few hours," Redling said. It was obvious what had really happened. Helicron had found himself a fixed game, then allowed himself to be fattened for the kill—only to be rescued, however inadvertently, by Teal's people.

Redling supposed that there were some very angry Choskey players in Plimbo City right now.

Helicron's eyes snapped open. "Leaving!?" he said. "We can't leave!"

"Well, we sure can't stay," Redling said, and then ignored the kid's spluttering protests.

He had other things to think about.

CHAPTER TEN

The *Gateway* was well on its way to Carstairs World and some six hours into its first Jump. Helicron Daas, fully recovered from his adventures in the various gaming dens of Plimbo City, had taken first watch, and Pikk Thyller was presumably deep in slumber by now. Redling and Dawn had completed their more pressing duties, and sat now in the ship's dining area, the same space where Redling had taught Helicron a thing or two about professional gambling.

Now, Redling had decided, was the time for him to learn the truth about Dawn F'Ral.

He was more than a little exasperated with the chain of events that had led him here. Each step along the way had seemed simple and obvious enough, yet none had taken him where he wanted to go. Instead, each had been a misstep or a stumble. The operation had begun as a simple enough exercise in subterfuge and deception, with the perfectly pragmatic goal of appropriating some pre-human artifacts from individuals who were obviously unqualified to appreciate them. Insatead, what should have been an easy trip to the Red Nebula had become something more tangled than a decades-old floogle vine.

Again and again along the way, Redling had found himself able to see only part of a picture, or none of it. Three times now, he had stumbled into events that were already in progress, and then been forced to move on. Mystery after mystery had presented itself to him, then passed from his life before he could resolve them, even to the minimal extent that he would have found satisfying.

That had to end.

Redling knew that he couldn't do much now about Chim Blork and Sascha, or about General Chilhoub (late of the Imperial Marines), but he could certainly do something about Dawn F'Ral.

She sat opposite Redling now, at the same uncovered table. She looked utterly relaxed, even tranquil, with her hands neatly folded on the table's top. Not for the first time, Redling was struck by the sense of understated self-confidence that seemed to radiate from the trim, attractive woman. The only time he had seen her genuinely disconcerted was during that chance encounter in the tavern on Draen, when he had interrupted whatever game she had been playing with the Guy-troy.

"So we're finally going to have our meal together," the seated woman said, smiling slightly. "Not quite as public as I would have wanted, but I suppose there's nothing to be done for that."

Redling didn't have anything to say to that.

"I thought you had forgotten about me, back on Plimbo," Dawn continued. "I waited hours for you, across from the Registry Hall."

"I doubt that," Redling said sourly. He thought again about the dead woman he had found at the warehouse district's borders, slain by a poison dart from a pneumo-gun, fired by an expert hand.

He rather suspected that the hand in question was one of the pair Dawn F'Ral had neatly folded in front of her now.

"You don't strike me as someone who lets herself remain idle for long," he continued.

Dawn smiled again. "I'll take that as a compliment," she said.

"Don't. It's just an assessment."

"How else do I strike you, then?" Dawn said. Her eyes suddenly looked remarkably intense as her gaze met his.

She was really very attractive, Redling realized, and obviously knew how to use her looks as a tool. Under other circumstances, he might be willing to play the game.

Other circumstances did not hold, however.

"I'm not here for that," he said crisply. "I'm here to ask questions, and you're here to answer them."

"And if I don't?"

"I'm the *Gateway*'s captain, Dawn, or whatever your name really is. I'm *your* captain. That means I can ask any questions I please of the crew and passengers." Fleetingly, and not for the first time, Redling wished that he had been able to replace her, back on Plimbo.

The somewhat awkward circumstances of the *Gateway*'s exit had precluded such an action, of course. He rather doubted that Inspector Teal would have allowed him to hold employment interviews.

He suspected that Dawn would have tried to prevent him from doing so, too. For whatever reason, she seemed determined to remain attached to the *Gateway*.

"If you don't want to answer my queries, I can place you under arrest and confine you to quarters," he continued.

Silently, he wondered how much luck he would have keeping her there.

"That would leave you without an engineer."

"We'd manage, I think. There are such things as emergency procedures and distress beacons," Redling noted. "And I don't think it would be a very good idea to resist arrest." He let himself smile, despite the unfamiliar tension that was gathering in his spine and neck.

"Really, Captain," came the reply. "There's no need to be so combative. We're here to talk, remember? Not fight." She displayed her nails again, ten neat crescents that glistened with a metallic sheen. "These are the only weapons I'm wearing, and that's because, as you pointed out, they're too much trouble to remove."

"Too much trouble for you, perhaps," Redling said. "I imagine I could do the job easily enough, though."

Dawn laughed, a sound like silver bells tinkling, a sound of amusement that sounded utterly sincere. "Oh, you are a confident one," she said. "It's difficult for me to believe that a man like you would ever let himself become a spazzed-out crystal head." She paused. "And it's even harder to believe that someone, anyone could come back from years on Euphorinol and remake himself into the cool customer I see before me."

Redling smiled now. "The rehab colony was very good to me," he said lightly. "They offered some remarkable courses."

"None of them are that good," Dawn responded. "But that doesn't matter right now, does it?"

Redling shook his head. "No, it doesn't," he said. He looked at her grimly, all banter gone from his voice. "I want to know who you are, Dawn—who you really are, and what you want with Ku-Ril-La, and I want to know now."

"My name is Dawn F'Ral," she said, sounding somewhat prim.

"I doubt that very much," Redling said calmly. "Unless it's yours because you bought it."

Dawn suddenly looked impish.

"But that's not what I asked," Redling said. "I asked *who you are*."

"A loyal subject of the Imperium, like any other," Dawn said. "Like you are, I hope."

Redling said nothing, but satisfied himself by glancing pointedly at the seated woman's fingernails. Bioenhancement processes like the ones that produced them were expensive, and embodied technologies that were controlled on most worlds.

Dawn caught the glance.

"Well, a subject like some others, at any rate" she allowed, smiling again. She drummed her fingers briskly on the tabletop, kicking up a small could of plastic chips. "This is going to take some explanation, and some background," she said.

"We have time," Redling said. "We have hours until watch-change, and days until we're out of Jump Space."

Dawn nodded. "Tell me, then," she said, "have you ever put much thought much into the Imperium itself? As an institution, I mean."

"Not really," Redling said truthfully. With a conscious effort, he let some of the tension ooze out of him, and settled back in his chair. Something about the tone of Dawn's voice and the look in her eyes made him think that the games were over, at least for now.

"It's the largest single sociopolitical construct in history," she said. "Tens of thousands of worlds, bound together by custom and commerce—"

"—and by more than a little military power," Redling interrupted. "Remember the esteemed General Chilhoub."

"—and it gets bigger every year." Dawn continued speaking, as if Redling had not. "What makes it work?"

"More than a little military power," Redling repeated. He had seen numerous world governments brought to their knees by Imperium troops, and entire competing systems overwhelmed by heavily armed Marines.

Dawn shook her head. "No," she said. "The Imperium is just too big to be held together by force of arms, especially when you consider the problem of communications. In some ways, it's similar to the situation on pretechnological planets, places like Nephlim."

Redling flinched.

"Entire regimes can rise and fall in the time it takes a Core Worlds directive to reach the frontier," Dawn continued.

"That's why some of the frontier worlds don't regard themselves as part of the Imperium."

"They're wrong, though. As long any of the human races occupy them, they're part of the Imperium, or they will be. If necessary, the Imperial Marines will remind them of that little fact of life, sooner or later. We live in a human cosmos, Redling, and the Imperium is the expression of that human dominance."

"Tell that to the Hivers, or the K'Kree, or the Denaar, or the Graytch," Redling said, rattling off the names of several of humanity's competitors for the stars. He had heard Dawn's line of argument too many times before—and faced too many members of the nonhuman races in armed combat to dismiss their species entirely. Life had taught him most of its messages on a personal, pragmatic scale, and he did not care much for rhetoric about species and destiny, or heritage and fate.

He had shaped most of his life with the sweat of his own brow, and saw little reason to share the credit with ephemeral principle.

"No," Dawn said emphatically. "Where we don't compete, we tolerate. Where we do compete, we dominate. The K'Kree and the Aslan and all the rest live at our sufferance. When we need their worlds, we will take them, just like we took the Droyne's."

Redling laughed. He knew a bit about the Droyne, if only because certain of their surviving artifacts were of such value. The Droyne had been humanity's predecessor in the galaxy, a nonhuman race that had mastered scientific disciplines that still remained mysteries to their heirs. Humans owned an enormous debt to their long-ago antecedents, even if the Droyne were no longer around to collect.

It was the Droyne who had collected hominid specimens from a prehistoric Terra, for whatever reason, and then proceeded to seed the stars with them. Thousands of generations later, genetic drift and the demands of new environs had worked changes on the descendants of those hominids, creating new breeds and strains, all of them nonetheless related. The Vilani, Zhodani, and other human races descended from those long-ago specimens, and the Solomani claimed their heritage somewhat more directly from old Terra, but all were of the same genus and could interbreed.

"As I understand it," he said, "we didn't so much

take the Droyne worlds as inherit them." He thought of certain items, awaiting his attentions within the boundaries of the Red Nebula. "We're taking them still, as a matter of fact," he continued. "The fact that the Droyne wiped themselves out and cleared the way for us made the job easier, of course."

For reasons that were likely to remain a mystery, the Droyne had declared war on themselves, and pursued the conflict with the same thoroughness and ingenuity that had enabled them to occupy much of the galaxy. The end result had been thousands of worlds, filled only with dead cities and other traces of the Droyne's passage.

In his rare, very rare melancholy moments, Redling wondered what traces his own kind would leave, once humanity's day was done.

Chief among the Droyne's *memento mori* had been Redling's ancestors, and Dawn's, along with those of the Vilani and the Zhodani and so many others. In short, the antecedents of most of the Imperium's current human citizenry had been left to fend for themselves among the ruins of the Droyne worlds. The major exception were the Solomani, whose forebears had made their own way from the home world millennia later, only to find distant cousins already waiting for them.

What had caused the end of the Droyne? What slight, or advance, or simple madness had led a galaxy-spanning race down the road to its own ruin? Scholars could debate it endlessly, but no one would ever know, Redling supposed.

Dawn F'Ral seemed less uncertain in that, as she did in many things. "The Droyne were doomed from the moment they landed on Old Terra," she said, as if answering his unspoken question.

She had a dogmatic tone to her voice now, and a fervor that Redling typically associated with religious fanatics and other zealots.

"The hardier species will always expand and occupy any available ecological niche to which they are suited, and the Droyne made theirs available to us," she continued, and grinned blackly. "Think about it. How could a race wipe itself out completely? All they really managed to do was weaken themselves enough that they could fall to their own pets, to the proto-men and proto-women who gave rise to our people."

"That's one way of looking at it, I suppose," Redling said. "I'm not a student of history, but I suspect that it's an unorthodox interpretation."

"But an accurate one. Humanity will expand to fill the entire galaxy, and the Imperium is the instrument of that expansion."

"I'm not as confident of that as you are. This is the *Third* Imperium, after all."

"The Ziru Sirka and the so-called Rule of Man—the First and Second Imperium—were false starts. Part of my job is making sure that this one isn't."

"So we're finally getting around to you, and who you are."

"Getting closer, at least," Dawn said. "Tell me, Redling, how do you think the Imperium rules?"

"I thought we had already settled that one."

"Good point," she said, and paused. "Put it a different way, then. How do the Core Worlds *administer* their rule? How do they govern individual planets or systems, and coordinate military initiatives, when years can pass between issuing a directive and acting upon it?"

Redling considered the question for a moment. She had a point, he realized, a point underscored by his own experience. His journeys from one world to another had been characterized by startlingly different approaches to implementing the broad outlines of Imperium policy. Some of those variations were the result of differing levels of technological achievement. Others, however, seemed to stem from less specific causes—if nothing else, from the obstinate desire of the average individual to do things "his (or her) way." The Imperium was a huge construct, to use Dawn's term, and it was composed almost entirely of elements that diverged from one another, to a greater or lesser extent.

Much of Redling's career had consisted of exploiting differences between those elements, but he had given little thought to the forces uniting them.

What held the together? It certainly wasn't the common good; Redling didn't believe in the abilities of nonexistent forces to accomplish much. Nor could it be simple commonality; as Dawn herself had pointed out, the Imperium, though dominated by humanity, was comprised of many different races with many different needs and priorities.

Redling viewed himself as a pragmatic man, if not a practical one. He believed in competition and conflict, and in the immediacy of life. The common good and simple commonality were nice to talk about, but if they weren't enough to unite a single planet of Plimbo's size, they certainly weren't enough to unite systems-spanning empire many thousands of times larger.

"How does the Imperium rule?" Dawn repeated.

"Loosely," Redling said slowly. He was unaccustomed to thinking much about such issues, but now that they had been pointed out to him, certain factors sprung into stark relief. "Local governments wield a great deal of power, and have considerable discretion, as long as they operate within broad parameters."

Dawn nodded. "The idea being that all policy is, ultimately, local policy. Each world gets to make their own mistakes, and find its own way," she said. "That's the strength of the system—but it's a rule of life that strengths and weaknesses tend to be bound up rather closely with one another. The same broad parameters that allow for success and freedom can also produce tyranny and repression." She paused. "Enough about the governors, at least for the moment. What about the military?"

Redling knew a bit about the Imperial Marines. "They answer to the Ruling Council, too, but the communications lag requires that they have some day-to-day autonomy, too. They're leashed, but it's a long leash and a loose one."

"What about Chilhoub?" Dawn asked, smiling yet again, but her eyes were humorless as they gazed at him. "It took him quite a while to come to heel. Chilhoub's an example of what goes wrong with that approach, isn't he?"

That was true; the Imperial military weren't supposed to insert themselves into member planet politics, for example, and Chilhoub, apparently, had chosen to do precisely that. Their charter dealt with suppressing rebellions, and countering extra-Imperium aggression, and policing the space lanes.

Redling shrugged, irritated. "I thought we were talking about you. We're getting pretty far off the subject, aren't we?" he said, annoyed.

"On the contrary; we're only now getting close to it," Dawn said. "Now, tell me: how does the Imperium administer its rule? Or enforce the alliance, if you prefer. How does it exercise specific control where specific control is needed, without discouraging the independence and initiative that make the Imperium work?"

Redling didn't say anything, but he abruptly had a bad feeling about the new direction that the conversation had taken. He was accustomed to dealing with planetary authorities and Imperial Marines alike, and more than accustomed to dealing with but if Dawn were saying what he thought she was saying—

Dawn slid her right hand into her tunic's pocket.

"Slowly," Redling said, tensing.

"Slowly, then," Dawn agreed, nodding. "But I told you I wasn't carrying any weapons, remember?"

Redling made no response as he watched her draw a familiar item from her pocket. It was a Universal ID, the standard identification device that all law-abiding Imperium citizens carried.

All who abided by the law, and more than a few who did not.

"It's just my Imperial," she said. She turned the device so that its familiar front panel faced him. "See?"

Redling nodded. In base mode, the identification device displayed an image of his navigation officer, along with sample fingerprints, DNA encoding data, and other identifying information.

Dawn reversed the ID and did something to it. When she reversed it again and presented it to Redling, something about it had changed.

The name beneath the image, spelled out in neat Imperial characters, was "Kob Thrommus."

Redling made a sound of disgust and plucked the ID from her unresisting fingers. Much as he had done with Ku-Ril-La's Universal, what seemed like a lifetime ago, he pressed the appropriate key and paged through the various certifications and seals that were stored in the memory cells of Dawn's, of *Kob's* Universal.

They passed before his eyes in rapid succession. Redling had seen most of them before, when originally interviewing Dawn for the role of engineering officer. Now, however, he noticed with some surprise that each bore the name she had now given as her own. It was Kob Thrommus who claimed full membership in the Guild, and Kob Thrommus whose passport fields were marked with visa-seals of a dozen planets, and Kob Thommmus whose file was flagged for personal weapons use. The substitution was perfect and consistent, and would doubtless pass muster in any court or jurisdiction within the Imperium's borders.

In short, Dawn's ID subverted the very notion and core function of a Universal. The forged IDs he stored in his own weapons kit were good, but this was better by far. Anyone who carried an ID like this one could hide, secure and safe, behind a variety of identities.

Redling wondered where he could get one for himself.

Aloud, he said, "Very nice. Can you change the picture, too?"

Dawn nodded, smiled. "Completely user-programmable," she said cheerfully, "but I'm not about to show you how. Keep going. You haven't seen what I want you to see yet."

Redling pushed the key again, and watched as a final image presented itself—a nearly abstract emblem, etched in dark blue against a white field. He had never seen the symbol before, but he knew with sudden certainty what it represented.

"Cobalt Division," he said softly.

This time, it was Dawn who was surprised. "You are well connected," she said, obviously surprised.

"I've heard the name," he said softly.

"Mind telling me where?"

"Yes," Redling said. "Yes, I would."

But he couldn't help thinking about the answer to her question.

How long ago had it been? Twenty years? Twenty-three? How long had it been since a very young man had awakened from Low passage, and found himself the lone survivor of the fourteen who had taken that desperate passage? Redling, moving through a dozen lives and a dozen local calendar systems, had long since lost track of the specific years and dates. They didn't much matter, anyway.

What did matter, he remembered well, with an immediacy and detail that even he found surprising.

Planetfall had been on Laumer, he recalled, a dirtball world with an agricultural colony with little opportunity to offer a youth with his then-nonexistent skills.

Laumer's moon had been another story, however.

That arid sphere had been the base of a pirate band, working the local spacelanes, fleecing the ships that carried money and goods between neighboring systems. Redling—or, rather, the boy who would one day call himself Navis Redling—had joined the buccaneers in fairly short order, quite pleased to find work that suited his bent and offered great promise for success.

Oleck, the fat old Vilani pirate who had founded the band, had taken Redling under his wing and schooled him in the basics of interstellar piracy. Redling, in turn, had worked hard to learn his lessons well—and schemed to make the band his own.

He suspected now that Oleck had known of his ultimate goals. Certainly, were there positions reversed, Redling would have.

Business was good; Laumer was close enough to the Imperium's frontier to benefit from the waves of expansion that swept through its sector. As neighboring, legitimate economies grew, so, too, did the less lawful one hosted by Laumer's moon. The host planet's government had taken a percentage of the booty, and Oleck had paid liberal bribes to the local Imperial Marines garrison to look the other way as he went about his business. Everyone profited, though Redling's gains had been measured more in knowledge than in credits.

That all came to an end during his second year with the Oleck's organization.

On one well-remembered Senday, Oleck had dispatched Redling on what should have been a simple enough raid—Redling's first operation as squad leader. A tipster had provided a copy of the craft's manifest, and the thick document's pages had fairly bulged with the promise of data and money. It had been a simple enough bit of tactics for Redling's craft to intercept the ship, fire on it, storm it—

And charge into the waiting arms—firearms and otherwise—of the Imperial Marines.

It had been a massacre, with Oleck's men finding the fate they had intended for the passengers and crew of the liner. The battle had been swift and merciless and ruthlessly efficient, far more effective than any other Marine handiwork Redling had encountered, before or since.

Of the men and women in Redling's squad, only Redling himself survived. Escaping the trap, he had made way back to Laumer's moon, seeking refuge, or, just possibly, revenge. Instead of either, he had found that things were much worse than he had dreamed.

Not only was he the only survivor at liberty of his own squad, he has the only survivor at liberty of Oleck's entire organization.

Another contingent of Space Marines, dispatched from a system beyond wily old Oleck's financial reach, had stormed the pirate stronghold and destroyed it. No one remained alive or at liberty to greet Redling upon his return.

Of the only home that Redling had known for more than a year, nothing remained but ash and mist.

In the long years since then, a chastened but still ambitious Navis Redling revisited those events more than once, both in his memories and in his research. Laumer's governor had been apprehended on that same dreadful day, he knew now, and the Marines general on Oleck's payroll had found himself court-martialed, cashiered, and sentenced to a penal asteroid. It had been easy enough for Redling to learn what had happened, but not why.

Why had such a sweet operation, well-designed and successful, gone so suddenly, so terribly wrong?

It was a question without an answer. The only clue

he had been able to find, then or in all the ensuing years, had been a whispered rumor, a name, two words that defied analysis.

The words had been spoken to him by a renegade data technician, a man who had made his living by stealing information from databases that were supposedly secure. He had "volunteered" the paired words only after some rather vigorous interrogation on Redling's part, but that was the price that to pay for linking one's fortunes to those of Redling's competitors. Those two words were the last the man had spoken, at least in this life, and had remained filed away in Redling's memory for many years, until uttered now, by his own lips.

Cobalt Division.

"So you're Cobalt Division, eh?" he asked. He kept his voice deliberately casual as he tossed tossing the customized Universal back to Dawn, who caught it in mid-trajectory and returned it to her pocket. "Is that supposed to surprise me? he asked.

"Yes," she said, sounding faintly puzzled. She looked at him speculatively, as if half-awaiting something.

It took Redling a moment to realize what. When he did, it was almost enough to make him laugh out loud.

More than once, he had thought Dawn might be a competitor in his clandestine business—a data pirate, or a syndicate member, or a freelance operator.

Apparently, she had entertained somewhat similar suspicions.

"Is this where I'm supposed to present my own Universal?" he asked, still wanting to chuckle. "Or a secret handshake, or a password or countersign?"

Some of the anticipation left Dawn's features, to be replaced by a different kind of tension. "Neither of those are very effective in this line of work," she said easily. "They're too hard to update on a timely basis. If you *were* Cobalt, you'd know that."

"I never said I was."

"True. And maybe the only truth I've ever gotten out of you."

"Strong words for someone with a programmable ID and a wardrobe of identities," Redling said.

Dawn nodded in acknowledgment. "Fair enough," she said. "It's just that you've displayed certain skills, certain disciplines..." Her words trailed off and she shrugged. "It wasn't very likely, I suppose, but it would have made things easier."

That was enough, finally, to make Redling laugh. It was an honest laugh, welcome and justified, that came up from deep inside him and burst from his lips before he could call it back. He laughed for longer than he had in memory, and let himself be carried away on the waves of mirth, if only for the moment. When the laughter subsided to a mild chuckle, he realized that Dawn—or Kob—was staring at him, a look of complete bewilderment on her features.

"Mind telling me what's so funny?" she asked.

"Easier," Redling said. "You said easier, and this entire trip has been anything but easy. In fact, considering the total effort expended, and the likelihood of return, I'd say this is the hardest endeavor I've ever undertaken."

"One of the hazards that comes with buying someone else's identity."

Redling made no response, verbal or otherwise.

"At least, that's what I think you've done," Dawn continued. "I can't be sure. It's too hard to research a situation like this."

"Is that so, *Kob*?" Redling said, stressing the name. "It must be terribly difficult, not knowing who you're talking to."

Dawn smiled at that one. "That's different," she said. "I'm a professional. And let's stick to the labels we know, shall we? I gave you my real name—my birth name—because I want you trust me, not because I want anyone else to know it."

"Trust you? Trust Cobalt Division? That's not a very attractive option."

"Keep it up," Dawn said, "and you'll convince me you really do know something about us."

Redling remained silent.

"Cobalt Division," Dawn said crisply, "is a top-level intelligence gathering and policy enforcement division. Our operatives enjoy considerable independence and answer directly to the Ruling Council."

"What's the meaning of the name?"

"Cobalt? It occurs in nature wherever silver is found. Silver is soft, but cobalt is hard," Dawn said. "Some people say that the Ruling Council is soft, but no one who knows about the Cobalt Division thinks we're anything but hard. We're the steel that gives strength to the Imperium's long leash. Our very existence is a closely guarded secret. We watch the watchmen, but we are unwatched in return."

"All that secrecy must make it hard to exercise whatever authority you have."

"Not really." She drew forth her ID again, and passed it to Redling once more.

Now, it identified her as one Ras Anderthall, Five-Star General in the Imperial Marines.

"Nice," Redling said. "How many other identities do you have hidden in here?"

"Enough," Dawn said, taking the ID again. "There are data files available to back up each of them, too. I can be whoever I need to be, just like you, apparently."

"So we're back to that?"

"Not really; I was just speaking out of professional curiosity. Under other circumstances, Redling, I would invest considerable time and effort in finding out just who you are. Right now, I don't have either to spare."

That was a bit of a relief, actually. Redling had become increasingly concerned with each new revelation. The minute amount he knew about Cobalt Division—and all of his experience with the operative seated before him—suggested that the mysterious organization was remarkably tenacious in its operations. Dawn's words had done little to dispel that impression, and much to augment it.

Redling really didn't want to think he had come to the attention of an agency—any agency—that reported directly to the Ruling Council.

He wondered if Oleck had taken part in a conversation like this, those long years before. The thought was almost enough to make him nervous.

"Instead," Dawn said, "I'm telling you more than I've told any other civilian, much more than my superiors would think it necessary for you to know."

"Which means I can expect a midnight visit from your coworkers some day?" Imperium secrets had a way of being kept, Redling knew.

Dawn shook her head. "Not if you keep a low profile," she said, "and I think you know how to do that. I've seen you at work, after all."

Again, she smiled.

"Why, then? Why are you telling me all this? You must want something."

"I want nothing from you—no effort, no interference, no getting in the way of my assignment. I want you out of my way and off my road. You're entirely too competent at some rather specialized disciplines, and I don't want you getting in our—in *my* way on Carstairs World."

"What happens there?"

"I take Ku-Ril-La into custody. Arresting someone of his rank will be difficult enough, without unwelcome interference from a misguided champion." She grinned. "I saw you in action, back on Plimbo, you know. Four men in as many minutes; very impressive."

"And how long did it take you to kill the people at the perimeter?"

"Approximately seven seconds longer than it took the sentry to hear me when I got too close. But then, I didn't have the advantage of a robot rat to scout the way for me," Dawn said. "At any rate, my associates are somewhat more capable than Kiggle and Chilhoub's other boys, but we don't like trouble."

Redling blinked at that. Dawn's words were a surprise, but not a total one; he had long since deduced her interest in the Guy-troy onboard, even if he had wondered about the nature of that interest.

Still, there was some wisdom in not letting Dawn know that her surprise was only partial.

"You're going to do what?" he asked, making himself sound surprised. "And why? He's a millionaire, and he's got a diplomatic immunity from most laws, planetary or otherwise!"

"That just makes it a bit more difficult, Redling, but certainly not impossible." She paused. "As I said, we enjoy great autonomy, ourselves."

"But why?"

"It's like I told you before, Redling, this is a human cosmos, and it's in the Imperium's interest to keep it that way. Flarge, it's in the interest of the K'Kree and the Aslan and Asym and all the rest, too. We keep the peace."

"From your viewpoint, at least."

Dawn shrugged. "The only one that matters," she said primly. "Not one that Ku-Ril-La shares, I suppose, but that's what makes gaming matches. He wants to change the situation a bit, and the Cobalt Division doesn't intend to let him do that."

"What's he done?" Redling asked slowly. It was difficult to reconcile Dawn's words with his personal knowledge of his most valued passenger. "What's he going to do?"

"I can't tell you much about that," Dawn said.

"Can't, or won't?"

"Both, actually. I know the nature of his aspirations, but not the specifics. He's putting something together," she continued. "Or did you really believe his line about the Grand Tour?"

Redling made no response.

"Think about it," Dawn said. "He's the head of the Kaal—the single largest privately held business concern inside the Imperium's borders, a combine that wields tremendous financial and political power. A sentient like that books passage on a tramp freighter? How likely does that sound?"

"What's your explanation, then?"

"He knew that someone on the *Spider* was riding his trail," Dawn said easily. "I don't think he knew it was me, because I wasn't me then. But he knew there was someone after him, someone who had gotten close." She paused, as if considering how much more to say. "He's putting something together, Redling, one piece at a time, and he's got a timetable. I wrecked that schedule when I made it necessary for him to leave the *Waltzing Spider*."

"'Made it necessary'?" Redling quoted. "That's not how he told the tale."

"There are two sides to every story," Dawn said. "After that, the *Gateway* was the best solution he could find. You just came along at the right moment, and you really aren't very hard to manipulate."

Redling wanted to say something, but didn't.

"I wouldn't put it past him to stir Blork's pot a bit, either," Dawn said, "just to make the situation more urgent."

"It seems to have worked well for you, too."

"Don't flatter yourself or this rustbucket. I'm here because the Controlled is here, and when he leaves, I'll leave too."

"That's the third time you've used that term. Explain it."

Until now, Dawn's voice had held at least a faint note of banter and playfulness, presumably some kind of interview technique that worked to her advantage. When she spoke this time, however, her tones held nothing but business.

"I can't tell you anything about that," she said. "Except to say that I used the term partly to see if you would recognize it."

"What does it mean?"

Dawn shook her head. "No," she said. "No more answers. All I want now is your cooperation."

"And what's to keep me from going directly to Ku-Ril-La now, and telling him what you've told me?"

"You won't."

"Answer the question."

"You won't," Dawn repeated.

Redling looked at her.

She looked back.

"You make it sound like a threat," he said calmly. "I don't respond well to threats." He grinned crookedly. "Maybe that's why I'm so easy to manipulate."

"I've made no threat, and I've played square with you. I've given you a great deal of information. Others in what I suspect is your trade would kill to know the things I've told you today, and I've answered all of your questions but one." She paused. "And I've made a statement of fact. Whatever Ku-Ril-La is up to, it ends on Carstairs World. That's the last stop on his so-called Grand Tour, and it's the first world on it with appropriate Cobalt Division facilities. I plan to complete my assignment before he finishes his, and you are not going to get in the way."

"It still sounds like a threat," Redling said.

"I prefer to think of it as a statement of fact."

CHAPTER ELEVEN

From Plimbo to Carstairs world was a three-Jump trip, thanks to the limitations of the *Gateway*'s engines and the distance that stretched between the two worlds' suns. Each of the Jumps was to take a week (ship's time) and cover approximately two parsecs of "normal" space. The *Gateway*'s engines required recalibration between Jumps, adjustments that took the better part of a day.

Ordinarily, such pauses did little to disrupt the tedium of shipboard life. Usually, all it meant was that an exterior video feed was available to the passengers, granting them a glimpse of stars and nebulae, rather than of the neutral nothingness of Jump Space. On occasion, in the more heavily populated sectors of space, the ship's communications matrix might pick up attenuated broadcasts from neighboring systems. Then, it could provide the passenger with outdated news and entertainment. Both starscapes and broadcasts tended to be boring.

Redling, at least on this trip, had come to savor the boring. The ship's monitor system had become his almost constant off-duty companion.

He was relaxing in his cabin between watch shifts when the call came. Some three light years to the port bow, on a semi-industrialized planet named Endymion, steamed seafood had apparently enjoyed some kind of vogue in the fairly recent past. Now, Redling's cabin monitor fed him images of a stocky man deboning a fish, the amplified echo of a years-past instructional broadcast. The stocky man had removed the fish's head and was scooping out its entrails when the call buzzer sounded. Redling thumbed the MUTE switch on his remote control and shifted the audio feed to an intercom frequency.

"Redling," he said, by way of greeting.

Dawn F'Ral's familiar—too familiar—voice flowed from hidden speaker and filled his cabin's spaces. "We've got a bit of a problem, Captain," she said.

"Precisely which 'we' are you talking about?"

Dawn laughed softly at that one; the two of them had spoken little since their tense confrontation some days before, certainly no more than was necessary for the successful operation of the *Gateway*. There had been no more conversation regarding their mutual identities, but the subject had never been far from Redling's mind.

He suspected that Dawn would have said the same, if put to the question.

Now, however, her amusement at his query did not fully hide a tone of concern in her voice. "'We' as in everyone on this ship," she said. "And it's not a big problem now, but it could become one. Could you join me on the bridge?"

Less than a minute later, Redling strode into the cramped confines of the ship's command center. Only Dawn was there to greet him, and the worried expression on her face matched the tone in her voice.

"I didn't call the others," she said. "I wanted to show you this, first." She gestured for him to take his station.

"What's the problem?" Redling asked, as he settled into the command chair.

As if in response, the main display at his station cleared itself, and then presented a new image. It was a complex array of interleaving sine curves, each annotated with narrow columns of numbers.

"That's a live display of the Jump engines' output signature," Dawn said.

"Not my favorite thing to look at," Redling replied. "It makes my eyes hurt."

What the screen showed was a two-dimensional representation of a four-dimensional wave form. He knew that it was as near as the computer could come to showing the effect that the Jump engines had on the neighboring space. Even in idle mode, the interstellar drive made ripples and eddies in the fabric of space itself. The effect was vaguely analogous to a radio transmitter's unmodulated carrier wave—always present, even when no information was being sent. Redling knew enough about warp mechanics to recognize the display, if not actually read it.

"What's the problem?" he asked.

Dawn did something more to her control station, and another display superimposed itself over the first one. "That's a computer model, based on the Helicron's and my input," she said. "It shows what we should be getting out of those engines; the first one shows what we are getting from them."

Redling examined the two elaborate, curving lattices. To his eye, the looked much the same, the second overlaying the first so precisely that it hid most of the live output from view. Even the columns of numbers were close matches; certainly, he could see no discrepancies in the first several columns.

Of course, Redling was no expert.

"You're going to have to provide a bit more detail," he said, "or a bit less. If I were a Jump expert, I wouldn't need an engineer."

In response, Dawn stepped closer to his workstation and pointed at a section of his screen. The tip of her steel-hard fingernail make a clicking sound as it touched the display's plastic surface, just to the left of its right hand edge.

"Here," she said. "The model and the live reading don't match, and they should." She pressed a button, and the section of the curves she indicated enlarged to fill the entire screen. "See? It's point-oh-oh-oh-three out of synch."

She was right. Now that the image had grown, he could see that the two curves drifted slightly apart from one another, and that several digits in the appended readings didn't quite match.

"Models are just that," he said slowly. "Models. How precise a match did you expect?"

Even as he asked, he knew the answer.

"Absolute," Dawn said crisply. "We're dealing with pure mathematics here. Any deviation from projections that the eye can detect is a significant one."

"Is there a problem with the engines? I thought you had them professionally recalibrated, back on Draen."

Dawn nodded. "Yes, I did. The engines are the only system on this bucket that work to perfection. Or should."

Redling gazed at the screen, thinking. He didn't much like things he couldn't understand, but he was well aware that almost no one had a full comprehension of the Jump drive's mysteries.

"Generally speaking," Dawn continued, "Jump engines either function properly, or they don't function at all. You can misuse them, of course, or feed them bad data—but the there's not much margin for operational error, practically speaking." She used her thumb and forefinger to indicate a space too small to measure. "Proper functioning and catastrophic failure are about this far apart. Jump physics is not a very forgiving discipline."

Redling knew that, and suddenly felt very cold. He had heard horror stories about failed Jump drives, and about drives activated without proper calibration. Explorers had found themselves cast deep into unknown regions of space, or had vanished, never to return. One whispered rumor, overheard by him in a beer-mill on Pepperdyne, told of one ship that had suffered sudden, disastrous Jump failure when its fusion pile failed. The drunken Marine claimed that the craft had re-entered normal space intact, and at its programmed destination.

But all of the people onboard had been turned inside-out.

"Can you fix it?" he asked softly.

He didn't like relying on things he couldn't understand.

Dawn shook her head. "No," she said, "and that worries me. I verified all of the readings and even reloaded the software, and every time I do, this, this discrepancy re-manifests itself."

"What now?" Redling asked. "Using conventional drive, we'd s still need at least five years to reach a starport. We could issue a distress call, but the chances of ship pausing between Jumps near enough to hear us—"

"Is nil," Dawn concluded. "Or nearly."

Redling thought for a long, silent moment, but couldn't' think of anything to say or do. Finally, he asked, "So what happens if we Jump?"

"Don't know," Dawn said simply. "I think—*think* —that we re-emerge in normal space, maybe six weeks out from Carstairs, under normal drive."

"But—the stories I've heard, everyone says—"

Dawn laughed again, a sound that Redling sometimes found amusing and sometimes found irritating.

It struck him in the latter capacity, now.

"Oh, Captain, Captain," she said. "You really should learn more about the ship you own. You're thinking about blind Jumps, aren't you? You're thinking about vanished ships and gross topological distortions."

"Well—"

She shook her head. "You need to learn how to read a screen," she said, pointing again. "This is gross power processing, not location or displacement factors. The *Gateway* is a Jump-2 ship—each Jump can carry us a two parsecs, under normal operating conditions. For whatever reason, we're only processing about ninety-seven percent of our normal power input; I don't know why. Whatever reason, every text I have says that should create a paralinear shortfall in Jump efficiency. If the status holds, we'll stop short."

"If."

"If." Dawn nodded. "That's why I'm so concerned. This worries me, but the fact that I can't pinpoint its cause worries me more. If the power distribution subroutine is failing, others could fail, too. They haven't yet, but—" She looked up at him, and smiled sweetly. "It's time for what we call a command decision, Captain," she said.

Redling thought for another moment, but this time he had something to think about. The options were simple: stay in place and starve to death waiting for aid; spend years under conventional drive to reach the nearest planet; or proceed under with an uncertain Jump.

But only slightly uncertain, apparently.

"What about after we Jump?" he asked. "What happens then?"

"I don't know," Dawn repeated. "But I don't think we have much choice but to find out."

Redling nodded. "Proceed, then," he said. "We'll have to chance it. If we're lucky, all that will happen is we finish wrecking our schedule."

"If we're lucky."

He looked at her. "Have you ever heard of anything like this before?" he asked. "In any of your various lines of work?"

"Only in theories and texts," Dawn said. "It's possible to calibrate a Jumper to work at less than peak efficiency, but I don't know why anyone would want to do it. Certainly, I've never heard of it being done. Like I said before, it's what I don't understand that worries me."

"I can understand that," Redling said dryly.

Two days into Jump Space, Redling dined with Ku-Ril-La in the Guy-troy's quarters. They ate better food than the *Gateway*'s galley could offer, retrieved from a stasis locker among the winged man's luggage.

"I can see why you'd be willing to travel on the *Gateway*," Redling said, lifting a forkful of pickled sand hydras to his waiting mouth. He chewed, savored, swallowed and smiled before continuing. "With provisions like these, you must be very nearly as comfortable as on the *Waltzing Spider*."

Ku-Ril-La nodded. "True enough," he said, taking a bite of his own meal. "But not my reason, of course. Yours was the only vessel available to me, and the needs of my Tour were fairly precise."

"I was wondering about that," Redling lied easily. "You've spent time in the Guy-troy enclaves—"

Ku-Ril-La shot him a look. Apparently, "enclave" was not a polite term.

"—in Guy-troy *neighborhoods*," Redling amended hastily, "on each of the worlds we've visited. Looking up old friends, or conducting Kaal business?"

"Either. Both. My reasons are my own."

Redling nodded this time. "Of course," he said. The desire for privacy was something he could understand, if not always honor. More than once, Dawn F'Ral's constant probes had offended him mightily, and he felt slightly chagrined to find himself mimicking her techniques.

More to the point, he felt chagrined at doing it in such an overt way.

"I had no desire to offend," he said.

"You have not," Ku-Ril-La said, and paused for a long moment as he studied the food on his plate. When he spoke again, there was a different note in his voice.

"I'm not accustomed to being in debt, Redling, and it occurs to me that I am very much in yours."

"Hmmm?" The comment surprised Redling. Since leaving Plimbo, the Guy-troy had been even more reclusive than usual, and Redling's mind had been occupied by other matters. Now, he found himself wondering the meaning of the winged man's words.

"You saved my life on Plimbo, at great risk to your own," Ku-Ril-La continued. "I have failed to thank you properly for your effort."

"That?" Redling asked, genuinely startled now. The thought had not even occurred to him. "That was no risk—a vigorous exercise, at most. And I had to get you back; Plimbo's authorities would have kept me planet-bound forever, otherwise."

"I do not believe that," Ku-Ril-La said. "At any rate, you will be rewarded."

Redling wasn't sure how to respond to the Guy-troy. His borrowed memories screamed exhortations of greed and delight, but his own mind was more sanguine about the situation. The Guy-troy was fabulously wealthy, he knew, and well able to afford gifts beyond even Redling's considerable dreams.

Of course, naked greed, the kind of avarice that his namesake would have voiced so eagerly, might prove counterproductive. Ku-Ril-La's gratitude might be an asset better exploited in a strategic, or at least tactful manner.

"That's really not necessary," he said.

"It is," Ku-Ril-La said, "but we will talk of it another time."

Somewhere inside Redling's head, an echo of the real Navis Redling's consciousness moaned in despair as a chance for sudden wealth ambled off into the distance.

Long moments passed in silence, broken only by the sounds of utensils on plates, and eating.

"The ways of our races are very different," Ku-Ril-La said. "I hope I do not offend—"

"No, no, not at all."

"—by what I am about to say," Ku-Ril-La continued smoothly. "Are you familiar with the term, 'cuckoo'?

"It's a kind of a bird, I think," Redling said. "Or a timepiece; I'm not sure which. It's an old word, and different worlds define it different ways."

"It's the closest I can come to an equivalent for a word in my own tongue," Ku-Ril-La said. He then emitted a rasping series of clicks, apparently a word in his own language. "The," he made the same sound again, "was a very important factor in the evolution of my people."

"Oh?"

Ku-Ril-La nodded, making the human sign of assent with practiced ease. "The cuckoo was a competing species that stole nest space from my forebears. Similar in size and coloration to the Guy-troy's progenitors, it laid its eggs in our nests, and fooled us into raising its young as our own."

Redling nodded, too. "An impostor," he said, unsure of the conversation's new direction.

"No. More intimate than that, I would think. Accepted as a family member, or a nest mate, perhaps," Ku-Ril-La said. "Or as a crew member."

Redling looked at him and set down his eating utensil. "You'd best explain that," he said.

"The Kaal is strong on Plimbo. My associates were most eager to investigate the unpleasantness surrounding my abduction, and were able to provide me with some interesting findings before we embarked again. Nothing definitive, but enough to suggest that one of your associates merits further study. Certain inquiries were made on Plimbo, certain offers, and word of them made its way back to my organization. As I said, nothing definitive, but—"

He meant Dawn, Redling realized.

Aloud, he said, "Who are you talking about?"

Ku-Ril-La told him.

The *Gateway* dropped out of Jump Space some six weeks from Carstairs world, confirming Dawn's projections and nearly doubling the distance that Redling had intended to cover before landing on the world near the Red Nebula.

Despite his current suspicions, Redling felt a wave of relief sweep through him as he realized that he and his shipmates had returned to normal space without harm. Then he forced the thought from his mind and turned to more pressing matters.

He glanced at his monitor screen, at the display it relayed from the defensive sensors that were controlled from another bridge station.

Three red spots gleamed there, blood-colored against a dark background that was overlaid with a distancing grid. Only one kind of ship could be waiting for them here, so far out from Carstairs. Only one kind of ship could have known to wait for them, and where.

Pirates.

"Pikk," he said. "Shields up."

The big man looked up from his weapons station, started by unusually commanding tone in Redling's voice. "Huh?" he said, sounding for an instant very much like Tithe, back on Farworld. "Don't need—"

Redling ignored Thyller's words. The giant's hesitation had been enough to tell him what he needed to know. Moving with Aslan-ish speed, Redling spun in his chair and raised his right hand. As he moved, he tensed the muscles on his right forearm.

This time, instead of a knife, a thud gun's butt filled his waiting hand. It wasn't his favorite weapon, but it seemed appropriate to the circumstances.

"Now," Redling said, one eye still on his monitor. The red spots were moving, swiftly, towards the screen's center.

Toward the *Gateway*.

"Shields. Up. Now." Redling barked the words.

Thyller made a curse in some language that Redling did not know, then stabbed a key on his control panel.

"Captain! What—" That was Helicron.

"Shut up," Redling responded. A milky overlay had appeared on the monitor display. The shields were up.

He didn't need Thyller anymore.

As Redling tensed his trigger finger, two things happened. First, a wave of shock and thunder roared through the *Gateway*, as meson bursts slammed against the craft's shielded hull. The force of their impact was enough to make the cabin shake and rock around Redling, enough to make him lose his aim for a moment and send his shot wild.

The second thing that happened was that a roaring Pikk Thyller erupted from the gunnery station and came surging towards Redling like a man-shaped tidal wave.

Redling shot him.

"Captain, what's—" Helicron said.

"Shut up," Redling answered. Thyller was still coming, so Redling shot him again, and said, "Dawn. Take the weapons station, please. Now."

Even the unflappable Dawn F'Ral seemed taken aback by the sudden turn of events. "But," she said.

"Now!" Redling snarled, and grinned wolfishly as he saw the attractive woman take Thyller's place behind the gunnery station. If anyone else on board could operate the station, it was she.

Redling shot Thyller a third time. Each of the thud gun's rounds packed approximately enough force to render a normal man unconscious. It was designed less to kill than to stun, but what had led Redling to use it today was the fact that the shots, if fired, were unlikely to damage any of the bridge equipment.

He was beginning to think he might have made a better choice.

"Not that easy," Thyller said, drawing closer, slowed but still moving. The man's vitality was incredible.

"Easy enough," Redling snarled. He dropped the gun, curled the fingers of his hand into a fist. As Thyller lunged for him, he drove his knuckles into the man's larynx.

There was a sound like meat being chopped.

Thyller fell to the deck. He gasped and wheezed, then shuddered once and lay still, apparently concentrating all of his remaining energy on forcing himself to breathe.

Redling ignored him, and leaped for his own station.

"Captain, I—"

"Shut up, Helicron," he said a third time. "You want something to do, find a tangler and secure Thyller. He sold us out, and now I've got to deal with who bought him."

The *Gateway* shuddered again, as another blast caught it.

"Status," Redling demanded.

"Fore cannon cycled, charged, ready," Dawn called

back. "Rear cannon cycled, charging—charged, ready now."

"On my command," Redling said, unlocking the computerized steering system and taking manual control of the ship's trajectory.

"On your command," Dawn agreed. "But I suggest—"

"Bearing seven-six-tree," Redling directed, firing port steering jets and sending the *Gateway* in a curving spin. "Lead attacker, five-second burst. Now!"

Again, his screen told the story. An incandescent diagonal traced the span between the screen's center and the first of the red dots.

Then the red dot wasn't there anymore.

"Not expecting us to fight back," Redling said. "Strictly a smash and grab, and we didn't get smashed." He was reasonably confident that the pirates had chosen to fire only when they saw the *Gateway*'s screens come to life. That must have been when they realized that their ploy of bribing the ship's gunner had failed.

Redling knew a thing or two about how pirates thought.

"They're expecting it now," Dawn said, her voice tense. The cabin light flickered and dimmed as another energy barrage smashed into the *Gateway*'s shields, prompting them to draw more power from the ship's reactor.

"Satisfy their expectations, then," Redling said. "Bearing nine-nine-six, aft. Now!"

More energy roared from the *Gateway*'s cannons, cannons that Redling had bought with considerable credits from a fat man named Tithe. At the moment, as the second red spot on his screen went dark, he did not begrudge the junkman his price.

"Third target's receding," Dawn said. "Breaking off the engagement. Prepare for pursuit? They'll Jump soon."

Redling looked at the dwindling point of light his screen displayed. He thought for a moment of a page from his own book of life, of that terrible moment when he had returned to Oleck's compound on Laumer's moon.

"No," he said. "Let them go."

"They'll be back," Dawn said. "If not for us, for someone else."

"That's someone else's problem, then," Redling answered. He glanced to his left, where Helicron Daas was winding band after band of tangler tape around the recumbent Pikk Thyller. He looked back at his screen, where the third raider had vanished, taking refuge in Jump Space.

The entire conflict, internal and external, had taken less than a minute.

"They aren't so brave without their stalking goat," he said.

"Stalking goat?" Helicron asked.

"An old story; I'll tell it to you some time. For now, just understand that your drinking buddy sold us out." Redling looked in Dawn's direction. "If you tear down the engines on Carstairs," he said, "I think you'll find some kind of bug in the operating system. Whatever it is, Thyller put it there."

Dawn nodded. "Then his cronies came ahead from Plimbo in faster ships and waited for us. The big man's got quite a story to tell."

"He can tell it to the Starport Authority," Redling said. He had been quite ready to kill Thyller, but not now. Fewer cadavers meant less explanation to make.

"Shields?"

"Keep them up," Redling said grimly.

"That's quite a strain on the engines."

"Keep them up," Redling repeated, "and keep me posted." He stepped towards the cabin door. "I've got passengers with nerves that no doubt need soothing."

He also knew that he had a choice to make.

Six weeks later, ships time, the *Gateway* limped into Carstairs World's main starport. It was met there by representatives of a half-dozen offices and authorities, each with an agenda of its own. In the days just prior to docking, the airwaves had been alive within back-and-forth messages, and the status of the ship and its occupants was well known.

The Starport Authority wanted to take Pikk Thyller into custody and imprison him for his crimes.

Representatives of he Jump engineer's guild wanted to inspect the *Gateway*'s engines, and determine what mischief had been done to them.

Agents of the Public Defenders office were equally eager to provide an advocate for his defense.

Customs officials wanted to inspect the Droyne artifacts in the *Gateway*'s hold.

The sector's Marine Garrison wanted to interview Redling regarding the salvoes his ship had fired it its defense.

Officers of the Diplomatic Corps waited to validate Ku-Ril-La's status as a plenipotentiary at large, and to announce a public function in his honor.

The list went on and on, reaching its climax with a heavily armed contingent of Kaal employees, waiting to escort Ku-Ril-La to secure quarters in the Kaal enclave on Carstairs World.

Dawn F'Ral watched the Guy-troy leave, then turned to Redling, cold fury in her eyes.

"You tipped him," she said angrily. "You tipped him, and now we can't take him without causing a major disruption."

"I didn't tip him," Redling said, which was true enough, at least by his standards. All he had done was hint to the Guy-troy that trouble might be waiting for him on Carstairs, and make the hint strong enough that the winged man had acted on it. He had said nothing about Cobalt Division, or about any of its operatives.

There were some secrets that it seemed wiser to keep.

"Why the flarge did you tip him? I told you—"

"You told me nothing," Redling said. "Nothing I could use, at any rate. It was Ku-Ril-La who told me that Pikk Thyller was up to something." He had been able to combine the time with some knowledge of his own, regarding pirates and their mindsets, and then deduced that some kind of trap had waited for them.

"How did he know?"

"The Kaal is strong on Plimbo," Redling said, in a fair approximation of the Guy-troy's tones.

"What kind of combine has its own intelligence-gathering division, especially one sensitive enough to pick up things like that?" The rage in Dawn's voice had become disgust now. "You've made a mistake, Redling, a terrible one, and I hope the entire Imperium doesn't have to pay the price for it."

"I've made mistakes before," Redling said softly. He had made an uncommonly large number of them on this trip. "But I never turn my back on a friend, no matter what the situation." He paused. "I hope I never do."

EPILOGUE

The first thing he realized was that he could not see.

Consciousness came to Redling slowly, in ripples and waves. He fought back the first few, but they built in strength until he could no longer resist their power, and found himself sprawled once more on the shores of awareness.

Awake, he could feel and taste and smell and hear again, but he could not see, could not even open his eyes. Something covered them. A blindfold? His first conscious thought was to remove it, but he found himself unable to make even the beginnings of the motion.

"Don't try to move yet," someone said. "I know you're awake, but the anaesthetic has not worn off completely. Be patient, and your motor control will return."

Anaesthetic?

That explained the sour taste in his mouth and the ringing in his ears, loud enough to distort and obscure the voice he heard now. Still, even with the masking overlay, there was something familiar about the voice, about its patient tone and the idiosyncratic way it shaped certain words.

"Where?" he croaked. The single word was all that he could force through still-numb lips.

"That does not matter, at least for now. Please, resist the desire to move; you cannot."

Redling concentrated, strained, struggled against the chemical bonds that held him immobile, but the only result his exertions yielded was a grim confirmation of the unseen speaker's words. The bones and muscles of his arms were dead things, and he had to concentrate in order to feel them at all. It was readily apparent that, even if he could force some meager bit of movement from his limbs, he would be unable to move swiftly enough to accomplish anything, especially if he had to contend with an adversary.

He rather suspected that such was the case.

How long would he have to wait for feeling and control to return? Minutes? Hours? He did not know, could not know, but he suspected that his captor did not know, either. Redling had been captured before and had been drugged before, and he knew from experience that he typically recovered faster than most.

How long did he have to wait, until sensation and control returned?

How long had he waited already, unconscious, paralyzed, and helpless?

"I mean you no harm," the voice continued. "Quite the contrary. You are a difficult man, Navis Redling. It took far more effort to apprehend you than it would have to slay you. My operatives would not have expended that extra effort, were my goal to cause you harm."

Redling thought about that. Since planetfall on Carstairs World, he had twice had the uncomfortable feeling that he was being stalked, paced by a person or persons unknown. The clues had been minimal, so minimal that he had not been certain they were clues at all. There had been a slightly familiar face in a crowd, and he had seen a discreet nod from a bartender that may or may not have been directed at someone behind him. He had been careful after that, and intensely alert, but no more hints had presented themselves to him. Things had gone well enough that he had dismissed the uncomfortable feeling as a result of his knowledge that he had come to the attention of Cobalt Division.

Now, in an odd sort of way, he was pleased to learn that his first impression had been the correct one.

Redling's line of work required an edge, and it was always good to confirm that he was not losing his.

"How?" he rasped. This word came more easily than the last one had. Some degree of sensation had returned to his facial muscles. He could feel his own flesh move, feel coolness as the sweat on his skin evaporated into the surrounding air.

And he could make one finger move.

He couldn't move it very far, but the nerves and muscles in his right index finger were his again, and he could make it shift and flex. Sensation had returned there, too, enough that he could feel cloth beneath the fingertip. The fabric had the distinctive, tight grain of a bed sheet; that, and his horizontal position, along with the faint medicinal scent that reached his nose raised a new likelihood and a new possibility, neither of which he liked very much.

He was probably in a hospital, or at least an infirmary; that meant that what he wore on his face was probably not a blindfold, but a bandage, instead.

What had been done to his eyes?

"How did we capture you? With great effort," the voice said. "On the local Star Street. You had just left your young associate, following a chance encounter at a gaming facility. You may remember a slight pinch or sting behind your left ear, like an insect's bite."

Redling didn't, but he didn't try to say so. He was conserving his limited energy on the twin efforts of reasserting control over his body, and putting a name to that damnably familiar voice. It was more familiar now, as the ringing in Redling's ears subsided, but he still could not identify it.

"You appeared to faint, then. The drug on the dart was a neurotoxin, fast acting but safe at the dosage you received. Its effect was somewhat like a *petit mal* epileptic seizure, a mild convulsion with some disruption of cognitive processes. Our collapse was enough to bring you to the attention of the city watch, and, ultimately, to my custody."

Redling's first guess was that Dawn F'Ral's office had abducted him, in order to make good on her threats, but two words made him think something else—"your species." From what little his erstwhile engineer had told him about her true employer, he was reasonably certain that Cobalt Division's ranks did not include any nonhumans.

Besides, he had heard those words spoken before, in those same tantalizingly familiar tones. He had heard that cadence, that voice before, heard it from—

Sudden realization exploded in Redling's consciousness, erupting like a supernova and banishing the last of the darkness that filled the corners of his mine. The realization was so sudden and emphatic that he felt his muscles twitch and spasm in response to the wave of energy sweeping though his nervous system.

He was pleased to realize that he could move all of the fingers of both of his hands now.

"This," he said slowly, "is a flarge of a way to pay me back for helping you, Ku-Ril-La." He spoke slowly, both because of some lingering numbness and because he needed time to consider his options.

And whether he had any.

There was a pause, and then the clicking was the sound that was Guy-troy laughter reached Redling's ears.

"Astute," the winged man said. "Very astute. You would make a dangerous adversary, Navis Redling. I do not want that to happen."

"You're not treating me like a friend," Redling responded, pleased to discover that he could speak almost normally now. The last of the paralysis was fading now, and only a hint of pins and needles lingered.

"Actually, I am. I have rewarded you this day, Redling, and made your future brighter than that of most of your species. When we are done here, you will be free to be on your way, free to pursue whatever endeavors you choose." The Guy-troy paused. "From what I know of your nature, your goals are unlikely to bring you into opposition with me and mine, especially if you are wise."

Redling tensed the long muscles of his arms and legs, just enough to determine whether they were bound.

They weren't.

"A new day is dawning, Redling, a day that will dawn in slow sequence across many words. Your own people have a saying about early birds and worms. I am the early bird, and more will follow me," Ku-Ril-La said, a new edge in his familiar voice. "Take care that you do not become one of the worms."

Redling's hands came up then, both of them. His left flashed to his face, where it clawed at the blinding bandage, and his right flailed almost at random, seeking a weapon.

His left was successful; his right was not. The familiar contours of a water carafe filled one hand while the other groped the strip of adhesive plastic that masked his eyes. As his fingers sought purchase on the bandage (and found none), Redling heaved himself forward, and threw his body in the general direction of Ku-Ril-La's voice. He didn't know much about the Guy-troy, but he knew that they were light, made mostly of hollow bone and taut-stretched skin, basically fragile stuff. If he could use the water bottle as a club—

Before he could more than a few centimeters, something slammed into Redling's chest, smashing him back into what he was now reasonably certain was a hospital bed. Other hands—strong hands, human hands, by the feel of them—clamped down hard on his wrists and held them.

"Don't touch the master!" another voice roared, so close that he could feel spittle splash on his cheek.

That voice was familiar, too, but it certainly didn't belong here. Redling wished desperately that he had been able to remove the bandage, so that he could see who had spoken. It sounded like—

It couldn't be.

"We spoke once of history," Ku-Ril-La said. "I told you then that my people knew little of such, because it did not interest us. I lied to you then."

"And it wasn't the first time, I'll wager," Redling said, still straining against the iron grip that held his wrists. He had already dropped the useless water carafe, but he paid that no attention. Instead, he twisted his body, drew one leg up against his flat stomach, and lashed out with the other one. From the direction of the new voice, and from the angle at which his arms were pinned, he knew the location of his new assailant. If he could just connect—

It was like kicking a stone wall.

Pain, sharp and real, surged up Redling's leg as the force of his own kick was turned back on him. For a moment, he thought could feel his own bones breaking, and then the tsunami of pain subsided and he realized that he was still intact.

For the moment, at least.

"True enough," Ku-Ril-La continued, implacably. "But what do you know of truth? What does your race? Your forbears stole our history from us, Redling, through subterfuge and genetic torture. Many thousands of your 'standard years' ago, our peoples met for the first time. Individually, you were not ready to meet the challenge we posed, so you overwhelmed us by force of numbers, instead. It has taken many years of research and study to learn what your ancestors did to us, and to undo it."

Redling kicked again, harder and higher, not because he thought it would break the grip that held him. Rather, he struck because he wanted to hear that new voice again, if only in a cry of pain.

His captor grunted, but did not cry out, as Redling's heel found his chin. Fighting blind wasn't easy, but Redling had done it before.

"Your struggles are useless, Redling, and pointless as well. I have no intent to harm you, in any way. You will only damage yourself if you continue."

"Pardon me if I don't believe you," Redling snarled. "I try to make each mistake only once."

He kicked again, and twisted his body, and then kicked a fourth time. The final blow landed in a spot somewhat lower and more yielding than chin or chest, the belly, and Redling was rewarded by a very familiar cry of pain, familiar enough to confirm the identity of who voice it.

Redling knew who held him now, though he could scarcely force himself to believe it.

The hand clamped around this right wrist relaxed a bit now, and Redling tore himself free. He hooked the fingers of his right hand and lashed out with them, seeking the eyes of the man who held him. Based on what he remembered of the other man's build, that should put them some six inches above the remembered location of his jaw.

He misjudged the distance, and found the man's mouth instead.

Now it was Redling's turn to cry out in pain as strong teeth ground down on his fingers.

"The world that gave rise to my folk was a harsh, competitive place," Ku-Ril-La continued, apparently unmindful of the commotion. "Evolutionary pressure gifted my people with a complex system of biochemical cues, pheromones that they could use to command and direct the activities of their flocks. We are all the products of our heritage, Redling, and those cues served us well as we struggled for dominance. They served us so well, in fact, that the first of your folk to find us fell under their sway, and became more loyal to our own species than to their own. That aptitude was taken from us, Redling, by genetic manipulation, and our history was stolen from us, to further obscure our rightful legacy."

Redling suddenly had a pretty good idea just what kind of puzzle pieces that Ku-Ril-La had gathered on his long journey. But from whom? From his own sources, or other members of the Kaal, or renegade scientists?

He supposed it didn't matter, at least not now.

Redling forced his hand up and back, ramming it deeper into his assailant's mouth, deeply enough to interfere with the other man's breathing. Even as he felt his flesh tear and blood trickle down his arm, Redling kicked yet again, even lower this time.

"Your people took that from us," Ku-Ril-La said. "The time has come for mine to take it back."

The biting jaw popped open, simultaneously releasing Redling's fingers and a scream of agony. The still-clasping hand released too, and there was a sound like thunder as the other man fell to the floor. Before another second passed, Redling had torn the bandage from his eyes.

What he saw proved his suspicions correct. He was in a hospital room, all polished white enamel and bright lights. The sudden radiance made his eyes sting and water, but he ignored the discomfort and looked hastily from side to side, eager and desperate to assess the situation.

He could still see, he realized with a rush of relief.

He saw a tiny room, brightly lit and well-appointed, but apparently designed for proportions somewhat different from his own. He saw Ku-Ril-La, comfortably seated in a chair built for his kind, and training an oddly shaped pistol in Redling's direction.

He saw a man he had never expected to see again, rolling on the floor and clutching his groin and retching.

He saw Pikk Thyller.

"All right," he said easily. "How did you do it? And why?"

"Do it?" Ku-Ril-La asked mildly.

"Get him, and get that that kind of loyalty out of him. Pikk Thyller never struck me as one to call another 'master,' and he's certainly never been particularly loyal."

Thyller had pulled himself together now, and glared angrily in Redling's direction, but the big man did not seem to recognize him.

"Stay, Thyller," Ku-Ril-La said, as his empty hand drummed on the chair arm again.

Thyller fell back obediently.

"Very good," Ku-Ril-La said to Redling. "Very good, indeed. To answer your question, Thyller became mine because I wished it, and the Kaal's power is sufficient that most of my wishes become reality. His loyalty became mine, because my scientists administered a synthetic version of the control pheromone to him."

"Why?"

"To punish him. To demonstrate to you the power I can wield over your ground-crawling kind, now that my researches are complete. As Thyller crawls before me now, so too will governors of entire worlds—perhaps even members of the Ruling Council. It has taken many years of hard work by many members of the Kaal, but we have pieced together the reality of my people's past." Ku-Ril-La paused. "Our past, and our future, and the nature of our vengeance."

Dawn F'Ral's vision of a human-dominated galaxy suddenly seemed much more attractive to Redling than it had when she voiced it. He began to feel a certain sympathy for the members of Cobalt Division.

"It will take many years to take your precious Imperium from you, Redling, and neither you nor I will live to see the process to its completion," Ku-Ril-La said. "Because of that, and because of your service to me, I can promise you the chance to live out your life, free and unmolested."

"This isn't unmolested," Redling said, "and sitting across from a man with a gun doesn't qualify as free." His hand was bleeding profusely now from the gouges cut in it by Thyller's teeth, so he took a cloth from the washstand beside his bed and improvised a bandage.

He was careful not to wrap the wound tightly, however.

Ku-Ril-La rustled his folded wings. "This is but a passing moment," he said. "I needed to place my mark on you. In the years to come, you will be grateful I did."

"Mark?"

"A minor signature tag in the iris of your left eye. Invisible to the human eye, but quite evident to mine. You are under my protection now, Redling, no matter what face you wear or what name you use. One day, all of your kind will wear such a mark, the label of your owner. For now, however, it is but an indicator of free passage," Ku-Ril-La said. "Provided that you behave."

"Why." Redling said the word flatly, not bothering to make it a question.

"It does you ill to question your better," Ku-Ril-La said. "Even allowing that I have a certain affection for you."

Until now, Redling might have said the same, but now—

Branded like a pet. The thought appalled him.

"You have an interesting way of showing it," Redling said.

"Show power, then mercy, or the mercy is worth nothing," Ku-Ril-La said. "Another adage."

Redling nodded. "Fool me once, shame on me," he said. "That's another."

He twitched his right hand, throwing the bloody washcloth at Ku-Ril-La to draw his fire, and then he threw himself.

Then the Guy-troy shot him.

A chirping signal from Redling's wrist com woke him, and he found himself in his hotel room once more. This time, he awoke easily and completely, so much so that he had to wonder if his last, jumbled memories were a dream.

Then he felt the pain of his injured hand, and realized that the memories were real.

Redling answered the com. "Wake-up call, sir," a too-happy voice said. "Can we provide you with any service this morning?"

"I think so," he replied. "Do you have a medic on staff?"

"Yes, sir. Do you need attention?"

Redling looked at his hand again. The bite marks were scabbed over, obviously had been, for some hours. Still, there was the matter of infection, and it was better to be safe than sorry.

"I think so," he said. "Mind telling me how I got here?"

"Sir?"

"Check the access log and see when and how I got here," Redling said, irritated.

"Um—seven hours, ten ago," the clerk responded. "Big fellow brought you in. Said you needed sleep."

That wasn't all he needed, Redling realized sourly, but he didn't say so. "Send the medic to my room in an hour, please," he said. "I've got some other calls I need to make."

He sat on the bed's edge for a moment, thinking. He thought about Ku-Ril-La, whom he had liked, and about what had been done to him. He thought about the mark he bore now, Ku-Ril-La's mark, and the terrible misstep he had taken by helping the Guy-troy. He thought about Cobalt Division, and the words Dawn F'Ral—or Kob Thrommus, or whatever she chose to call herself—had spoken to him.

Redling was not a man who spent much time looking at the big picture, but even he recognized that some pictures were too big to ignore.

Not really wanting to, and fueled by some sort of desperate frustration, he raised his com again and entered the one code he had for Dawn F'Ral.

He could only hope she answered.

TO BE CONTINUED...

THE TRAVELLER
SCIENCE FICTION ROLE PLAYING GAME

The **Traveller** role-playing game, originally published in 1997 and now in its fourth edition, is a comprehensive science-fiction system which describes a vast future universe in which mankind has already reached the stars and conquered thousands of worlds, but still faces the never-ending struggle to conquer more worlds and wrest more secrets from the universe.

Based On A Role-Playing Game. The **Traveller** science-fiction role-playing game is a set of rules which detail the fundamental principles of the universe...how people interact, how starships fly, how guns work, how businesses operate, how worlds are defined. Using those principles, any activity is possible, and players attempt most of them. Over time, the adventures of players and the ideas of writers has helped to create the future **Traveller** universe.

Dice. When playing **Traveller**, there must be some device introducing the element of unpredictability. **Traveller** uses dice. Players need at least two six sided dice (as found in most board games). The Two Dice Chart shows the probability of rolling a specific number using two dice. For example, the chance of rolling exactly 7 is 17%; the chance of rolling 7 or less is 58%, and the chance of rolling 9 or greater is 28%.

TWO DICE (All N = 36)

Roll	N	N%	N -	N -%	N+	N+%
2	1	3%	1	3%	36	100%
3	2	6%	3	8%	35	97%
4	3	8%	6	17%	33	92%
5	4	11%	10	28%	30	83%
6	5	14%	15	42%	26	72%
7	6	17%	21	58%	21	58%
8	5	14%	26	72%	15	42%
9	4	11%	30	83%	10	28%
10	3	8%	33	92%	6	17%
11	2	6%	35	97%	3	8%
12	1	3%	36	100%	1	3%

There are 36 possible outcomes of throwing two dice (they range from 2 to 12).

THE CHARACTER IN TRAVELLER

Fundamental to **Traveller** is the instrument by which players can interact with their universe: the character. Characters are the focus of **Traveller** adventures.

A player is the actual person participating in the game.

A character is the gam persona. A character has six basic characteristics, a variety of skills, a background based on schooling and education, and may have a prior career which has produced additional experience.

Player Characters (PC). A PC is a character actively used by a player; the major characters within each adventure.

Non-Player-Characters (NPC). An NPC is a character manipulated by the game master as it interacts with the player characters. NPCs are often reasons for adventures; the means by which the game master communicates plot details.

CHARACTERISTICS

The six basic characteristics are:

Strength (Str) indicates physical power and ability.

Dexterity (Dex) indicates body and eye-hand coordination.

Endurance (End) indicates personal determination and physical stamina.

Intelligence (Int) indicates natural mental ability to think and reason.

Education (Edu) indicates an equivalent level of schooling (although not necessarily attendance).

Social Standing (Soc) indicates social class and the level of society from which the character comes.

ROLLING CHARACTERISTICS

The player rolls two dice for each characteristic. For example, for the character's Strength, roll two dice: the result is his or her Strength. Notice that the maximum characteristic that can be rolled is 12 and the minimum is 2. Higher and lower values for a character may become available through later events in the game system.

THE AVERAGE CHARACTER

A perfectly average character has average characteristics: Str 7, Dex 7, End 7, Int 7, Edu 7, and Soc 7. This typical person is used in the examples throughout this module.

THE UPP (Universal Personality Profile)

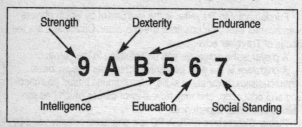

HEXADECIMAL NUMBERS

Base10	0	1	2	3	4
Base16	0	1	2	3	4

Base10	5	6	7	8	9
Base16	5	6	7	8	9

Base10	10	11	12	13	14
Base16	A	B	C	D	E

Base10	15	16	17	18	19
Base16	F	G	H	J	K

Hexadecimal (base 16) numbers express digits greater than 9 using only one space. The value is that columns of such digits can be written with their places aligned.

The system originally went to 15 (hence hexadecimal); it was extended to cover higher numbers as the game structure has evolved.

I and O are omitted to avoid confusion with 1 (one) and 0 (zero).

PHYSICAL VS. MENTAL

Physical Characteristics: Strength, Dexterity, and Endurance.

Mental Characteristics: Intelligence, and Education.

Social Characteristics: Social Standing.

FOR EXAMPLE

The character UPP shown above indicates was generated with two dice for each characteristic.

He (assuming the person is a he) rolled 9 for Strength. Since 72% of those rolling the dice will roll less than 9, that places this character at at least the 72 nd percentile in Strength.

The character's Dexterity (10) is shown in hexadecimal format, as is his Endurance (11).

The UPP for an average character would be 777777.

STRENGTH

Str	Equivalent
0	Incapacitated.
1	Almost Incapacitated.
2	Very Weak.
3	Somewhat Weak.
4	Weak.
5	Below Average.
6	Average.
7	Average.
8	Average.
9	Above Average.
A	Strong.
B	Quite Strong.
C	Very Strong.
D	Remarkable
E	Extraordinary
F	Superhuman

Strength is the ability to apply physical force. Loads in association with Strength are calculated in kilograms.

1 x Str = Load which can be carried all day long.

2 x Str = Load which may be carried until collapse. This is **Double Burden.**

3 x Str = Load which may be carried until collapse. This is Triple Burden.

5 x Str= Load which may be carried for under 7 (or End x) minutes no more than once per hour.

10 x Str = Load which may be lifted (not carried) for under one minute.

15 x Str = Load which may be dragged for under 7 (or End x) minutes.

Double Burden. When carrying a 2x load, reduce Strength, Dexterity, and Endurance by -1 until half an hour after the load is shed.

Triple Burden. When carrying a 3x load, reduce Strength, Dexterity, and Endurance by -2 each until half an hour after the load is shed.

Burden Modifiers. Some equipment (and some weapons) have a burden modifier (ranging from - 5 to +5). Reduce or increase Load by Burden Modifier before calculating Burden.

FOR EXAMPLE

An average character (by definition a character with Strength 7) can carry a load of 7 kilograms or less all day long. This might include a back pack, a weapon and ammunition, and some sort of instrumentation.

This same character could carry a load of 20 kilograms (Triple Burden) and would be reduced (temporarily) from 777777 to 555777 after a half hour and to 333777 after an hour. After 90 minutes, the individual would collapse from the strain.

This average character could carry 35 kilograms for up to 7 minutes once an hour).

DEXTERITY

Dex	Equivalent
0	Paralyzed
1	Extremely Clumsy
2	Very Clumsy.
3	Clumsy
4	Unhandy
5	Below Average
6	Average
7	Average.
8	Average
9	Above Average
A	Adroit
B	Dexterous
C	Very Dexterous
D	Remarkable
E	Extraordinary
F	Superhuman

Dexterity indicates body and eye-hand coordination, and reflects an ability to manipulate objects and to throw accurately.

BALANCE

In a circumstance in which a character risks losing his or her balance, roll two dice: if the result is greater than the character's Dex, the character falls or trips.

ACCURACY

In a circumstance in which eye-hand coordination is called for, throw two dice: if the result is greater than the character's Dex, the effort fails.

FOR EXAMPLE

An average character (777777) confronted with a balance situation, would lose his balance (throw greater than 7 on two dice 42% of the time). If a balance situation is imposed for stepping over a curb, the results would be ludicrous: characters would routinely fail simple walking situations nearly half the time. Instead, the game master must judiciously impose a situations with an awareness of the likelihood of success or failure.

A typical situation calling for balance is walking a narrow log across a gorge: the character to select to go across first would be 7B7777 rather than 737777. Character 7B7777 could pull a rope with him and the others could follow with the support of a safety rope. If any of the subsequent characters lose their balance, the rope prevents a long fall.

It would probably be a good idea to have B77777 control the rope because of his strength.

Accuracy: Similar concepts apply to determining when to impose situations which call for accuracy.

ENDURANCE

End	Equivalent
0	Comatose
1	Very Poor Stamina
2	Poor Stamina
3	Very Easily Fatigued
4	Easily Fatigued
5	Below Average
6	Average
7	Average.
8	Average
9	Above Average
A	Above Average
B	Great Stamina
C	Very Great Stamina.
D	Remarkable
E	Extraordinary
F	Superhuman

Endurance is a measure of personal determination and physical stamina.

BASIC ENDURANCE

1 x End +9 = Number of waking hours until fatigue begins.

(1 x End +9) + End = Number of waking hours until collapse (Endurance becomes 0).

FATIGUE

A character is fatigued after 9 plus 1 x End waking hours. Once fatigued, -1 from End after each hours.

Collapse: If End reaches 0, character collapses and must sleep.

Rest. Undertaking no tasks (cat-napping) in a 2 hour period halts loss of End and regains 1 point. One to 3 hours sleep returns End to one-half normal, but fatigue restarts immediately. Four to 7 hours sleep resets the fatigue clock to normal.

FOR EXAMPLE

An average character begins to feel fatigued after 16 hours, at which point his or her End begins to decrease. At -1 End per hour, the character would collapse from fatigue after 23 hours.

A high Endurance character (77C777) would feel fatigued after 21 hours and collapse after 33 hours.

On the other hand, a low Endurance character (772777) would feel fatigued after 11 hours and would collapse after 13 hours (this person would benefit from a series of naps during the day.

INTELLIGENCE

Int	Equivalent
0	Instinctual
1	Very Low
2	Very Low
3	Very Low
4	Low
5	Below Average.
6	Average.
7	Average.
8	Average.
9	Above Average.
A	Superior.
B	Gifted.
C	Very Gifted.
D	Genius.
E	Extraordinary
F	Superhuman

Intelligence indicates natural mental ability to think and reason.

USING INTELLIGENCE

There are times when a **player** has a **character** who is smarter than he is (or a **player** has a **character** who is less intelligence than he is). Intelligence is used to resolve what the character is capable of.

Solving Puzzles. When a character is confronted with a puzzle, the throw to solve it is Int or less. The game master manipulates this basic process to reflect harder puzzles, simpler situations, or other complications.

FOR EXAMPLE

An average character acts normally all of the time: there is no need to resolve situations such as dressing oneself, filling out forms, or driving a vehicle. But there come times when the character is confronted with a challenging intellectual problem: detective work based on clues, understanding cryptic notes, or puzzling out a new device. In such instances, the player may understand immediately, but the character may not. The key to the player understanding the situation is his Intelligence.

The character rolls two dice to resolve the puzzle or understand the answer. If the dice roll is equal to or less than the character's intelligence, then the character understands.

The Game Master's Call. If the governing characteristic is uncertain, the game master may declare that Intelligence or Education or either may be used.

The game master may declare that one governs and the other may be used with a negative modifier. For example, Intelligence may govern, but Education may be used with a subtraction of -2 (or -3 or -4).

EDUCATION

Edu	Equivalent
0	Instinctual.
1	Illiterate.
2	Basic Reading.
3	Grade School.
4	Education Certificate.
5	High School.
6	Associate (2 years).
7	Bachelor's Degree.
8	Master's Degree.
9	Advanced Work
A	Doctorate.
B	Independent Research
C	Independent Research
D	Independent Research
E	Independent Research
F	Independent Research

Education indicates an equivalent level of schooling (although not necessarily attendance at an educational institution).

THE ALTERNATIVE

Education is the alternative to Intelligence. In **Traveller**, they are decoupled: they are unrelated, and it is possible for a very intelligent person to have a low Education (or a very high Education person to have a low intelligence).

Solving Puzzles Based On Education. An average character act normally all of the time: there is no need to resolve situations such as reading or writing because the character is assumed to be able to do so (very low Edu characters can't do some of these activities, which adds to the interest in role-playing them). But there come times when the character is confronted with a challenging intellectual problem: scientific problems, questions of historical knowledge, or even understanding details of philosophy.

The key to the player understanding the situation is Education.

The character rolls two dice to resolve the puzzle or understand the answer. If the dice roll is equal to or less than the character's Education, then the character understands.

The Game Master's Call. When the governing characteristic is uncertain, un unclear, or ambiguous, the game master may declare that Intelligence or Education or either may be used to resolve the puzzle.

In some cases, the game master may declare that one characteristic governs and the other may be used with a negative modifier. For example, Education may govern, by Intelligence may be used with a subtraction of -2 (or -3 or -4).

SOCIAL STANDING

Soc	Equivalent
2	The Dregs of Society
3	Lower Low Class
4	Middle Low Class
5	Upper Low Class
6	Lower Middle Class
7	Middle Class
8	Upper Middle Class
9	Lower Upper Class
A	Middle Upper Class
B	Upper Upper Class
C	Remarkable
D	Extraordinary
E	Extreme

Social Standing indicates social class and the level of society from which the character comes.

NOBLE TITLES

The Imperium issues noble titles which are reflected in personal social standing.

B	Knight.
C	Baron.
D	Marquis.
E	Count.
F	Duke.

There are ranks above F, but they are generally reserved for non-player characters

G	Archduke
H	Emperor

SUPPORT

Social standing determines the cost to that individual for basic living.

Cr250 x Soc = Typical cost of monthly support (food, clothes, lodging, basic entertainment).

FOR EXAMPLE

An average character (777777) requires about Cr1,750 per month in order to live in a style which is comfortable and satisfying. A lower class person (777773) needs only about Cr750 per month (mostly, one would suppose, for food). An upper class character requires about Cr3,000 per month.

In every case, this requirement is for the necessities: food, lodging, or other details. An upper class character might find personal communicator service a necessity, while a lower class character might not.

HUMAN HEIGHT & WEIGHT

	kg Wt	cm Ht	pds Wt	in Ht
-4	41	1.20	90	47
-3	43	1.28	95	50
-2	45	1.35	99	53
-1	47	1.43	103	56
0	49	1.50	108	59
1	51	1.58	112	62
2	53	1.65	117	65
3	56	1.68	123	66
4	59	1.70	130	67
5	62	1.73	136	68
6	65	1.75	143	69
7	68	1.78	150	70
8	73	1.80	161	71
9	78	1.83	172	72
10	83	1.85	183	73
11	88	1.88	194	74
12	94	1.90	207	75
13	100	1.93	220	76
14	106	1.98	233	78
15	113	2.03	249	80
16	120	2.08	264	82
17	127	2.13	279	84
18	135	2.18	297	86

Weight is in kilograms. Height is in centimeters (for convenience, weight is also shown in pounds and height in inches). Determine height and height separately using the **average** of Strength, Dexterity, and Endurance +D -D, and using all available DMs and modifications.

Weight vs Mass. Technically, the value shown is **mass**.

FOR EXAMPLE

The average character (777777) has an average of Str + Dex + End of 7.

Determining Height. To determine the character's height, the player takes the average of Str + Dex + End (which is 7), rolls one die and adds that to the average, and then rolls one die and subtracts that from the average. Assuming the + Die is 3 and the - Die is 5, the result is 7 +3 -5= 5. Reading the height table, this character is 1.73 meters (or 68 inches or about 5' 8" tall).

Determining Weight: To determine the character's weight, the player takes the average of Str + Dex + End (which is 7), rolls one die and adds that to the average, and then rolls one die and subtracts that from the average. Assuming the + Die is 6 and the - Die is 2, the result is 7 +6 -2= 1. Reading the height table, this character is 88 kilograms (or 194 pounds).

The Purpose of Knowing Height and Weight: Height and Weight add interest and dimension to a character; they help the player visualize him (or her) in his mind. It also helps if someone else has to carry this character.

CHARACTER CARDS

The basic information about a character is recorded on a character card. Not all information boxes are necessarily filled in or used.

1. Basic Characteristics. Roll the six characteristics (2D each): Strength, Dexterity, Endurance, Intelligence, Education, and Social Standing. Character beginning age is 18 years old.

2. Basic Details. Decide on basic details (this step may be delayed until the end of the sequence).

A. Name. Decide on this character's name.

B. Race. Determine the race of the character (characters are assumed under this system to be human). Default is Imperial Human.

C. Gender. Determine gender of the character (default is the same sex as the player).

3. Physical. Determine character height and weight. Other Details. The remaining details are produced in other aspects of the game system.

Name			UPP	Str	Dex	End	Int	Edu	Soc
Service and Rank			Race						Sex
Enlisted	Discharged	Served	ColdSleep	Birthdate					
Skills				Birthworld					
				Homeworld					
Possessions and Money				Height			Weight		
				Degrees					
Comments									

Str ☐☐☐☐☐ ☐☐☐☐☐ ☐☐☐☐☐ Int ☐☐☐☐☐ ☐☐☐☐☐ ☐☐☐☐☐
Dex ☐☐☐☐☐ ☐☐☐☐☐ ☐☐☐☐☐
End ☐☐☐☐☐ ☐☐☐☐☐ ☐☐☐☐☐

Character Card   Form 11

This form may be photocopied for use with the Traveller game system.

PLAYING TRAVELLER

Traveller is played in two distinct and different ways:

With Others: One player is a game master who resolves the various game situations as the players tell him what actions their characters are taking. This is the traditional view of role-playing games.

Alone: The alternative is playing **with Traveller.** The player uses the game rules to create characters (or, using other modules, to design ships or create worlds)

EXERCISE 1
GENERATE CHARACTERS

With two dice and copies of the Character Card, create a group of five characters.

EXERCISE 2
GENERATE MORE CHARACTERS

Roll one die twelve times. Using this sum as a point pool, create a character by allocating these points to the various characteristics. Create five new characters.

EXERCISE 3
ANALYZE THE GATEWAY CHARACTERS

Using the text of Gateway, and copies of the blank Character Card, reverse engineer the details of the various human characters in Gateway (and cite text in support of your conclusions).

Name			UPP	Str	Dex	End	Int	Edu	Soc
Service and Rank			Race						Sex
Enlisted	Discharged	Served	ColdSleep	Birthdate					
Skills				Birthworld					
				Homeworld					
Possessions and Money				Height			Weight		
				Degrees					

Comments

Str ☐☐☐☐☐ ☐☐☐☐☐ ☐☐☐☐☐ Int ☐☐☐☐☐ ☐☐☐☐☐ ☐☐☐☐☐
Dex ☐☐☐☐☐ ☐☐☐☐☐ ☐☐☐☐☐
End ☐☐☐☐☐ ☐☐☐☐☐ ☐☐☐☐☐